Arrivederci and Hello

A Journey of Farewells and Greetings

RINA AUCIELLO

ARRIVEDERCI & HELLO

Published in Australia, 2023

This book is entirely a work of fiction. Some parts of this story are based on historical events, but have been adapted. References to real people, events and establishments are intended only to provide a sense of authenticity. All other characters and incidents are drawn from the author's imagination and are not to be construed as real.

ISBN: 978-0-6458182-0-8 (Paper back)

ISBN: 978-0-6458182-1-5 (ebook)

Website www.rinaauciello.com.au

To my two angels in Heaven A & M.
There isn't a day that goes by that you are not in my thoughts.
You live on through me and the people who love you.

CHAPTER 1: ARRIVEDERCI

"Hello?" whispers Mario into the desilvering mirror hanging from a frayed string attached to a crooked nail. A small suitcase sits open on an old chair in the corner of the room, next to three single beds that are crammed together with just inches between them. Two people sleep soundly as the sunlight sneaks in, around and under the rudimentary coverings on the windows. Mario looks at his brothers, listening to the sounds of slumber, then turns back to the mirror. He has his father's once-upon-a-time good looks and his mother's slight but sturdy frame. His shirtless body reveals a very toned and muscled torso, a by-product of his military service.

He moves around the room slowly, not wanting to wake his brothers, and carefully arranges the items in his suitcase—a few toiletries, a brush and comb, some clean but well-worn undergarments and two neatly folded white shirts. He picks up a small Italian/English dictionary he borrowed from an army friend when they were stationed in Trento, which he conveniently forgot to give back when he left the military. He flicks through the pages to the bookmark with an image of Saint Anthony, which his mother gave to him so long ago he can't remember. He kisses it and places it back between the pages.

The dictionary is his most important possession. He carries it everywhere and uses it constantly, to teach himself English. His brothers would laugh at him when he stared at himself in the mirror and conversed with his own image in English, something he often did. They would shout offensive remarks, and he would respond with a few English swear words—his brothers quickly learnt some of the more colourful words of the English language. The dictionary represents change and opportunity. It gives him the ability to make his fortune and help his family—after all, he is the eldest, and it is his responsibility to improve the family situation. Neither the wine-making skills learnt from his father nor the army drills of his twelve-month military service help, and he has limited possibilities for further education. Mastering English and seeking work outside of Italy is his only chance to change the situation for himself and for his family.

Dictionary in hand, Mario returns to the mirror. "Hello, how are you?" Mario asks his reflection, a little louder, a little more convincing this time. His English has improved, the reflection thinks, and it answers, "I'm very well, thank you."

"Sta zitto scemo!" mumbles one of his sleeping brothers—(Shut up, you idiot!)—as a flying shoe just misses Mario's head and clips the mirror. Mario steadies the swinging reflector as a few more Italian profanities are expressed. The mirror back in place, Mario looks to his reflection and smirks to himself as he pushes back his thick, wavy hair and brushes down his secondhand suit. He picks up the immigration papers scattered on the side table, flicks through them one last time, then places them in the inside pocket of his jacket.

He thinks, *This is the right thing to do. Yes, it is.* It will give both him and his family a better future, and he'll be able to restore the cantina to its former glory. The man in the mirror, however, looks unsure as he places his hat on his head. Mario takes off his hat and puts it on the nearby side table. He takes the Saint Anthony bookmark out of his dictionary and wedges it in the ribbon of his hat like a decorative feather. It remains on the side table as he leaves the room.

"Boungiorno a tutti!" Euplio, Mario's father, tilts his head and holds up his arms in an exultant manner as he addresses his audience. The donkey and the cow seem uninterested, but the chickens cluck around, frightened by his thundering voice. The ruins of the once popular cantina in which he stands, in the village of Bovino, used to welcome many paying customers, but now houses only the donkey, the cow, five chickens and the odd visiting rat family.

Euplio Lanzani's cantina was once a thriving business. People would come from all the surrounding villages and even from the capital city of Foggia to buy the well-crafted produce—the olive oil, small goods, cheese and bread—but what everyone really came for was the wine. Euplio was a master winemaker but is now a master wine drinker. Both of these skills have been handed down to Euplio by his father. Withered grapes hang from the few remaining vines, a cruel reminder of a once abundant life. The vineyard has made way for hay production, as animals need to be fed, and Euplio can sell, swap or barter the hay.

Sadly, wine is no longer an affordable luxury. Antonietta warned him against giving credit, but he trusted his customers, who were loyal to him until the day they were asked to settle their accounts. Suddenly, it seemed no one could, or would, pay him. With debts mounting and no money to buy goods, the cantina has become no more, and the rows of the finest Sangiovese grapes have been replaced with herbaceous plants for animal fodder.

Euplio, his erstwhile handsome face barely visible under his long grey curls and worn features, shuffles over to a crevice in the wall, hidden in the shadows of the cantina. He readjusts his fallen brace up onto his shoulder and slicks back his hair, which immediately falls into its original position. He reaches into the crevice to pull out a dusty bottle of wine. He removes the crumbling cork and holds the bottle aloft to his animal audience. *"Saluti!"* he toasts. The animals look up for a second or two and then resume their activities. He watches the donkey as it drinks from the trough. Euplio mumbles something to himself and grabs a handful of hay.

"Vieni...vieni," Euplio calls to the donkey as he waves the hay to lure it closer. The donkey finishes his drink, raises his head and ponders.

"Vieni," Euplio says again, summoning the donkey. (Come.)

The donkey takes a step towards Euplio, who takes a step back, still waving the hay. Looking into the donkey's eyes, he feels for the bridle, which is hanging somewhere on the wooden pillar beside him. The donkey inches towards him. Euplio locates the bridle and slowly takes it down from its hook, his gaze never faltering. When the donkey is in reach of the hay, he gives Euplio an innocent gawp and then takes the hay from his hand. The bridle is placed around the donkey, and then with one large slap of his hand across the animal's head, Euplio leaves the donkey braying and kicking as he laughs malevolently.

"Ciuccio, sei troppo fiducioso!" He smirks. (Idiot, you're too trusting!) The other animals join in the biophonic symphony

as Euplio plays the conductor, to his continuing amusement.

It has been seven years since the end of World War II, and even though Bovino never witnessed any action, the aftereffects of the war shroud the village like an invisible cloak. Poverty lurks in every ruin of the once quaint Italian village. The evidence of husbands and sons who died fighting for their country can be seen in the many women dressed in black, mourning their loved ones. The Lanzanis are one of the lucky families. Euplio was too old and his sons too young to join the Axis forces. Although he did, for a while, have great respect for Benito Mussolini, he was never going to fight even if he were called up—he would have found a way out somehow. Euplio managed to avoid military conscription for a while thanks to his conveniently forgetful father, who did not register his birth. The Italian authorities made him register well into his twenties, but he missed any WWI action completely, which makes him very happy. He is a lover, not a fighter, and he fathered eleven children to prove that.

Antonietta looks older than her forty-five years and much frailer than she actually is. She came from good stock and survived nine pregnancies; unlike Euplio's first wife, who died during childbirth along with her twins. Antonietta lost her first three children to natal complications, but in the end, she managed, whilst also working in the cantina, to bear six healthy children. Time was on her side—her husband was too old for the war, and her eldest son, Mario, was too young. But now her beloved Mario, who has just returned from his military conscription, is leaving again, but this time, he is going thousands of miles away and God only knows where. Economic forces are much greater than any military ones, enough to tear a son away from his mother. A single tear follows the trail of others she has desperately tried to keep hidden. She reaches for the pot of water on the stove.

"Ohhhhh!" She pulls her hand away abruptly. Now she has another reason for tears. She reaches for the pot again, with a rag in hand this time, and carefully pours the water into two cups placed on the worn wooden table. A homemade tea bag is quickly dunked two times in each cup and then placed on a stained plate until its next use.

Antonietta scoops half a teaspoon of sugar and carefully divides it between the two cups of tea. She stirs both of the teacups, then places the spoon next to the limp tea bag on the resting plate. Mario walks in, and she starts to cry.

"Mamma," Mario says sympathetically as he hugs her, drawing in as much of her maternal love as he possibly can. She wonders if he can feel her heart beginning to rip in two. He is her first surviving child, and it is he who mended her broken heart after the loss of her first three children. She has always known that one day he would leave, but wonders why he must go so far away. She manages to tear herself away from him and offer the prepared cup of tea. He shakes his head, which triggers another bout of crying from her. She offers him a piece of toast. He doesn't dare refuse.

Mario and Antonietta sit at the table near the smouldering fireplace. She holds one of his hands; he uses his other hand to eat the toast. The only sound is his crunching as he stares at his mother's hands clasped with his own.

"Mario...Mario...*andiamo!*" Euplio shouts from outside. Mario looks to his mother's tear-soaked face, takes a deep breath, then releases his hand from her grasp as respectfully as he can. He puts down the half-eaten piece of toast and picks up his suitcase. With a gentle kiss on each of his mother's cheeks,

Mario leaves in silence. No words are needed, everything expressed in his mother's heavy sigh.

Euplio sits on a small cart harnessed to the donkey. His loose trousers are held up by one brace over a worn shirt, the other brace fallen to the side. He pulls the brace up onto his shoulder again.

The air is cold but not fresh as the donkey defecates onto the gravel road. Euplio reaches for his new jacket, which seems out of place with the rest of his attire. He puts his jacket on and slicks back his greying curls. He shouts again, his loud, thundering voice hurrying his son. The donkey bucks and brays in a pointless protest as Euplio pulls on the reins.

"*Fermati, cretino!*" (Stop, you cretin!)

Mario races to the cart and jumps in the back. He finds the cleanest spot available and settles in. Euplio asks Mario if he is ready to go, and Mario's preoccupied smile tells him it is so.

With a flick of the reins, the donkey pulls away, and the wheel of the cart runs over the fresh droppings. Mario looks back at the indented shit and wonders, *Is that a metaphor of change and what is being left behind...or is it just shit? And is there more to come?*

Mario looks up to see his mother receding slowly in the distance. She stands on the dirt track, waving and crying, until Mario is well out of sight.

Antonietta walks back into the kitchen, where her cold tea and dried-up toast awaits. She slumps into a chair and takes a sip from her cup. She looks at the family photo before her, showing sixteen-year-old Mario with his five younger siblings. Her thoughts turn to her other children. One day, she knows, Mario will be back, but in the meantime, she vows to remain strong, the rock that's needed for the family. She must lead the way so that they will follow—including her husband, for he is the biggest child of all.

She finishes her toast, kisses the photo and heads towards the bedrooms, shouting at the family to get up, for there is work to do. Her remaining two daughters and three sons scramble out of bed, including the five-year-old. Nobody wants to disappoint their mother.

In the cart, Mario and his father pass scenes of lush green Bovino countryside. The beauty of the land does not reveal the true hardship of village life. Mario waves to Angelo, their neighbour, as they pass. Angelo is leaning on his plough, taking a well-deserved break from turning the land. He waves and shouts to Mario, "Where are you going, Mario, all dressed up like a toff?"

Euplio answers in his usual thundering voice, in a particularly harsh Italian dialect.

"We are going to mind your own business!"

"OK, and you, Euplio, can go to hell!" Angelo retorts.

Mario chuckles at the normal daily banter between the two neighbours.

"And you, you bandit, stop stealing water from my well!" Euplio yells.

"The well may be yours, but the water belongs to everyone!"

"Cretin! My donkey has more brains than you!"

Angelo takes a large handful of his pants around his penis. "Euplio! Suck on this!"

Mario can't stop himself from roaring with laughter as he waves and shouts to Angelo, "Ciao, Angelo!"

"Ciao, Mario! Good luck, you're a good kid. It must come from your mother's side."

"*Vaffunculo!*" is Euplio's response.

The cart is now out of earshot of Angelo, and his response is inaudible as he makes obscene gestures.

Mario's face is pensive and uneasy. He hangs on to the cart as it navigates increasingly vicious bumps. Finally, the cart stops at the Foggia train station. Mario clutches his suitcase and jumps out to face his father, who is holding tightly onto the reins. Euplio towers over Mario as he stays firmly in the seat of the cart, no handshake or fatherly concern forthcoming, only a reminder that Mario is not wearing a hat and must think about the family. Mario knows exactly what 'think about the family' means.

Mario daydreams on the train journey to the Port of Naples, and in what seems like five minutes, he finds himself looking up at an enormous ship awaiting his embarkment. He stands with many other passengers on their way to encounter Miss Destiny. Mario, though, will not succumb to her strong, persuasive ways—his companion is Mr Time, who is all Mario needs to achieve his goals and to walk his path in life.

"*Arrivederci* for now!" Mario says quietly to his home country. Many travellers, mostly young men, restlessly line up to board. Mario is the only one not wearing a hat.

CHAPTER 2: HELLO

Mario and his companion Mr Time ride in a bus filled with different languages. He doesn't mind the sudden bumps in the road; they are much better than the constant seasickness he experienced on the ship. One hand holds on to his suitcase, and the other holds a wooden rail as the bus momentarily flies through the air and lands with a particularly nasty thump. Iterations of "Bloody hell!" in various languages ricochet around the bus. Mario turns to the man on his right, thinking, *This man is more scared than I am.*

"Hello?" Mario says, determined to use his English and maybe impress the stranger. The man just stares and blinks.

"Italiano?"

The man nods with an looming smile. Mario offers his hand. The stranger shakes it nervously, and Mario tries to put the man at ease by speaking to him in Italian.

"My name is Mario."

The man still just stares and blinks, so Mario stares back, waiting for him to speak. After a short, awkward pause, the man finally says something.

"P-P-Pietro," the man stutters, embarrassed.

Mario gives Pietro a comforting smile. *This man is going to need a friend—he speaks a different language with a stutter. But then again, he's quite tall and buff, so he might be able to look after himself.* He asks Pietro where in Italy he comes from. Pietro hesitates but eventually stutters out: "Ch-Ch-Chieti."

"Oh, you're from Abruzzo?"

Pietro nods again as the bus hits another bump, resulting in another round of complaints being thrown around in different languages. Mario and Pietro laugh, and the tense situation subsides.

"I'm from Bovino," says Mario, looking at Pietro. Mistaking his blank expression for ignorance, he explains, "La Puglia!"

"I know," responds Pietro, his stuttering becoming less prominent as his comfort in Mario's company increases. He looks towards Mario's hair.

"Have you lost your hat?"

"No. I left it at home."

Pietro is silent. No respectable man goes out in public, let alone travels to the other side of the world, without his hat.

"A man w-w-without his hat is a g-gypsy," Pietro finally blurts out.

Mario hangs his head and shuffles in his seat uncomfortably, pauses, and then looks into Pietro's eyes.

"Yes, right now I am a gypsy, but the day will come when I return home, and I will wear my hat again!"

"I'm n-n-never going b-back!" Pietro replies.

Mario purses his lips and then asks, "A woman?"

Pietro nods. "And her h-husband!" he adds.

A judgmental laugh comes out of Mario's closed mouth, his eyebrows raised. Pietro's silence does not hide his guilty and devilish demeanour. The bus is full of chatter and laughter in between the bumps and swerves.

"OK, then," Pietro eventually says, "I will c-c-call you Mario sensa Capello!"

With a shrug of his shoulders, Mario answers, "OK, I will call you...Pietro Pistola." Mario makes gun sounds, imitating Pietro's stutter. Pietro's tense stare leaves Mario wondering if the joke has offended his new friend. After a few seconds, which seem like minutes, Pietro's mouth starts to turn up and a roar of laughter exits his mouth as he slaps Mario warmheartedly on the back.

Mario joins in on the laughter, relieved to discover that Pietro has a good sense of humour.

Their chatter diminishes as the sun sets on the convoy of buses. All that can be seen is faint lights in the distance as the passengers—some sleepy, some pensive, some bored, but all quiet—sense the beginning of a new life, or at least a new chapter in life.

The buses slow down as they enter the camp gates, passing a dimly lit sign: "Commonwealth Immigration Centre Bonegilla." A few more bumps, and the buses stop in front of the administration block. Passengers are guided by uniformed officials towards the large reception hall.

There is the drone of people chattering. Children, and even some adults, are crying, whilst others sing comforting songs to ease the tension. Mario and Pietro step off the bus, and an unexpected chill hits them. It sends a shiver through Pietro, and he looks puzzled as he comments that he had been told Australia was hot.

Mario shrugs as he pulls up the collar of his coat for some protection. They are shuffled along in the darkness, not even a moon in the sky to shine any kind of light upon where, exactly, it is they have landed.

Official immigration papers are shoved into Mario's hands

as he enters the reception centre. He reads the heading on the first pamphlet: *Happy in a New Homeland*. Right at this moment, he is happy just to be out of the cold.

Uncertainty veils every face as they enter the great hall and find a camping chair to sit on, a wall to lean against, or just a piece of floor to claim as their own for the time being. The hesitancy slowly eases into suspicion as the uniformed officials close the doors behind the last entrants. Some of the officers station themselves in front of the doors, whilst others walk to the anterior of the hall.

Mario and Pietro stand amongst a group of Italian nationals congregated together, all conversing in their native tongue, guessing what is going to happen next.

Genaro and Stella, newlyweds from Naples, hold each other closely, looking into each other's eyes; six or seven single men, also from Naples, complain loudly in their animated and distinctive Neapolitan dialect. Within the mix of single men stand Alberto and Matteo. They are both married and have left their wives in the homeland looking after their children, with the promise of a better future as a result of this temporary separation. Being married, however, is not stopping them from ogling every young girl of consenting age.

An older man in a neat, well-fitted dark grey suit walks up to the microphone at the front of the hall. There is an agonizing screeching sound. The noisy buzz in the reception hall is hushed as one of the other officials scrambles to adjust the audio system. The man in the grey suit approaches the microphone again.

"Good evening, everyone, my name is Mr Dobson, I am the director here at Bonegilla, and I would like to welcome you all to Australia, your new home."

Genaro pokes Mario in the ribs.

"*Che dice...che dice?*" Genaro questions. (What is he saying?)

"*Benvenuti* in Australia," Mario interprets as a crowd of Italians gather around him, nodding in approval.

The director continues with his customary inspirational speech in a soothing English accent.

"Australia is a wonderful country full of opportunity for people willing to work and contribute to society. You are all New Australians now and hence must learn to speak English as soon as possible."

Genaro gives Mario another poke.

"*Che dice?*" he says, along with the others in the crowd asking the same question.

Mario turns to them. "*E fammi sentire!*" he says. (Let me listen!) He turns towards Mr Dobson, concentrating.

"Bonegilla is about the future and not the past."

Mario parrots the director's words in Italian. Collectively, the group gestures with their hands; some in agreement, others indicating that it will be hard.

"We are happy to have you here and hope that your new life in Australia brings you health and happiness. I will now pass you over to the camp supervisor, Brigadier Sinclair, and after his address, you will be given some dinner," concluded Mr Dobson.

Mario again translates for the crowd behind him. They all agree that Mr Dobson is a good man, and the babble crescendos to a loud buzz as excitement and hope envelopes the room.

A lanky redheaded man in an army uniform walks in, looking like he's trying to hold a nugget between his bum cheeks, aloof and awkward. He approaches the director, who offers him the microphone. He takes it, but the microphone is redundant as he shouts, "Quieeeeeeeet!"

The hall immediately stands to attention in anticipation of what this tall, mean-looking man has to say next in his Australian English accent.

"Right, you lot...you may be our guests for now, but while you are all here, you need to fall in line. May I remind you of how lucky you are. My own grandmother didn't have the luxury of travelling to the countryside on a train or a bus, she had to walk. A few rules for you! No smoking inside the dorms, no cooking outside the mess hall, no drinking allowed, no fishing allowed..."

Mario repeats what he can understand in Italian. There are increasingly animated responses from the crowd, agreement that this man is a '*bastardo.*'

Brigadier Sinclair continues. "No inappropriate behaviour will be tolerated, and under no circumstance will you leave the camp without permission. There are clipboards to the back of the hall. After your meal, look at them to see where you will be sleeping. Follow the maps and you shouldn't have any problems. You will all be processed tomorrow. Good night." With that, Brigadier Sinclair leaves without making any eye contact with the crowd whatsoever.

Mario wraps up his interpreting as the crowd is ushered towards the mess hall. They move with mild confusion as they complain about the brigadier, calling him derogatory names and illustrating them with inappropriate gestures.

Everyone slowly enters the mess hall, looking more like a flock of sheep than welcome New Australians, each lining up to collect their plate of food. Mario and Pietro sit with the other Italians as they all stare down at the dried-up mutton and what look like three different vegetables that share greenish-brown characteristics. Mario knows he should be grateful for this food, but as he picks through the vegetables, his hunger and revulsion are in disagreement.

"I—I—I can't eat this, it is disgusting," complains Pietro. His sentiments are mimicked by almost all the surrounding Italians.

Mario suggests that Pietro should be grateful and eat his food, and says that perhaps it will be better tomorrow. Pietro watches Mario pick at his own plate and reluctantly place a piece of mutton in his mouth, chewing very hard for nearly a minute before swallowing.

After the meal, Mario and Pietro walk in the dark, cold air towards their assigned accommodations, still without a clue of where they are and what actually surrounds them. They enter the dimly-lit hut crammed with six small, wire-framed army beds. There is not much room between them and absolutely no partitioning or privacy. Three of the beds are already taken by sleeping occupants, leaving the three closest to the window—and closest to the cold night air. The mattress on Mario's bed is no thicker than a folded blanket, and atop it sits two actual folded blankets, sheets, a pillow and a towel. Resting on the towel is a silver tray with melamine dinnerware stacked in a pile. He slides his suitcase under the wire frame and attempts to make his bed. Pietro does the same without a word of complaint. Mario wonders whether he is in shock or just too tired to care. At that moment, Genaro bursts in, swearing in Italian.

"Quiet, there are people sleeping!" whispers Mario.

"Ma, mi parla in inglese?" Genaro demands. (What, you speak to me in English?)

"Sì...yes, you must learn English now."

"*Vaffunculo a te, e tutto l'Australia!*" (You can get fucked, together with all of Australia.)

"*G-G-Genaro, c-che c'e?*" Pietro says. (G-Genaro, w-what's wrong?)

Genaro explains in Italian with intermittent grunts: "I'm here with you all, when I should be with my wife. I nearly hit the bastard when he said no men and women together. I know now why they need more people in this country, if the men and women are all separated."

From one of the other beds comes an abrupt response: "*Sta zitto, dormi, domani ci pensiamo.*" (Be quiet, go to sleep, worry about it tomorrow.)

Mario gestures with his head towards the remaining empty bed.

"*Yamm, Genaro vatt' a dormi.*" (Come on, Genaro, go to sleep!)

"*E mo, mi parli in italiano, deciditi!*" Genaro retorts. (Now you speak to me in Italian! Make up your mind!)

Mario shakes his head and sighs, making a typical Italian 'let's call it a day' gesture with his hands. Genaro, now a bit calmer, gives in to his frustration and tiredness and slumps on the empty bed, not even bothering to make it. He pulls the blankets over himself and immediately falls asleep.

"*M-ma quisto e p-p-roprio Napoletano!*" Pietro scoffs towards the sleeping Genaro. (This one's a real Neapolitan!)

Mario lies in his bed, his suit still on as it is no warmer inside the hut than outside. With one blanket on his body and the other over his head, he watches a large moth, as big as a small bird, suspended on the ceiling near the light.

Loudspeakers blare "Lights out!" in English and German, the two languages that the Bonegilla administration considers the most important. With that, the moth disappears, and Mario lies in complete darkness. He struggles to sleep amidst the sounds of sobbing coming from nearby huts and the snores and grunts of his fellow occupants.

* * *

The breaking dawn wakes Mario from his three-hour long sleep. He is the first to rise. He looks around his living environment: nothing more than a rudimentary timber-framed army barrack, with unlined corrugated walls and a low-pitched galvanised roof. The army barracks back in Italy were five stars compared to this. Mario looks out the window as Pietro stirs. All that he can see is a vast open space with knee-deep dry yellow grass and a line of barbed wire surrounding the camp. He takes a second look just to be sure.

"My God, this is a concentration camp!" he exclaims to himself.

"You have no idea what a concentration camp is, you over-privileged Italian arsehole," barks an unfamiliar voice. Both Mario and Pietro turn towards the scruffy man dressed in Australian-issued army greens rising from his bed and rubbing the sleep from his eyes.

"Overprivileged? I escaped poverty to be here!" protests Mario.

"Ha! I escaped death!" counters the stranger.

"Well, you can die from starvation," Mario retorts.

"Not as quickly as you can from a bullet!"

Mario is stumped by this response, but offers his hand to the stranger. The man takes it.

"Mario," he introduces himself. "And this is Pietro."

"Alesky Gulan. Who is the loudmouthed Romeo over there?"

"Genaro," responds Mario with a smirk.

"He will need to find another way, they won't allow women and men to sleep in the same room," Alesky informs them.

"Yes, maybe we can help him," Mario says as he gives a questioning look to the other two sleeping roommates.

"They belong to you lot—overprivileged, complaining Italians," says Alesky.

There is a faint *clang-clang-clang* coming from the direction of the mess hall, signalling breakfast. Mario looks down at his crumpled suit.

"I should probably wash first."

"No, you should probably eat first. Who knows what we find and how much?" responds Alesky.

Mario agrees as he puts on his shoes and turns to Pietro.

"Let's go."

As the first rays of Bonegilla sunshine hit Mario's face, he hears the the extraordinary sounds of magpie warbles and the kookaburras that seem to be laughing at them. Even though the air still has a chill, it smells smoky, like the embers of the fireplace from home. With cutlery in their hands, Mario, Pietro and Alesky walk across the frosty grass towards the mess hall. In the distance is a lagoon surrounded by sparse gum trees and the odd rabbit scurrying across some greener grass. It reminds Mario of an oasis in the desert, and his attitude towards this new land begins to warm up, like the day.

Breakfast offerings amount to plain porridge and white square bread, toasted or untoasted, with butter, jam or honey, tea or hot cocoa. Alesky piles his plate with as much porridge as he can fit, and some spillage occurs. Holding the plate with one hand, Alesky grabs four slices of toast with the other and carefully places the toast on top of the porridge, leaving a free hand to carry a cup of cocoa, and then looks around for an empty space to sit. Mario and Pietro forego the porridge for a couple of pieces of square toast with butter and jam, and a cup of cocoa.

Alesky dives into his porridge like a man possessed, while Mario and Pietro cup their cocoa, feeling the first bit of comfort since their arrival in Australia.

"Questo e' b-buono," says Pietro with long-awaited satisfaction.

Alesky takes a brief break from devouring his porridge to look up at Pietro.

"You need to speak English. No English, no job," Alesky says. Pietro stares at Alesky without saying a word.

"You speak English, Mario. Where did you learn?" Alesky asks.

"I taught myself," says Mario proudly.

"Mmm, bravo. I speak six languages, they all taught me! You'd better teach your friend, Mario, but I don't know how that will go with his stutter?"

"He will manage."

Pietro, understanding the context of the conversation, directs his frustration towards Alesky. *"Parli italiano?"* he inquires.

"Sì," answers Alesky.

Pietro shows Alesky his middle finger as he says, *"Vaffunculo!"*

"Ahh, Pietro, you don't stutter when you're angry," Alesky says.

Everybody starts to laugh, except Pietro.

The speakers blare out more instructions, first in perfect English and then in imperfect German.

"Would all new arrivals please make their way to the processing hall. I repeat—all new arrivals to the processing hall." About a quarter of the men in the room pick up their dinnerware and exit the mess hall.

A Commonwealth Employment Service (CES) officer sits at his desk in the administration block, with three interpreters positioned behind him. Brigadier Sinclair and some of his patrolmen walk around, on alert, as if there's likely to be trouble at any minute. The row of New Australians with immigration papers in their hands starts to grow. The CES officer looks very busy, ignoring the increasingly agitated crowd.

"Hurry up!" shouts a voice from the crowd.

"Have ya got somewhere else to be?" retorts the CES officer. The patrols have a laugh at the remark as the three interpreters look at each other awkwardly.

The crowd, which remains silent for about two minutes, soon begins to voice their annoyance to each other, but loud enough that the patrol personnel can hear.

"Alright, alright," shouts the brigadier finally.

The CES officer indicates he is ready and rises from his chair to speak.

"Have all your papers ready and then go to the hospital and get a medical checkup. Don't bother giving me any papers with qualifications, 'cause we know they're all fake. None of you are doctors or lawyers or anything else—even if you were, you're not now! Alright, who's up first?"

The CES officer sits back at his desk, and the crowd is processed one by one. Almost an hour goes by before Pietro's turn has come. Mario stands alert, concerned about how Pietro's speech impediment will be received. Pietro walks up to the CES officer and stands in silence. The officer looks up at Pietro's imposing figure.

"Name?" he asks.

"P-P-Pietro...M-M-Maan-cini," Pietro spits out.

"Are you from Italy...P-P-Pietro?" The officer bursts into laughter. He turns to the Italian interpreter. "What's 'P-P-Pietro' in English?"

"Peter," says the interpreter, approaching the desk. "I'll take it from here." The interpreter calms Pietro down with soothing Italian words, and assures him he is going to be fine and that not all Australians are like this. Ultimately the CES officer stamps Pietro's papers and he is free to go.

"Hey, P-P-Peter, don't forget your p-p-papers!" The officer laughs at him.

The interpreter snatches the papers from the officer's hands and gives them to Pietro. The interpreter shakes Pietro's hand, then shoots the CES officer a disgusted glance, which is totally ignored. The officer and Brigadier Sinclair laugh.

"Fuck me, a stutter and an accent? He's not going to last long," sneers Brigadier Sinclair.

"Next!" shouts the CES officer.

Mario steps up to the desk, annoyed at the treatment of his friend.

"Mario Lanzani," he says.

"Haven't asked yer name yet!"

"I thought, maybe, it would be useful," Mario says snidely. The interpreters at the back finally smile.

"Your English isn't bad," the officer says.

"Yours is," Mario replies.

"Where did ya learn yer Eng-a-lish?"

"Dick taught me."

"Dick who?"

"Dick...Chenary."

"Dick Chenary? Dictionary!" At this point, the interpreters are shaking with laughter. The same can not be said about the CES officer, who realises he has borne the brunt of an unwanted riposte.

"So, you're a smart-arse, huh?"

"No, I'm Italian."

"You're a dago, a fucking smart-arse dago, that's what you are!"

"E tu si un figlio di puttana," Mario replies. (And you're a son of a bitch.)

The CES officer turns to the wide-eyed Italian interpreter, who just shrugs his shoulders.

"Don't you speak your fucking dago lingo to me. You're in Australia now, mate, don't forget that. Do you want your papers stamped or not?"

Mario nods sheepishly. The officer stamps Mario's papers with such force that the ink blurs. He shoves them back to Mario as he turns to Brigadier Sinclair.

"You better watch out for this one, mate!" His attention reverts back to the line.

"Next! Name?"

"Alesky Gulan."

"Where did you come from?"

"My mother's vagina."

Everyone that understands roars with laughter, and the ones who don't join in anyway.

"Another fuckin' smart-arse, this time we have a Balt one.

23

Listen here, all you wogs and reffos, you're all here thanks to the gracious courtesy of the Australian government, and you're damn lucky, you better understand that." He turns to the interpreters. "Tell 'em in their own language how lucky they are."

The Italian interpreter speaks his mind to the officer: "I think you should treat them with a little more respect. They are in a different country, confused and scared, and you are treating them very badly."

"You're not paid to think, you're paid to interpret, so interpret!" the officer snaps back.

The officer stamps Alesky's papers and calls, "Next badly treated New Australian! And you watch yourself too, Balt!"

Silent awkwardness fills the room as Alesky sidles out to Mario and Pietro, who are leaning against the wall, smoking.

"Your mother's vagina has caused some trouble." Mario smirks.

"He can tell a joke, but he can't take a joke," Alesky says. "Anyway, you made him mad before I did."

"Yes, we need to watch ourselves now," Mario says.

"Nah, I've avoided smarter men than that."

"Where and when?"

Alesky steals Mario's cigarette and walks off, offering only a sly laugh as his answer. Mario turns to Pietro and steals his cigarette, takes a puff, shrugs his shoulders and then offers it back. Pietro instead walks off. Mario is left wondering about both of them.

CHAPTER 3: LET'S PLAY

Another day passes much like the rest. All are gathered in the mess hall, and again, Mario stares down at another serving of dried mutton and vegetable surprise, this time drowned in tomato sauce—sweet Australian tomato sauce, certainly not the kind the Italians are used to.

"I can't eat this!" says Mario in disgust.

Alesky slides Mario's plate over to him. "Give it to me, then, you overprivileged Italian."

"How can you eat so much shit?" Mario asks, incredulous.

Alesky's mouth is full and he does not respond. Pietro also slides his plate to Alesky. Both he and Mario look outside towards the lagoon, watching the birds fly around the treetops and the rabbits that scurry away at the slightest noise. Mario and Pietro turn to each other, smiling, knowing exactly what the other is imagining—rabbit cacciatore!

It is a fine, sunny afternoon, and most of the camp residents are sitting outside to soak up the warmth of the sun's rays. Alberto, one of the married men, appears with a soccer ball he found under one of the recreation huts, which looks as if it has been there since the landing of the first fleet. He shows his find and rallies enough interest within the Italian congregation to make five on each side. As is the Italian custom, most people, when they are at a familiar stage of knowing each other, are called by their nicknames instead of their proper names. This makes it easier for people to be identified.

The opposing captains are Genaro "Napolitano" and Alberto, nicknamed "Mussone" (Big Lips). They choose their team members one by one. None of them really look like soccer players, with their long trousers rolled up to their knees, white singlets and dress shoes.

On Genaro's team is Franco "Trippa Nero" (Black Belly), Rocco "Spaccone" (Showoff), Augusto "Parapalle" (Equal Balls), and Ciro "Patatone" (Big Potato).

On Alberto's team is Matteo "Bottiglia" (The Bottle), Giovanni "Calze Caggato" (Shitty Socks), Antonio "Puzzone" (Stinky), and Biaggio "Chiachiarrone" (Chatterbox).

Genaro shouts in Italian to Mario, who is sitting with Alesky watching Pietro set up his rabbit trap.

"Oi! *Sensa cappello*, Pietro Pistolla, come play with us!"

Mario looks to Pietro, who shakes his head no and continues to prepare his trap.

"Come on, Alesky, you play?"

Alesky shrugs his shoulders. "OK."

They strip to their singlets, roll up their trousers to the knee, and walk across the field to join the others.

"Pietro Pistola?" asks Genaro.

"He's busy, Alesky will play."

"I can't bloody understand you, speak to me in Italian!" complains Genaro in his thick Neapolitan accent.

"Genaro, don't break my balls," Mario replies in Italian. "I want to speak English. If you don't understand, that's your problem."

Genaro ignores Mario's comment as he commands Mario to

be on his team and Alberto to take Alesky, who he nicknames: *Che ne saccio?* (Who knows?). Everyone laughs at Genaro's nickname for Alesky. Chairs, benches and other inanimate objects determined the field boundary, with two wooden two-by-fours used as goalposts at each end of the field.

The game begins without an umpire. Rocco "Spaccone" performs his soccer ball tricks, but he is not quite as good as he thinks and Antonio "Puzzone" easily takes the ball off of him, dribbles it towards the unattended goalpost, and scores. They all realise that each team has not designated a goalkeeper, and argue amongst themselves until Augusto "Parapalle" becomes the goalkeeper for Genaro's team, and Giovanni "Calze Caggato" for Alberto's. Goalposts manned, the game begins again as a small crowd of spectators gather, including the Area Patrol, which is made up of mainly German-speaking personnel working for the Australian government.

Genaro, who is quite skilled, begins to dribble the ball as he eyes Stella, who smiles in approval. He easily bypasses Alesky "Che ne saccio" (Who knows), who knows nothing about soccer. As Matteo "Bottigglia" and Biaggio "Ciaciarrone" approach him, he passes the ball to Franco "Trippa Nero," who stops the ball successfully, but trips over it, sliding across the dusty red ground. He lies on his back with his hands on his head, his singlet concertinaed up to his armpits, and everyone can see why his nickname is the Italian for "black belly"—his entire front torso is carpeted in thick black hair. Genaro gives him a helping hand up while scolding him for tripping and wasting a good pass; meanwhile, Alberto "Mussone" has the ball and is heading towards the other side of the field. Alberto is chased by Mario, but he is much faster, and easily outruns him, only to be intercepted by an awaiting Ciro "Patatone", and falling to the ground.

The crowd erupts in protest as Ciro holds up his arms in question and passes the ball to his goalkeeper. There is now a melee in the middle of the field between all the hotheaded players, except for Mario and Alesky; they laugh at the situation while also watching Pietro set up his rabbit trap in the distance, which makes them laugh even harder.

Pietro carefully places a Y-shaped stick under the wooden half-crate he permanently borrowed from the kitchen. Around the stick, wound very tightly, is a piece of brown string. Pietro takes an apple out of his pocket; he bites into it to produce little apple pieces. He places some under the wooden box, with the other pieces dropped around outside the box. He cautiously unravels the string about a hundred metres and settles himself behind a small bush to wait patiently for his unsuspecting prey. Twenty minutes go by; three rabbits hover around the box, unperturbed by the soccer shouts in the distance. Pietro tightens his grip on the string in anticipation, mindful not to accidently pull it and ruin his plan. The rabbits nibble at the outside pieces of apple, inching closer to the box. His plan is working—closer and closer they come. Pietro readies his position—a couple more hops, and there will be rabbit for dinner. Almost there...

BANG! A soccer ball hits the wooden crate, and the rabbits scurry off faster than the blink of an eye.

"Noooooooooo!" screams Pietro as he punches the ground, then gets up to wave his fist and shout obscenities at the soccer players. The players stand in amazement, mostly because they didn't think that Alesky could kick that far.

"Sorry, Pietro, I was going for the goal...truly!" shouts back Alesky.

Pietro stands with his hands on his hips, shaking his head. He angrily paces back to his rabbit trap and collects it all, knowing that the rabbits won't come back today; he will try again tomorrow.

The game continues. Genaro's skills are on show as he dribbles the ball down the flank, swerving and passing all the opposing defences. As Genaro approaches the goal, he sees the goalkeeper running away. He stops, puts his foot on the ball, and shouts: *"Calze Caggato, dove vai?"* (Shitty Socks, where are you going?)

With his stomach rumbling like a small volcano, he runs on his tiptoes as he answers in Italian, "If I don't reach the toilet in time, I really will have shitty socks!"

Giovanni "Calze Caggato" is followed by six of the other players, all wanting to avoid the same fate, and suddenly the match is over. The bad food is the ultimate winner.

* * *

Night falls on a quiet camp as Mario and Alesky play cards. Pietro lies in his bed, still annoyed about his failed rabbit trapping—but, determined to succeed, he thinks about other foolproof rabbit-catching plans. Genaro is worn out from the soccer match, and sleeps soundly, as do the other two occupants, Augusto and Ciro. From the corner of the cramped hut where Pietro lies comes a beautiful rendition of the Italian ballad "Mamma". It is sung with feeling and, in the operatic harmony of a first-class tenor, the words flow with effortless conviction.

"Mamma solo per te la mia canzone vola...Mamma sarai con

me, tu non sarai piu sooolllaaaa...Quando ti voglio bene...Queste parole d'amore, che ti sospira il mio cuore...Forseno s'usano piuuuuuuuuuu...MAAAMMMMMA!"

Mario and Alesky glance at each other, tears pooling in their eyes as they listen.

"Jesus Christ! He can't speak, but he can sing!" says Alesky, not quite believing what he is hearing as the song continues.

"Mamma la conzone piu belle sei tu...Sei tu la vita, e per la vita non to lascio mai piu Maaammmma mai piuuuuuuuuu."

Pietro stops singing, turns himself around and settles down to sleep, leaving Mario and Alesky quite stunned and emotional. The card game between Mario and Alesky ends without a word. The overwhelming sentiment has caused Alesky to retreat to his bed and prompted Mario to write home.

He writes the first four words on the blank page—*Caro Mamma e Papa*—and stops. He stares down at the words with his elbow positioned firmly on the edge of the makeshift table, the palm of his hand holding his wilted face. A single teardrop falls onto the words and smudges the ink. More tears follow until Mario screws up the paper and leans his whole head into his folded arms. He quietly sobs, making sure that no one is awoken by his heartache. As the sobbing subsides, and his fatigue takes over, he is suddenly startled by Alesky's screams.

"Noooo! Noooo! Ljubica...Ljubica, forgive me! Please forgive me...Ljubica!"

Mario watches, transfixed by the scene before him as Alesky thrashes around, pulling at his hair and hitting his head against his pillow and the wall. The others in the hut begin to wake as the screaming continues.

"Ljubica! Forgive me! Ljubicaaaaa!"

Mario isn't sure if it is a good idea to wake someone from a nightmare, but he doesn't want to see his friend in such pain. He slowly approaches the aggressive Alesky and gently places his hand on his shoulder, easing the thrashing. When Alesky is in a calmer state, Mario softly pats his face, which wakes him up in a fright. He breathes heavily in a semiconscious state, finally recovering.

"What?" He asks Mario.

"It's OK, you just had a bad dream."

"So you decided to wake me up?"

"Yes, I didn't want you to hurt yourself."

"Next time, mind your own business!" Alesky snaps.

"Next time, I will!" Mario retorts.

Alesky abruptly turns, and Mario storms back to his bed, calling Alesky derogatory names in Italian.

"Mario, I can understand you!" Alesky says, annoyed.

"I know," responds Mario.

* * *

By midmorning, Mario is alone in the hut finishing the letter he began the night before, without the tears.

Caro Mamma e Papa,

I have arrived in Australia after a long journey. I didn't imagine it was so far away. It's very different here—the trees, the sounds, the animals and the people. Nothing like the pictures they show you in the immigration brochures. The Australians are different; they speak a kind of English that is sometimes hard to understand, you know, a different dialect, like the Calabrese. They call us wogs and dagos, we just call them stupid. I haven't seen a kangaroo yet, but plenty of birds, rabbits and animals they call possums, which sometimes keep us awake at night when they play on the roof. I forgot the flies—too may flies, they drive you crazy. We stay in a camp while we wait for the government men to give us work; it's taking longer than I thought. There are many Italians, and other people from all over Europe, and also some families. The children play happily outside, but often, as I pass the huts, I hear the adults crying. If only the children could gift their hopeful innocence to their parents. The food is terrible, but don't worry, Mamma, I am eating what I can, and if my friend Pietro catches a rabbit, we will cook it the Italian way. I can imagine it now, Mamma, how you make the roasted rabbit with the onions and potatoes—so delicious. As soon as I get work, I will send money, some for you and the family and the rest to save for when I return. Please be at ease knowing that I am well, and one day I will see you all again, hopefully much wiser and richer.

Your loving son,
Mario

Alesky walks into the hut, reaches for a packet of cigarettes, and offers one to Mario. He politely declines Alesky's peace offering but gives him a smile. Alesky sits on his bed and places his cigarettes back into his pocket.

Genaro and Stella walk into the hut, kissing and giggling like two teenagers. He pins her against the wall and begins to kiss the cleavage of her large breasts tenderly. She moans with pleasure, breathes deeply, and then spots Mario and Alesky. Genaro turns sharply and stares the pair down, clearly giving the signal that he would like some privacy.

"Come on, " says Mario to Alesky.

"Fucking Italians," retorts Alesky.

"*Sì.*" Genaro smirks.

"We'll wait outside; it shouldn't take long," Mario says.

Genaro and Stella ignore the comment as he closes the door with his foot, burying his face into Stella's chest.

Alesky and Mario sit on the step outside their hut; in the distance, they see Pietro setting up his rabbit trap again. Just as he's finishing, he is approached by a patrolman who orders him to dismantle everything and move on. Mario and Alesky laugh at Pietro as he kicks the box and tangles himself in the string. Two Hungarian girls walking by also find the situation hilarious. They eye the two men, and one of them gives Mario a wink and a smile. Mario smiles back at her as she continues to walk on, giggling, with her friend.

"You should go for that, Mario."

"No, I'm not marrying anyone from here. I'll go back to Italy once I've made enough money."

"Who said anything about marriage?" Alesky opens up his jacket to reveal a variety of goods, including condoms. Mario declines.

"You shouldn't be so stubborn in your ideas, you don't know what destiny has in store for you!" advises Alesky.

"Destiny has no say in it, all I need is time. I know what I need to do, and nothing will stop me."

"Destiny and time are bedfellows."

Mario squints. "What are you saying?"

"What I'm saying is, you don't know how things will work out, you need to have an open mind."

"My mind is very open, clear, nothing blocking it. I know exactly what I must do—make money, get home and restart the family cantina!"

"We have very different ideas of what an open mind is."

"What are your plans?" Mario asks.

"No plans for me. Plans are for the inexperienced and hopeful."

"You speak rubbish. Are you saying that you live day to day with no hope for the future?"

"I'm saying you can't plan everything in your life and expect it to turn out exactly as you envisaged, you need to adjust for change."

"Nothing will change my mind about going home. What else do you have in that walking shop of yours?"

Alesky opens up both flaps of his jacket. Mario inspects the goods on offer.

"How much for the chewing gum?"

"Two pence."

Mario hands him the money. "Can you get olive oil?"

"Mmm, I think so. Why do you want olive oil?"

"For the rabbit cacciatore...if Pietro ever catches one."

Banging noises, moans and groans continue from inside the hut. Mario shifts around uncomfortably as Stella and Genaro reach their climax. Alesky reaches inside his pocket.

"Cigarette?"

Mario takes the cigarette happily.

Alesky lights it up. "This one is free, the next one will cost you," quips Alesky.

Kiehl Scheiberrne, a patrol officer, approaches the two men smoking on the steps. Without his uniform, he would not be notable—balding, and with eyes that seem to have no colour. He speaks with a German accent.

"What's going on in there?" he asks.

Alesky answers him in perfect German. "None of your concern, Boches!"

Kiehl is taken aback at the word 'Boches,' a nickname that was used for a German soldier during World War II.

"People are allowed to have some privacy," Alesky says, almost shouting. Kiehl stares him down, but Alesky wins the standoff, and the patrol guard walks away.

"What did you say to him?" asks Mario.

"Something that makes me believe he has a guilty conscience," Alesky replies.

"What is a guilty conscience?"

"It's when your mind reminds you that you have done something wrong in your life," Alesky explains. Mario looks puzzled.

"Look, Mario, all I know is they arrested many war criminals, but many more went free."

"You think he is a war criminal?" Mario asks, shocked.

"I don't know, but if you find a weakness in a man, you use it."

Mario ponders Alesky's last statement, and after a short period of silence, he asks, "Who is Ljubica?"

"No one you need to know about, my friend."

Genaro and Stella exit the hut, looking satisfied.

"Where did you get the cigarettes?" asks Genaro in Italian.

"Six pence a packet," replies Alesky, also in Italian, as he opens up his jacket store, revealing the contraband offerings. Genaro looks to Mario for approval. He nods his head as if to say, "You can trust him." Genaro hands over the money. He unravels the packet, takes a cigarette out and lights it up as he notices Pietro in the distance, again struggling to set up his rabbit trap.

"What the fuck is Pietro doing?" He takes a drag of his cigarette and passes it to Stella. "He is all brawn and no brains!"

Genaro grabs a nearby stick and walks in Pietro's direction, determination in his eyes. He would show everyone how to catch a rabbit.

Stella sits next to Mario on the step and takes a drag of the cigarette as all three smile at Genaro stomping across the field with the stick in his hand, ready for battle.

"Mario, will you help me with the business?" Alesky points to his jacket. "I'll give you thirty percent."

Mario looks to Alesky, then to Stella.

"Stella, would you like to buy something?" he asks in Italian.

"Do you have chocolate?" Stella asks.

Alesky shakes his head.

"How about some chewing gum?" Mario says.

"OK, how mucha?" says Stella in her broken English.

"Two pence," answers Mario, impressed by her attempt at English. Mario and Alesky watch as Stella delves into the crevasse of her large breasts, pulls out a small coin purse, takes out the two pennies, then places the coin purse back into her cleavage; the men's eyes never drift as the purse is swallowed up and disappears. She gives the coins to Mario, and Alesky hands her a packet of chewing gum. Mario hands Alesky one of the pennies.

"Fifty percent."

"Forty percent," replies Alesky.

"Fifty percent if you want the Italian market!"

Stella rises from the step. "Ciao!" She blows them a kiss and walks away.

When they finish watching Stella and her swaying buttocks, Mario turns to Alesky.

"OK. Fifty percent. Fucking Italians!" Alesky says.

"When you find a man's weakness, you must use it!"

Alesky, unamused, shakes Mario's hand, and the deal is done.

* * *

A gathering of New Australians forms near the shower block, where Alesky and Mario do a roaring trade in the sale of contraband items that no other jacket shop has: top-quality alcohol, personal items, cigarettes and sought-after condiments. The crowd only disperses when the Area Patrol is in sight. What they do not know is that Kiehl and the camp supervisor, Brigadier Sinclair, are watching and monitoring from afar, identifying black market culprits.

Father Kelly, the local Catholic priest, walks by the crowd and waves at them. Giovanni calls him over.

"What can I do for you, my son?"

"Father, can you talk to your boss?"

"Mr Dobson?" asks Father Kelly.

"No, no—God. Can you ask him to give us good food to eat?" Everyone laughs at the request.

Luca Locatelli now joins the conversation. "Truly, Father, we are here in this place, with bad food and bad houses. We were promised jobs, but no jobs are available. Some of us have been here for over three months, can't you do something about it?"

"Have faith, my son, things will improve." He cuts off at the sight of a stretcher with a body covered by a sheet, carried by two hospital interns. The priest makes the sign of the cross as the body passes.

"In the name of the Father, and of the Son, and of the Holy Spirit."

All the Catholics in the crowd join in with the ritual sacramental blessing and collectively say, "Amen."

"What happened to him?" asks Mario.

"He died of natural causes," replies Father Kelly as he leaves to follows the body.

"Bullshit!" says Luca. "There happen to be a lot of people dying of natural causes lately."

"What do you mean?" Mario asks.

"That was not natural death. It was suicide." There is a shocked silence. "People are so desperate. They came out here to build a future, and look what we get! I'm going to arrange a meeting with the consulate. If the Australian government isn't going to do something, I will."

"I read in the newspaper that there's a recession in Australia at the moment and the government is working towards creating more jobs," Mario says. "Maybe we need to be patient?"

"No!" says Luca forcibly. "We have been tricked and I have no patience left. The recession is not our problem. I don't trust what government men say, and if they can't give us what they promised, then they should send us back home. Why can't they at least do that, instead of leaving us here suffering, away from our families? I'll let you all know when the meeting is on, we need to do something!"

Everyone nods their heads in agreement, but are distracted when Pietro and Genaro walk by holding two dead rabbits up in the air, very satisfied with themselves, oblivious to what has just transpired.

* * *

A group of men and women are gathered in front of the washing line around block thirteen. Accordions and harmonicas are being played in harmony with makeshift drums and tambourines while Pietro sings "Reginella Campagnola". People are dancing, laughing, happy and joyful, sharing this little piece of home together, all of their troubles and boundaries forgotten for the moment. Behind and between the rows of washed bedsheets drying in the sun, Genaro, Stella, Mario and Alesky watch over the carefully prepared rabbit, which is cooking with tomatoes and onions in a pan on an illegal kerosene Primus stove. Finally, the much-awaited gastronomic dream will become a reality.

Mario reaches for a small bottle of oil from his jacket, and Alesky pulls out a bottle of wine. Genaro takes the oil and wine; he carefully pours just the right amount from each bottle, in just the right way, taking so much care it is as if his life depends on it. The singing and dancing Italians serve as a decoy for the patrolling camp guards. Mario sneaks a peek through the hanging sheets at the joyous spectacle and sees Pietro loving the attention he is receiving from his adoring fans—mostly women—as his wonderful voice fills the air with hope and happiness. Mario understands that Pietro doesn't want to return to Italy, because of his romantic entanglement. The singing Pietro is very different from the insecure and stuttering one, and Mario is in awe of him.

Mario's smile turns into a frown as he spots Kiehl approaching, looking as suspicious and autocratic as ever. "It's the Boches, he's coming!" he whispers.

Stella unbuttons her cardigan, revealing her weapons of mass distraction. "No worry, I fix," she says and dramatically slides herself from behind the hanging sheet.

"Brava," says Genaro, still overseeing the rabbit as if it is a needy infant.

The music plays, and the participants clap and dance as Kiehl approaches. Stella grabs Kiehl's hand and dances in front of him seductively. He is transfixed, and she leads him as far away from the makeshift kitchen as she can. He finds it very hard not to stare at the bouncing bosoms in front of him. Everyone joins in, encouraging the unlikely dancing couple, and they clap with excitement at the sight of the stoic guard almost enjoying himself. Mario reports: "Looks like it's working, he can't keep his eyes off Stella."

Genaro turns the rabbit pieces to ensure they are all covered by the simmering sauce. "Thank goodness he's not gay!" Genaro comments in Italian.

Mario laughs, but Alesky breathes a deep, pensive breath. To Genaro, nothing at this moment is more important than the rabbit, even if another man is halfway molesting his wife, which usually would result in a punch-up.

Eventually, Kiehl composes himself, remembering his position. He nods his head, gives Stella a polite smile, and leaves. The music continues; now they are playing the even more upbeat folk song "Finiculi Finicula", sung with gusto by Pietro and with help from the entire crowd. Genaro, Alesky and Mario have their noses over the rabbit, salivating as they bounce their bodies to the infectious music.

Suddenly, the sheets are thrown open, and the three cooks stand in shock as they stare at a frowning Kiehl, his mouth now turning up at the corners.

"Did you think a good set of tits could fool me? Cooking outside the mess hall is not permitted!" he shouts, and then kicks the Primus, causing the rabbit to fly out and land on the ground. Genaro cries in agony as he lunges to save as much of the stew as he can. The music stops, and Stella rushes to the sheet, unveiling the situation to the crowd behind her, all gasping at the spectacle as Kiehl continues to reprimand them.

"No cooking is allowed, do you not understand? Don't kill any more animals. Eat what they give you to eat and be grateful about it!"

Mario and Alesky hold Genaro back, preventing him from lunging at Kiehl. Many sets of angry eyes stare directly at the guard, who adjusts his collar nervously.

The air is thick with tension, but the angry eyes start to twinkle as two other Italian men walk by with a dead sheep propped up on their shoulders. Everyone starts to cheer and clap, to the bemusement of the two sheep thieves. Kiehl, whose joy has turned to frustration, walks away, not daring to confront the rowdy crowd. Alesky leaves Genaro to salvage as many rabbit pieces as possible, helped by Stella. The crowd voices its disgust and makes various crude gestures after Kiehl.

"Hey, Boches, stop...stop!" shouts Alesky.

Kiehl turns to eyeball him. "I'm Polish! Just because I speak German doesn't mean I am German!"

"Just because you're Polish doesn't mean you're innocent," Alesky responds. Kiehl's neck and face turn from a pale pink to bright red as he grabs Alesky's shirtfront.

"I know who you are—I have known many like you!" says Alesky.

Kiehl relaxes his hold on Alesky. "What would you know? Just watch yourself." He walks away, almost jogging towards the administration block.

Mario reaches Alesky. "You OK?"

Alesky answers with an unconvincing, "Yeah, but I think you

lot are going to find cooking the sheep a bit hard to hide."

Mario puts his arm around Alesky as they walk back to the gathering. The rabbit is ruined, but the dancing and singing continue.

CHAPTER 4: WHAT RULES?

Dobson and Sinclair sit in their comfortable quarters drinking a smooth port and smoking even smoother cigars, soft classical music playing in the background. They discuss the current issues of the camp, which include the emerging black market, the lack of order and obedience within the community and the arrival of more immigrants even though there are no jobs available.

Brigadier Sinclair reports: "There is quite an unrest developing, particularly amongst the Italians, who were expecting to be placed in jobs within a few weeks of their arrival, but instead, most of them have been in the camp for more than three months."

"The Italian consulate is coming next week," Dobson says.

"What for?"

"To talk about the job situation. He's had reports from some of our guests that they are not happy."

"Bloody communists!" complains Sinclair.

There is a knock on the door. "Come in," says Dobson.

Kiehl enters. "Hello, Director...sir."

"Hello, Kiehl."

"I would like to let you know about the situation at hand, sir."

"Have you been able to confirm any black market activity?"

"Still working on that, sir. However, some of the Italians have been cooking rabbits outside the mess hall. I caught them today."

"Bloody hell...why don't those bloody wogs listen?" scoffs Sinclair.

"That's not all, sir." The two men sit silently in anticipation. "They also stole a sheep from a nearby farm, and I daresay they're looking to cook that as well."

"Bastards, I'll have their nuts!" shouts Sinclair.

After a deep sigh, the director says, "No, leave it...Find the farmer and give him money for the goddamn sheep, we don't want to escalate the situation before the consulate gets here. Those spaghetti munchers complain about the food so much, we should let it rest for now."

"Yes, sir, but don't you—"

"That will be all, Kiehl."

"Yes, sir." Kiehl leaves.

The two men adjust their positions in their chairs, and the warmth of the burning fire makes them sweat more than it should. They begin to discuss in earnest the Italians' disrespectful behaviour, their apparent lack of interest in learning English, their national and personal characteristics, and how these qualities are not going to make them good workers, let alone good Australians.

* * *

Mario leans against the outer wall of his hut, staring into the vast horizon. The eerie dusk sky leaves him with a sense of wonder. It's such a different landscape than home, and it seems to be ever-changing. A noise startles him, and he blinks twice; he is confronted with the vision of a large kangaroo. It seems so close, but, in fact, it is quite far behind the fencing. The kangaroo stares at Mario as if to say, "What are you doing here?" Mario is in awe. He has only ever read about this animal, and it has such an endearing and wondrous face; the sight transfixes him.

Mario rushes into his hut.

"Pietro! Pietro! Quick, come with me!"

Pietro gets up, but he is annoyed. *"What?"* he demands.

"Quick, come—a kangaroo!" Immediately, Pietro follows him to the fence line, but the kangaroo is nowhere to be seen.

"W-w-where is it?" asks Pietro.

"It...it was here, then it...it...Ahh, now it's gone."

"Hmm, w-what does kangaroo tastes like?" Pietro wonders.

"Go back inside," retorts Mario, almost offended that Pietro could say such a thing about the majestic animal he just encountered.

"W-what are you doing out here?" Pietro asks.

"I'm waiting for Alesky."

"Mario, I—I am n-n-not sure about him. I don't like him."

"He's OK, don't worry. Go back inside."

Pietro shrugs his shoulders and leaves.

Mario looks to the horizon, again wondering if he imagined it all. A bird whistles, and Mario turns and is nearly hit with a hessian bag as it's hurled over the fence. He avoids another and then picks up both bags. They are heavier than usual. He drags them into the hut and places them on his bed. Mario opens one bag and fishes for the cigarette packets, then sees why the bags are so heavy; several cans of paint are scattered amongst the other items. Alesky enters with two other bags.

Mario doesn't ask any questions. He retrieves four packets of cigarettes to give to his roommates as hush money.

There is a knock on the door, and Luca enters the hut. "Did you get it?"

"Yes," answers Alesky as he hands over two cans of paint, then holds his hand out for the payment.

"You should donate the paint, it's for a good cause!" says Luca.

"It's your cause, not mine."

Luca pays him. "There will be a meeting tonight, are you all coming?"

They all nod except for Alesky, who is disinterested, too busy replenishing his jacket shop.

Kiehl watches the steady flow of people entering and exiting Alesky and Mario's hut from afar, careful not to be noticed. He hangs around for about an hour and a half, tallying the amount of customers. He sees Alesky and Mario exit the hut and immediately knows they are on the move to sell their goods around the complex. Kiehl will need to wait a couple more days; timing is crucial.

* * *

Alesky and Mario have had a couple of good days selling their wares. They are now crouched at the back of their hut, digging under the exposed stilts, retrieving more stock from their hiding place to replenish their jackets. Alesky crawls backwards, grasping the hessian bag full of goods, and spots two pairs of shoes at his eye level. He turns to Mario, who continues to dig, and kicks him. Mario now sees what Alesky sees. The shoes belong to Kiehl and Sinclair.

"Well, well, well...the dago and Balt corner shop," Sinclair says mockingly. Kiehl laughs. Mario and Alesky scurry to stand up. Alesky offers Sinclair a packet of cigarettes; he takes it and says, "Turn out your pockets." They hesitate.

"You heard him!" shouts Kiehl.

Mario looks to Alesky for some sort of guidance. Alesky reluctantly takes out the contents of his pockets, mainly cash, and hands it over to Kiehl as directed. Mario does the same. Sinclair grabs the hessian bag full of contraband from Alesky's hand.

"See you round, cobber."

"Do you know who you're working with?" blurts out Alesky, pointing at the patrol guard. Kiehl stops in his tracks; the supervisor looks at Kiehl, and then back to Alesky.

"I don't care!"

Alesky stares Kiehl down. "Maybe other people will care," he says.

Sinclair walks away as Kiehl approaches Alesky.

"Shut your mouth, or you're going to find yourself in a lot more trouble," Kiehl says coldly.

Mario holds Alesky back, and they look to each other in frustration, but they're both glad to see the back of Kiehl and the supervisor.

"We have to stop now, they're going to tell the big boss," Mario says.

"Don't be stupid, Mario, they are going to keep the money, and they won't tell anyone else."

"Fucking *barstardos*...even the Australian is a greedy thief."

"Oppressors come in many languages, my friend."

"All that hard-earned money, gone!"

"Mario, Mario, Mario...you need to always be a step ahead,

you overprivileged Italian."

Alesky reaches down the back of his pants into his underwear and fishes for something. He produces a wad of notes; he divides it into two and offers one half to Mario, who hesitates to take the cash.

"Well, do you want it or not?"

"I don't know, Alesky...I think my black market days are over. Maybe God is trying to tell me something."

"It will be OK, trust me, Mario."

"I trust you."

"That's your first mistake, you shouldn't trust anyone."

"You don't trust people?"

"Oh, I trust people—I just don't trust human nature."

Mario smiles. "I think I need to listen to the Australian God!" he says, pointing his finger to the sky and sliding down the side of the hut until he reaches the sandy ground.

"I didn't think you were religious, Mario."

"Well, I don't mind God, I just hate priests."

Alesky throws the money into Mario's lap. "Don't let this one little mishap get you down."

"No, that's it for me, no more." Mario tries to return the money.

"Keep it as a redundancy package."

"What is a redundancy package?"

"It's a retirement gift. See you around, cobber. I've got losses to make up."

Mario watches Alesky dance a little tarantella and then skip away, just as happy as he was before. Mario accepts his redundancy package and puts the money in his pocket; he decides he's not that righteous after all. He is homesick, however, and memories of his youth come flooding back to him as he basks in the rising sun peeking through the dark clouds.

* * *

The quaint little cantina just outside the centre of Bovino, nestled in the mountainous region of Puglia, is alive with customers. Business is booming, and a bust is looming: people are buying but nobody is paying. In the middle of a world war, money becomes increasingly scarce. Bovino doesn't ever see any fighting—it does, on occasion, host the odd group of German army officers, who are arrogant but never hostile—however, many wives and mothers have paid the price for Mussolini's allegiance to Hitler.

Antonietta, heavily pregnant with her fifth child, scurries around as best she can, serving customers, replenishing stock, preparing the orders and doing anything else that's needed to streamline the operations of the cantina. Euplio is around, but he mostly just complicates things, so she leaves him to liaise with customers, bark out orders, and, at times, do some of the heavy lifting that has become increasingly difficult for her. Euplio never verbalises his admiration for his wife—he takes advantage of her good nature and excellent work ethic, and she is very much an asset to him. In return, Antonietta never verbalises her contempt of her husband—most times, he is a liability, and his stubbornness, narcissism and libido are only just tolerated.

Antonietta is tired, and there are signs that the baby is ready to see the world. She wearily closes her eyes. *The children will be home from school soon, and they will help me*, she thinks as she takes a well-earned five-minute break, leaning over the counter for some needed rest. Two local priests soon interrupt her.

"*Buongiorno*, Signora Lanzani."

Antonietta respectfully exchanges greetings with Padre Domenico and Padre Crescenzo.

"We are here to collect for the less fortunate," says Padre Domenico.

"The less fortunate," repeats Padre Crescenzo.

The Lanzani family has fallen on tough times, but nowhere near as tough as most of the villagers, who can't even put food on the table for their families, so when the clergy come around asking for donations, Antonietta is more than happy to oblige. She never tells Euplio about the donations, as he inherently dislikes the church. She and Euplio often argue because he gives credit to dubious people in the hope of being paid, while she knows the church will help people in need. Euplio doesn't see it that way—in his opinion, giving things away for free will never get a return, emotional or otherwise. At least with credit, there is the intent to pay. Antonietta doesn't understand his logic, and neither does she try to reason with him; she just goes about things her own way and tells him as little as possible.

Padre Domenico peruses the wares around the cantina, calculating in his head what he will need.

"Some pecorino and burrata cheese, olives, a prosciutto, two or three capocollo and sausage, some focaccia and loaves of bread, and a dozen or so bottles of wine...That should do. For the poor!" he decides.

"For the poor," Padre Crescenzo repeats.

"Of course," responds Antonietta, sweat appearing on her brow. She is happy to donate, though she can't help but think the poor have very good taste; they are about to receive some of the best produce in the cantina, and most probably in the region.

"*Grazie*, Signora. Could you deliver it to the rectory, as I have a bad leg?"

"Yes, of course, Father Dominic."

"*Mille grazie.* God bless you."

"God bless you," repeats Padre Crescenzo.

Antonietta watches Padre Domenico limp out of the establishment with his walking stick, helped by Padre Crescenzo. She runs her hands over her belly.

When eleven-year-old Mario and his three siblings return from school, they bustle into the cantina to find their mother, unusually, sitting in a chair in the corner of the room. She is exhausted, but this does not stop her from barking out instructions to her children—after they each give her a kiss—which they all obey.

"Mario, sweetheart, come here."

"*Sì*, Mamma," he says as he goes to her and takes her shaking hand. "What's wrong, Mamma?"

"Nothing, I just need you to bring the cart to the rectory."

Mario looks to the handcart full of produce prepared by his mother. "All that for the priests?" he asks.

"It's for the poor. God watches everyone, it's right to do good for others."

Mario picks up the handcart full of produce and does as his mother asked.

"Don't say anything to your father!" she remembers to add.

Mario nods his head and begins his journey to the rectory. When he reaches the church, unsure where he is to deliver the goods, Mario knocks on several doors and windows; there is no answer, but he looks through a window at a large table, beautifully set, ready for a function. He looks around again, but sees no one, so he sits on a step with the cart next to him, waiting. The noise from his rumbling stomach reminds him of his hunger. He takes a piece of focaccia and wraps it around some cured sausage; after all, it is from his family's cantina, so it isn't stealing. On his second bite, Padre Domenico spots him through the window and shouts to Mario to stop eating the food, which belongs to the church. Mario takes one more bite and then puts the half-eaten focaccia back. Padre Domenico opens the door for Mario and shows him where to store the donations, continuing to berate him about taking something that doesn't belong to him. Mario feels the priest is out of order, but he doesn't make his feelings known—instead, he does as the priest asks and unloads the cart in the cellar, exactly as instructed.

To Mario's surprise, the cellar is full of all sorts of small goods: preserved fruit and vegetables, cheeses, and more wine than his father's cellar. Mario may only be eleven, but he is suspicious. Why is the food and drink allocated for the poor locked away in the rectory basement? Padre Domenico shows Mario the way out, not with a "thank you" but with an abrupt: "*Via!*"

Mario returns to the family cantina to find his mother sitting on the floor with her back against the wall. He rushes to her. Antonietta assures him that she is alright, she has been through four previous births, she knows exactly what is happening; all she wants at this moment is for Mario to just hold her hand, which he does.

"Mamma, how many gods are there?" Mario asks.

"What are you saying? There's only one."

"It seems to me that the Italian God isn't watching the

priests here in Bovino."

Antonietta chuckles. She squeezes Mario's hand during a contraction, and manages to ask between gritted teeth: "Why do you think so?"

"Because they have all the food for the poor locked away."

Antonietta squeezes his hand again as another contraction rolls through her. "Perhaps you're mistaken."

"No, Mamma."

"They are the messengers of God, but they are still human, my love." Another contraction, and the floor is flooded with watery liquid.

"Do you want me to call Father?"

"No! For the love of God, call Aunt Teresa."

Antonietta gives Mario a forced but reassuring smile, and he kisses her hand and then rushes off to call his aunt. He isn't worried about his mother—he has seen it all before, and understands that he is about to get another brother or sister.

After calling his aunt, Mario goes back to the rectory, just to make sure he isn't mistaken. He isn't. Through the window, he sees priests, German officers and some nicely dressed women enjoying some of the food and drink he delivered. Mario's confusion turns to antipathy as he watches Padre Crescenzo carve the prosciutto with precision while conversing and laughing with the guests, who are freely enjoying the flowing wine.

Smack! Mario is hit on the side of his head by Padre Domenico's walking stick.

"What are you doing here? Get out of here, you piece of shit!"

Mario collects himself, once his ears stop ringing, then runs away.

It begins to drizzle at Bonegilla, and the memory of Mario's

53

experience at the rectory fades, but the sting of Padre Domenico's walking stick remains.

CHAPTER 5: THE LESSSON

"English lessons for all blocks in fifteen minutes in the learning hall!" blurts out the Bonegilla loudspeaker. It repeats the announcement again in German. The block supervisors round up the migrants who don't speak English or German. They are all herded towards the hall, passing the Italian block number thirteen. Mario and Alesky start to follow. Genaro scratches his head and asks in his loud Italian voice, "Where are you two going? You know how to speak English."

"What else have we got to do? Come on, come with us," says Mario.

Just then, Stella arrives.

"I've got better things to do. Go to your lessons, and don't come back for at least one hour!" Genaro tells them. Stella and Genaro enter the hut and shuffle all the occupants out before shutting the door.

The hall is full of people scattered everywhere in a state of confusion. The place looks more like a cattle auction than an educational facility—there are Australian flags, Union Jacks, and pictures of the queen hanging in prominent positions, the only traces of considered civilisation. Three teachers stand on the stage, and are introduced to the crowd by the head language teacher. The head teacher writes a simple sentence on the board: *Cat sat on the mat.* He instructs the ones who can understand what's written to follow the teacher holding the notice that reads "ENGLISH SPEAKING", and the German-speaking people to follow the teacher holding the notice that reads "GERMAN SPEAKING". The rest are instructed to stay in the hall. This process is meant to grade the ones who can speak English, the ones who can speak German and the rest; however, when nobody is left in the hall, it is clear that the ones who cannot understand what is being said—such as the Russians, Italians and Greeks—just blindly follow the moving crowd. It takes a little longer to organise by language barriers than had been anticipated. Finally, the groups are sorted, and as the English- and German-speaking people move out, the others all join in with a very out-of-tune, comical version of "Three Blind Mice".

The English classroom consists of mainly displaced Eastern European persons who came with a good knowledge of the English language from the English-run camps in Europe, and people of other nationalities who either arrived with knowledge or have been at Bonegilla long enough to pick up a basic understanding. Mario and Alesky sit with about thirty Italians who have been at the camp for over two months; victims of the 1951 recession, which constricted the job market but not the moral obligation that the migrants felt they were owed.

Each participant is given a book prepared by the Commonwealth Office for the Department of Immigration titled *I Can Read English.*

The teacher welcomes the motley crew of students with the introduction of a film that shows people that are important to Australia, such as the queen, governor general and prime minister, and also Australian wildlife, which includes the Aborigines. The film aims to explain Australian cultural heritage and the cohesive nature of Australian society—which applies only if you can speak English without an accent, it seems, and if you are white. They are then taught to recite poetry such as "The Man from Snowy River" and "I Love a Sunburnt Country" to immerse them in the Australian psyche, but the truth is, they are just words and mean nothing to the misplaced immigrant guests of Bonegilla. Songs like "Roaming in the Gloaming" are sung, which entice the singer to roll the R's, so they could relate and adjust, but another truth is that the vast difference between the English and Australian accents only causes confusion. It is quite a hurdle to jump, and not easily done with just a few English lessons taught with haste and with as much enthusiasm as a sloth hanging from a branch.

However, the teacher does ask if anyone has any questions, to which one of the Italians blurts out: "Bonegilla sounds Italian...Is it?"

"No, it's not," says the teacher. "Bonegilla is an Aboriginal word for 'meeting of the waters', and your time here will mark your first steps towards settlement in Australia." This was said with some pride.

"Well, that cannot happen if every day you go to employment office, and everyday there is no job!" came the response.

The class all agree, most of them protesting and voicing their dissatisfaction, the decibels rising. Sensing the mood turning slightly hostile, the teacher barks, "The lesson is over!" and abruptly leaves.

Mario and Pietro walk back to their hut and find Genaro leaning against the wall, one leg propped up, head hanging down, inhaling and exhaling his cigarette with deep, long breaths. They exchange greetings, but Mario notices that Genaro is not his usual animated self.

"Everything OK, Genaro?"

"Yes...but, you're right, Mario, I need to learn to speak English," he answers in Italian.

"Good, that's very good, it will make life a lot easier for you. Why did you change your mind?"

"Umm...I don't want to be Australian, I want to be Italian."

Mario reverts to speaking Italian as he realises that Genaro does not fully understand what he's saying.

"You will always be Italian, Genaro."

"Yes, but my child will be Australian, and I need to help Stella."

Mario is overjoyed by the news that Stella is pregnant and congratulates the father-to-be. He thinks Stella is a smart woman who is already starting to speak English and probably doesn't need as much help from Genaro as he thinks she does.

Genaro looks at Mario. "How do I learn English?"

Mario instructs Genaro to wait as he goes inside the hut to retrieve his Italian/English dictionary. He shoves the dictionary into Genaro's hand along with his copy of *I Can Read English* and explains the mechanics of English, warning him that it won't be easy but that he needs to persist. Mario tells him that he must read—the newspapers are a good start, even if he doesn't understand the words—and listen when someone speaks English, and look at their mannerisms, as this can give you a clue as to what is being said.

Mario continues to advise an attentive Genaro to think the words in Italian and then think them in English. He needs to think in English, but he will always be Italian, and if someone teases him, Mario says not to worry and get mad. He will come to recognise the sound of the language, and when he is bilingual, he will have an advantage because he will understand Australians but they won't always understand him. Mario rationalises that most Australians can only speak one type of English but that Europeans can often speak more than one language.

"We need any advantage we can get, right?" says Genaro, revealing his vulnerability for the first time.

Mario gives him a comforting smile.

"This is a good decision for you, Stella, and your child," he says.

"You know what scares me? When my child is three years old, he will speak better English than me!"

Mario shakes his hand and pats him on the back. He says in English, "It will all be good...mate!"

Genaro gets the context of Mario's statement and nods his head. They join the others and immerse themselves in the routine Italian banter. The gathering increases in size as they are joined by other migrants, who discuss current affairs. The conversation mainly revolves around food quality but also encompasses employment prospects, money matters, dreams of the future, and failed expectations.

Luca Locatelli and Nicola D'Angelo approach the group with papers for all of them to sign. They explain that their signatures are needed so that the petition can be presented to the Italian consul when he arrives. Everyone signs without hesitation, and the discussions resume with even more vigour and conviction.

The Commonwealth Employment Service office has an obligation to be operating, even though jobs are scarce. This is not the fault of the immigration centre but rather a problem of a government system that allows little room for flexibility, coupled with the continuing recession. This is not fully understood by the migrants, and their handicaps of little or no English, feelings of constraint, little independence and no sense of control over their futures were leading to an ever-increasing, emotionally fuelled environment—not to mention the inherent volatile passion of the Italians.

Nevertheless, each day, most of them would stand in line at the CES office, hoping this day would be different; each day is no different, many of them thumping the officer's tables and exiting the CES hut cursing the day they decided to come to Australia.

One day while the job seekers are standing in the line, a couple of men who look like peasants, but are actually farmers from the surrounding area, walk up and look over the prospective employees. The farmers are in need of seasonal help, and they stop at Luca Locatelli, looking him up and down, and then proceed to touch him to see if he has any muscles. Luca immediately steps back, brushes off the farmers' hands, and says, "Take your dirty hands off of me or I will flatten you! Do you think I am cattle? I'm not cattle, and if you don't want to employ me, then send me back to Europe!"

The farmer is perplexed—not because of Luca's reaction but due to the fact that he can speak English. In his frustration, Luca picks up some stones and starts throwing them at the farmers. Although the stones hit the farmers as they run away, no harm is done. Luca then turns his attention to the CES office, and soon, others follow him in stoning the wooden building.

Mario and Alesky, who have witnessed it all, try their hardest to defuse the situation and calm everyone down. By the time the Area Patrol has come, everyone has dispersed and a shell-shocked CES officer is staring at two broken windows and a dented wooden wall.

* * *

Two days after the CES office attack, Paulo Tereni, the Italian consul, arrives in Bonegilla. A crowd of over two thousand Italian immigrants waits as patiently as it can for the consul to address the audience. He quickly flicks through the pages and pages of signatures on the petition he has been given, then fumbles with his pen and scribbles a few words on his notepad and whispers to his assistant. There is no microphone, and he isn't sure how he will be heard over the noise of two thousand people. Paulo wipes the sweat from his brow as his assistant dispenses soap, razor blades, socks, woollen jumpers and gum boots to the crowd, which seems to appease them somewhat. It is early July, and even though winter is well underway, the supplies are welcomed. Some of the men are particularly happy with the gum boots, as now they can play soccer on the muddy makeshift sports field.

"*Buongiorno fratelli e sorelle!*" Paulo announces.

The hall becomes silent. His speech continues in their native language.

"I know we are all here to discuss your concerns, and I am here to help you." The crowd claps and cheers.

"I realise there are no jobs at the moment, but the Australian government is working to fix this."

"Why did they bring us here if there are no jobs?" Nicola shouts out. Paulo has no answer, but even if he did, Nicola isn't going to be interrupted.

"This emigration is a swindle! We were promised jobs, and they told us it would take no longer than ten days, but we get here and one week passes, then two, then three—one month, then two, and still no work for us. They give jobs here to the Slavic, the Polish and the Russians but not for us! We're not used to this land of meat and three veg—we don't like porridge for breakfast. It's OK if you are used to it, but we are not. Most of us come from families who are used to cooked food, and our own bread. These Australians don't know how to cook!"

There is an eruption of cheers as Nicola continues.

"There is nothing to do here, we are wasting our time, and many of us have families waiting for us to send them money. We are sick of being pushed around and treated like nobody's sons. We are workers, and very proud of that honour. We are not beggars; many of us are mechanics, electricians, builders, but these skills don't matter! We want to let the Australian authorities know of our humiliation, and that we are human beings with souls. We want work or repatriation!"

The hall explodes with a deafening cheer. The Italian consul holds up his hands, nodding and trying to silence the masses, but it takes a while. Eventually he is able to speak.

"I understand, and I want to help you all. Firstly, I suggest you elect a representative for each block, and that you report to me every week so I know what's going on. When you have delegated your block commissioner, organise some peaceful demonstrations. The director has been forewarned, and has no objection, but please be patient, and no more throwing rocks!"

Paulo is pleased with how the crowd welcomes his sugges- tions, not knowing the looming storm he has helped to create.

Later, Paulo sits formally in the director's office, waiting for him to finish perusing the petition from the Italian migrants. Brigadier Sinclair stands at attention near the doorway. Mr Dobson continues to flick through the many pages; Paulo interrupts the silence.

"There are over two thousand signatures, sir. I had no idea there were that many Italians here. Is there anything that can be done?"

Dobson sighs. "I've been on the phone with the immigration minister, Harold Holt, and he tells me that there's not a lot that can be done at the moment, but they do recognise that the current situation is less than desirable. But the Italians need to be patient—throwing stones at the CES office isn't going to make things better for them. We don't get this sort of trouble with any of the DPs, and the Dutch, they are model citizens!"

"Sir, they just want to be heard and for their contracts to be honoured. You need to write to Holt and Menzies, as more needs to be done for the morale of these young men. Many are still teenagers who feel betrayed by the country they have chosen as their new fatherland. Maybe return the unemployed back to Italy."

"We both know that they wouldn't be here if their situation back in Italy weren't dire; they need to be appreciative of what's being done for them!"

"And we both know that they wouldn't be here if Australia didn't need migrants to do the jobs that nobody else wants!"

"Well, as soon as jobs that nobody else wants become available, they will get them!" This statement is followed by a silent intermission. The director, now wanting to soften the situation, eventually says, "Look, Paul..."

"Paulo," responds the Italian consul.

"Pa-llo...I'll do what I can, but you know my hands are tied.

Yours are too."

Paulo nods at this, the mood much less partisan. He shakes the director's hand and proceeds to leave.

"Pa-llo!" calls the director. "Can you be available for the next week or so? I might need your support as well."

"Sure, but write to Holt and Menzies, anyway, because my letters are not being answered."

"OK."

As soon as the consul leaves, Dobson turns to the head of patrol.

"Commission the sentries to guard all entries to the camp. No one that is not residing here, or without authorised permission, is to have access, especially the media. No media! We don't want them escalating this out of proportion."

At dinnertime the mess hall is full of chatter, as most of the Italians are deep in conversation about their plans to protest. Smelly mutton and vegetables are dredged out of terrines of water and sloshed onto each plate, and then smothered with sweet tomato sauce—a special treat for today. Most of the food remains untouched.

Alesky joins the table and sits next to Mario. Sporting a cut eye and scratches and bruises on his face, Alesky drives his fork into his meal and shovels it into his hungry mouth. His beaten face does not go unnoticed, but no one says anything.

Alesky breaks the silence.

"How are your protest plans going? It's been good for business—I'm selling a lot of paint. You sure you don't want in again, Mario?"

"No," responds Mario. "Alesky, what happened to you?"

Alesky shrugs the question off with a dismissive gesture. Pietro becomes increasingly agitated as he directs his stuttered concerns to Mario.

"*P-p-perche stai impegnato c-con quisto? C-cosa sai di lui? Parla sei lingue, ma c-chi parla sei lingue. Non e sospetto? Forse e un criminale.*" (Why do you hang with him? What do you know about him, except he speaks six languages. Who speaks six languages? Isn't that suspicious to you? He's probably some criminal.)

"I can understand you, Pietro," says Alesky with a mouth full of food.

"W-wella...wella are you? Are you *un criminale?*"

"Depends what side you're on," answers Alesky.

Nicola and Luca, together with some other irate fellow countrymen, approach just in the nick of time.

"*Vieni, raggazzi...*the protest starts now."

Everyone from the table rises to join the mob exiting the mess hall, except for Mario and Alesky. Mario stares down Alesky, who totally ignores him as he finishes the last bits of sloppy vegetables.

"What happened to you, Alesky? Is Alesky even your real name?"

"No, it's not," is all Alesky says. He takes an envelope out of his pocket and slides it across the table to Mario.

"Do you want me to post this for you?" questions Mario, looking at the letter, which has no address.

"No. If anything happens to me, send it to the Victorian police."

"Are you in trouble?"

"No, it's just insurance. Why are you not joining the others?"

"I'm more of a philosopher than a fighter"—Mario chuckles—"and I haven't been here as long as most of the others. I think we will have jobs soon enough."

"What are you going to do when you find a job?"

"I will work hard, make as much money as I can, and then go back home. I don't belong here. Australia is using me, and I am using Australia—we both win. How about you?"

"I've already won. However difficult things may get here, it's a paradise compared to the places I've been. Don't be in such a hurry to get back to Europe, Mario!"

"But I have family—a mother, father, brothers and sisters, and I can't see a future for me here. Do you have family?"

"No mother, no father, no siblings...no children."

"A wife?"

"And no Lubijca!"

A mob of around two hundred men, chanting, *"MANGIARE! LAVORE!"* (*FOOD! WORK!*) march towards the director's residence, fuelled by their disgust at the night's dinner. The director instructs his family to lock all doors and windows. The mob is relatively peaceful in its approach, with just a few bangs on the walls, but this still frightens the occupants, and the director, although very annoyed, thinks quickly to appease the pack. He picks up the phone.

"Tell the kitchen master to cook some spaghetti for these fucking Italians, and come here and get rid of them."

The chanting continues but becomes quieter when the patrol guard approaches.

"Alright, fellas, back to your huts. We heard ya. The director has ordered spaghetti to be cooked for you soon, so off ya go now."

Pacified by the news, the men scatter back to their lodgings, much calmer than before, and happy about the prospect of finally eating some pasta—a bit of home in a melamine bowl.

CHAPTER 6: THE PROTEST

The protests continue each day; the men are loud and persistent but relatively peaceful and organised. Separate demonstrations include marches to the administration block, the CES office, the block supervisor's office, the post office, the learning centre and even the church. Father Kelly, hoping for divine intervention, has been inwardly praying for rain to send them all back inside. Occasionally he addresses the protesters with words of religious verse, which are wholly disregarded by the majority of them.

Chants of *"Mangiare! Lavoro! Mangiare! Lavoro!"* continue. Various placards are waved, which read "We want jobs!" and "Your barbaric system is only worthy of stone age!" and "No work? Send us back home!" as well as some asking for better food.

The Area Patrol is scattered strategically, ready for any trouble, tentatively watching on, as are the other non-Italian migratory residents, some agreeing with the Italians and others shaking their heads in disapproval, but at least they are all being entertained. The director keeps a watchful eye from his office in the administration block. He is joined by the Italian consul, who has come for another meeting with the elected Italian block representatives. The meetings become increasingly heated, the representatives feeling that their efforts are being largely ignored by the authorities, and accusing the consul of not doing his job properly.

"Can't you sort this out?" Dobson directs his frustration towards the consul.

"I'll try my best, but I'm afraid this is a job for government policy reform."

"Well, we know that reform is a very blunt pair of scissors cutting through a lot of red tape, so right now, you will need to find a way. Tell them about the damn spaghetti!"

Paulo leaves the director's office and heads towards the protesting mob, targeting Luca Locatelli and Nicola D'Angelo, who seem to be the ringleaders.

Mario inwardly supports the cause but prefers to stand on the sidelines with Alesky and watch the circus roll by rather than participate directly—that is, until Luca drags him into the micro-meeting with the Italian consul. Mario occasionally darts frustrated glances at Alesky, amusing him to no end.

"You should not associate yourself with that communist mob," says Kiehl, sneaking up to Alesky.

Alesky does not show his surprise or his contempt. "They are not communists, you know that as well as I do. They just want what they were promised, and if any unfortunate accident should happen to me again, my Italian friends have a letter to give to the police."

"What, are you going to tell them about something I might have done to you?"

"No. I've told them what you might have done ten years ago."

"Ten years ago was another life, another time. We had to survive."

"Yes, but the stench of that life follows you no matter how far away you are."

Kiehl quickly departs, not wanting to continue the conversation, and avoiding the temptation to attack Alesky in broad daylight. Alesky revels in his small win against Kiehl as he continues to watch Mario's animated meeting.

"What is happening about our situation?" asks Nicola, shouting over all the commotion.

"Brothers, you must be patient!" pleads the consul.

"Brother, brother! What are you doing to fix things, brother?" Luca demands as he grabs the consul's jumper and twists it around his fist, almost turning it into a polo-neck sweater. Mario pulls Luca away.

"Come on Luca, you want to be repatriated, not deported." The consul gives Mario a grateful nod as he adjusts his jumper to its original shape.

"Just a friendly brotherly spat, hey, Paulo?" Luca sarcastically replies.

Paulo could deal with Luca's outburst, but as an growing crowd moves around him chanting, "We need help from the consul!" he begins to look attentively from side to side as his face turns a grey shade of white.

Mario shouts at the crowd: *"Vattene!"* (Go!)

At the nod of Luca's head, the crowd turns its attention towards the administration block.

"I'm doing all I can, you need to believe me," implores the consul.

"You will need to do more—who knows what this crowd is capable of?" responds Nicola.

"Yes, look, I know. The kitchen is serving pasta for you all soon, so they are making an effort...Please, you must be patient, you are being heard. I must go now... *Ciao, fratelli.*"

The consul's fast walk turns into a jog, leaving Luca's and Nicola's faces still shrouded in distrust. Mario is ecstatic about the pasta and tells anyone that will listen.

* * *

There is another day of peaceful but rowdy demonstrations, which mask the underlying festering pool of lava waiting to erupt. For the time being there is a sense of appeasement because, finally, the Italians are to be served the pasta they have all wanted for so long. At last, they would be eating a version of their mamma's food, and the comforting memories of home would be welcomed.

The Russian kitchen hands, overseen by Australian cooks, prepare the large pots of spaghetti and sauce. The Australian cooks do not notice when the Russians add sugar, instead of salt, and so the memories of home are to be unknowingly thwarted for the Italians.

The spaghetti is served. Initially, the Italians are just happy to see pasta on their plates instead of the usual mutton. The overcooked spaghetti floats in a grey-coloured sauce without a tomato in sight. There is no smell of any garlic either. The sauce is thin and has a sacrilegiously sweet taste, while the texture of the pasta resembles wet chalk. Mario can't help screwing up his nose as he drops cutlery into his plate and pushes it away. Across the table, Pietro does the same. The clicking and scraping of more abandoned cutlery from aghast diners fills the hall, the outrage escalating. Angry eyes lock on to each other, and only one word from Luca is needed.

"Andiamo!" And with that, a couple hundred hotheaded Italians pick up their plates of spaghetti and march to the director's office. One by one, the plates of spaghetti are aimed at the door until it is completely covered by the grey spaghetti slurry.

Inside, the director is becoming increasingly incensed, and in exasperation, he pops his head outside an adjacent window and shouts to the crowd, "I don't even eat spaghetti, and I never will!"

If he thought this would stop the crowd, he is very much mistaken. Instead, the emotional Mediterranean volcano has erupted. Two hundred turns into more than two thousand insurgents. They are even joined by many of the non-Italian onlookers, targeting all the buildings except for the hospital; even the church isn't spared. As the rioters approach the holy structure, Father Kelly stands in front with both arms in a halt position. For a moment, the group pauses as the priest announces, "Stop! My friends, please, have patience. God is with you."

A voice from the crowd responds: "Well, if God is with us, then he can help, come on!"

The church is stormed and set alight. Father Kelly gets out of the way in a hurry.

The Area Patrol can not break up the demonstration; there are just too many people hurling rocks at windows and striking buildings with wooden clubs. It is anarchy.

"Jesus Christ," is all Dobson can say, until he composes himself and shouts to his assistants: "Get the consul here now! Get Holt on the phone and call the army, in that order!"

The camp patrol retreats from an uneven brawl, but Kiehl's timing is off and Alesky takes the opportunity to king-hit him from behind, knocking him out cold. Mario stares at Alesky disapprovingly, and gets help from Pietro and Genaro to shield Kiehl from being trampled.

"This is getting out of control," exclaims Mario.

"He had it coming, Mario!" sneers Alesky.

"Maybe, but this is not right."

"Do you still have the letter?"

"Yes."

"Give it to me."

Mario finds the letter and hands it to him. Alesky shoves it in his pocket.

"I'm going, Mario," Alesky says as he starts to run off.

"Where are you going?"

"To Melbourne. I'll get my own job!"

"Take care, you troublemaker Balt, hope I don't see you too soon!" he says with a cheeky smirk.

"Me too, you overprivileged wog. *Arrivederci!*" He gives Mario a wave.

"Ciao, my friend." Mario waves to a disappearing Alesky.

"Thank God he's gone," grunts Pietro.

Mario's attention now turns to the unconscious Kiehl. "Come on, let's get him to the hospital."

"Wait," says Genaro, giving Kiehl a good kick in the guts, then continues in his best English: "That isa for the rabbits." He turns to Mario. "Did I say that right?"

"*Sì!* Come on, let's take him to the hospital."

Pietro picks Kiehl up, flings him over his broad shoulders with seemingly little effort, and pushes his way through the crowd towards the hospital building, followed by Mario and Genaro.

Alesky runs through the gates without any resistance, passing rudimentary signs placed next to the official Bonegilla sign, displaying the words "CAMP OF NO HOPE" and "WE WANT WORK OR BACK TO EUROPE". Alesky laughs to himself as he disappears beyond the horizon.

* * *

"The minister for immigration for you, sir," says the director's assistant, holding up the phone receiver. Dobson rushes to seize it.

"Harold, I've got a riot on my hands, the bloody Italians have gone crazy. You need to get them jobs now."

"I'm trying my best, Bob," responds Harold Holt.

"You're going to have to try harder. You and Menzies are going to have to sort out your immigration policy, quick!"

"Surely, things can't be that bad?"

Dobson opens a window and holds the receiver towards the chanting crowd.

"NO WORK, BRING US HOME. NO WORK, BRING US HOME!" It becomes louder and louder, mixed in with screams, smashing glass and endless thumps and bumps.

"Did you hear that?"

Holt is silent.

"Are you there?"

"Yes. Have you called the police?"

"I've called the army. They want work, Harold. What's being done about that?"

"Just very bad timing; I'll make it a priority. And keep the media out of this."

He puts the phone receiver down just as the Italian consul is escorted in. Dobson has never been so happy to see him.

CHAPTER 7: LJUBICA

Alesky stands at the ticket office on the station platform; there is movement from army personnel all around as they rush onto army truck convoys bound for Bonegilla.

"Where to?" asks the ticket master.

In his best Australian accent, Alesky says, "Melbourne, mate, one way."

"One ticket?"

Alesky nods.

"The train might be a bit late today, there's trouble at the camp. The dagos have gone crazy, I've heard."

"Thanks," says Alesky, as he exchanges money for his ticket to freedom. He sits patiently on a station bench, not particularly worried as he knows all the attention is directed towards the camp and not towards an unassuming, Australian-looking man without luggage.

* * *

"Brothers!" blares the loudspeaker. "Please stop! Calm down before somebody gets seriously hurt. Let's talk about this, please!" The message is repeated several times in Italian,

English and German.

The crowd suddenly quiets. It's not the words of the consul from the loudspeaker that make them stop—it's the sight of four tanks with machine guns rolling in with a convoy of two hundred fully armed troops, swarming like bees. Some of the anarchists flee, but most just stand still, clearly frightened and waiting for what will happen next. The army is really only there to scare the protestors, and it certainly does. The mood is subdued, and a more respectful manner prevails. The collateral damage of the protests is three burnt huts, a half-burnt church, quite a few broken windows and dented buildings, but no serious injuries.

Now that everyone is somewhat calm, the Italian consul addresses his compatriots in the hall. He feels embarrassed and annoyed that his countrymen have conducted themselves in such a manner; after all, he represents them and sees it as a reflection on himself. He taps on the microphone to ensure he will be heard, and he begins his speech in his native tongue.

"You are all very fortunate to be in a country like Australia. The way you have disrespected her, you all should be ashamed of yourselves."

No sooner had he finished that fateful phrase than the main ringleaders of the protest storm the stage and target the consul in a ferocious attack, threatening to kill him. The police intervene and rush him through the back door to safety. The consul is safe, but his car is not—he later finds it turned over onto its roof with all four tyres let out.

* * *

The swaying of the train on the tracks sends Alesky into a

restful sleep. It is what he needs but not what he wants. He dreads it, as, each time, it renders memories and not dreams.

It is a frosty dawn, no different to any other, but this morning could be the last one they see in their beloved country. A young man no older than twenty-one and his pregnant wife run through the forest, the sound of barking dogs becoming louder and louder. She slips and holds her stomach but forces herself to carry on.

"I'm taking you home," he says softly to her.

"No, where you go, I go."

He looks at her with admiration, takes her hand, and they continue on. The couple eventually reach a gravelled road that will lead them to the border, and to safety.

"Rest behind the tree while I see if it is safe," he instructs.

She obliges, happy for the rest. He takes out a canister and drenches her with the citrus liquid he has made to ward off the dogs, then crawls to the side of the road. He looks up at the midmorning sun. It is such a beautiful day—possibly too beautiful, too stark, to risk the journey. He decides they will rest until dusk. Moving in the twilight will make it safer to escape. He scurries back to the tree in anticipation of finding his wife softly sleeping. Instead, she is flanked by two men and their dogs, who are nosing around the base of the tree. The man's defeated eyes meet her sorrowful red ones. One of the pursuers whistles to the dogs and commands them to sit as he cocks his gun and aims it at the pregnant woman's head. She is still and silent.

"Let her go, it's me you need. Please! Let her go, and I will come without a fight."

"So you thought you could escape with your new family, and not pay any price for what you have done?" barks one of the pursuers.

"Let her go, and I will cooperate! I am unarmed, and she is pregnant—not even you pigs could be that merciless."

The captor now throws the woman towards Alesky, and both guards aim their guns at the couple. He kisses her forehead and then her hands.

"Go...go now."

She shakes her head no.

"Please," he pleads with her.

"Go, we don't need you," shouts one of the men.

She slowly tears herself away with tears streaming down her face.

"We don't need you, and neither does he!" the man says as he shoots the woman. She slumps to the ground. Alesky relives what he has just witnessed in slow motion. The laughter of the men fuels his rancorous trance into a fateful response, and in a matter of seconds, the men are disarmed and shot. Both the men lay dead along with their dogs. Alesky, bearing only minor scratches, scrambles to his wife and holds her in his arms. So much blood gushes, he doesn't even know where it's coming from. His tears mix with her blood-soaked face.

"Go...leave!" she whispers to him.

The voices of more shouting men come closer, no doubt following the noise of the gunfire and commotion between Alesky and the two men. His wife is now so weak she can't speak; he lays her down softly and says, "Forgive me, Ljubica... forgive me."

Alesky awakes from the vivid memory.

"This is the end of the line, you will have to get off,"

commands the conductor.

"Yeah, sure...sorry," replies Alesky.

"You were having some nightmare, mate."

"Yeah. Thank you."

Alesky steps off the train onto the platform, and looks up at the sign: "MELBOURNE FLINDERS STREET." He wipes his sweaty forehead and heads towards the exit sign, leaving Bonegilla and the riots behind as he walks into the welcoming arms of Miss Destiny.

* * *

Culprit or victim, the viewpoint depended very much on where one stood politically in the wake of the riots. On the part of the migrants, the demonstrations were not political, and were never intended to become violent. Fuelled by a few zealous young men, driven by a mix of testosterone, disillusion and frustration, it got out of hand, and although the method was not ideal, the results were: they finally had the attention of the authorities. Dobson and the Victorian police commissioner initially focused more on the punishment of those involved, and the likelihood of a communist underbelly, than the intrinsic reasons for the discontent of the migrants. Harold Holt and the immigration department vehemently repressed reports coming out of Bonegilla, but they could not stop the rumours and journalistic innuendo that made it to press. Issues of false advertising, unemployment, and provocation were taken up briefly by the mainstream media. Defensiveness was the administration's response to any questioning of its procedures.

Even though Dobson had threatened firm action against the main culprits, no one was formally charged, and life tentatively continued on as usual in the camp. The migrants agreed to repair and rebuild the damaged parts of Bonegilla, and the Italian consul did not take any action in regards to his written-off car; even Father Kelly found forgiveness in his heart, as the church was reconstructed, bigger and better than before. Whether it was the result of the uprising, the full attention of the Menzies government, or the natural progression of Australia's economic recovery—or possibly a mixture of them all, no one really cared—within two weeks, thousands of migrants were working. The New South Wales Snowy Mountain Scheme, the Queensland sugar cane fields and the rail transport industry gave many New Australians the opportunity for employment, fulfilment of their contracts and a sense of security for the future.

For Mario, Pietro and some of their other compatriots, they chose to work for the South Australian railways, committing two years of their lives to working in the middle of this vast country. Genaro and Stella found work in the kitchen at Bonegilla, and the food finally improved.

CHAPTER 8: MACUMBA

Mario, Pietro and a group of six other Italian countrymen stand on the platform of the Tintinara railway station, awaiting the arrival of a representative from Commonwealth Railways. They have been contracted for the next two years of their lives to upgrade regional train lines and develop infrastructure for emerging country towns. Tintinara is situated in the Mallee region, in the southeast of the state of South Australia. The landscape is very similar to that of Bonegilla, but the weather seems to be milder, and there is a sense of sweetness in the air—or it could have just been relief to finally be out of the immigration camp and feeling as though they had some kind of future.

They wait patiently, for what else could they do in the middle of who knows where? A freight train passes by with cargo carriages full of jumbucks, crammed in like sardines. The stench is crippling. Finally, the train has gone, but the smell still lingers. The men wave their hands in front of their noses, trying in vain to breathe in some semblance of fresh air.

Across from the railway lines, there is a cloud of dust and the sound of an idling motor. The sound stops, and the dust settles to reveal a man dressed in shorts and a singlet, exiting a Ford pickup truck. He leans on the open door and looks in the direction of the Italian men, who are still bitching about the lingering jumbuck smell. He puts two fingers in his mouth and gives a sharp, loud whistle. This gets their attention. He waves them over, and they pick up their menial belongings and cross the railway lines to reach him.

Jimmy 'Willy' Williams is forty-two years old. He stands at about five feet ten inches, and is very lean and muscular. His hair is an unruly reddish blond, as are his eyebrows and eyelashes; his blond stubble is hidden by a dirt tan that seems to cover the whole of his body. He greets the new employees.

"G'day! Yu the new EY-TY blokes?" The Italian men glance at each other as Willy continues. "Getcha gear 'en arses in back of the Henry."

"Is he speakin' the English?" Giovanni asks Mario.

"I don't know," answers Mario.

"Blimey, you fellas look more confused than a pickpocketer in a nudist camp!" says Willy. He grabs a roll of toilet paper from inside the truck and waves his arm in the direction of the truck tray. "Go on, in ya go."

The Italian men now understand that he wants them to climb into the back of the truck, and they do so, settling down on the rudimentary seating.

"Just wait here while I go an' give birth to a politician." Willy leaves the bewildered Italians and finds a bush, the roll of toilet paper in his hand. After a while, a relieved Willy returns.

"Righto, fellas, off weee gooo, an' watch yer nuggets on the bumps," he instructs them, as he imitates a bump and then grabs his testicles. The migrants don't really know what he's implying until they hit the road.

Fifteen minutes into the journey, they stop at the railway camp, a tent city situated on the edge of Lake Indawarra. The setup is comprised of around twenty smaller tents surrounding a much larger one, operating as the dining and social space for the forty or so workers of various nationalities. Unlike Bonegilla, there is much more camaraderie and empathy between the inhabitants, as well as the management team, which consists of Willy the supervisor, who has doubled up as the head cook; Richard "Dick" Robbins, the engineer; and Robert Cocks, the administrator. Willy escorts the new workers to meet Dick and Cocks, who are in the dining part of the large tent; he describes them collectively as the "three penises." Everyone laughs at Willy's quip, even the Italians, though they don't really get the joke.

Cocks, the administrator, hands the men some paperwork and tells them about their rates of pay and various organisational procedures. Dick explains the kind of work they will be undertaking, which is mostly replacing the old narrow-gauge railway with new standard-gauge railway, in an attempt to make the Australian railway system uniform. With Mario's interpreting skills, and the fact that Dick and Cocks spoke more understandable English than Willy, all the men are as informed as they can be and feel comfortable with their new work environment.

"Yu blokes must be knackered, go'an, getsum tucker inta ya. The thunderbox is over there next to the yabbie tank, watch out for the Joe Blakes," says Willy.

Mario looks to Dick and Cocks. Dick translates. "You must all be tired, go and get something to eat. The toilet block is near the lake, watch out for snakes. Don't worry, you will eventually get to understand him."

They all shake hands, and the Italians make their way to the servery for a much-appreciated meal.

Gary "Gazza" Walker mans the servery, and greets the men. "G'day, you must be the new EY-TYs. Me name's Gazza."

"Gazza?" repeats Mario.

"Yeah, Gazza, it's me nickname, you blokes have nicknames?"

"Oh yes, they call me Mario 'Sense capello', this is Pietro 'Pistola', Giovanni 'Calze caggato', Matteo 'Bottigllia'—"

"Whoa, whoa, whoa!" interrupts Gazza. "I'm just gonna call you Mars, and you Pete, and the rest of ya...well, we'll find you good Aussie names, don't worry about that! I've tried some of your grease frisbees when I was in Melbourne. Delicious!"

"What is that?" Mario asks.

"Oh, I think you call them pizza."

"Oh yes, yes, pizza, very good."

"Sure is." Gazza gives them a plate each of assorted sandwiches. "You can get some cloud juice over there."

"Cloud juice?" questions Mario.

Gazza laughs. "Water, mate, water, you know, cloud juice?" Gazza points to the sky, still laughing.

The Italians finally get the joke, then nod and laugh with Gazza, but continue to look at each other dubiously.

* * *

The bushman's clock wakes up all the workers, and they arise to a laughing kookaburra each sunrise. Every sunset, it laughs them to sleep. Two months into their tenure, the Italians are becoming increasingly comfortable with their new life in Australia. The work is hard and mundane, and tent life very elementary, but they don't mind, as they can feel their self-worth increasing, and they enjoy the weekly cash payments they have travelled so far to attain. During the day, they are in Australia, but at night, they are back home in Italy.

It's a Saturday morning, but not an ordinary one, for today is the grand final between the Geelong and Collingwood football clubs, and there's a buzz in the air, particularly amongst the Australians. Willy has instructed Mario to take the Henry and pick up some supplies from Tailem Bend, the closest main town. Willy often sends Mario on errands to Tailem Bend, and a couple times, he's even sent Mario to Adelaide. His ability to speak and understand English is a great advantage, and he is frequently chosen for various errands, which he really enjoys. It allows him to discover different parts of Australia; the main thing he has discovered is that his new, temporarily adopted country is varied, even within itself. He is beginning to understand the Aussie slang spoken by most of the white Australians he works with, although he still gets tripped up at times. Once, when Mario didn't feel well, Willy asked if he was "crook". Mario, slightly offended, said that he was not a crook; he was a very honest man. Willy burst out with laughter and then explained the meaning of "crook"—as in sick, not dishonest—although it could mean that in a different context. Mario was reassured.

The day is quite warm, not typical for the time of year, but Mario does not mind at all; he loves the heat, although, some days, the hot Australian sun shows them all who is boss. Nevertheless, he is glad he has chosen Australia and not Canada to emigrate to, as he hates snow and the cold and wet weather; it makes him feel gloomy. Many of his friends from the village have gone to Canada, and his mother wrote to him about his sister Catarina, who is to be married to Antonio Mastrangelo, a man who emigrated to Toronto a year before.

His mother explained that she is sad and happy at the same time for her eldest daughter, but the hope of seeing him, her beloved firstborn, come home from such a faraway land is what keeps her going.

Mario does not have a hat, as he refuses to wear one until he returns home, so on this particularly hot day he makes himself a substitute hanky hat, which serves the dual purpose of providing shade as well as acting as a sweat absorber.

Mario drives down the dusty road, on the lookout for his beloved kangaroos, which he sees in abundance now that he resides in the Australian bush. They continue to amaze him, and he loves it when he spots a baby joey poking its head out of its mother's pouch. Today there are none to be seen. What he does see in the distance is an Aboriginal man walking along the road. He has cutoff Western-type trousers on, no shirt, and is carrying a spear. Mario often sees Aboriginal people in the distance, but not walking along the road. He slows down the truck as he approaches the Aboriginal man and stops, reaches over to the passenger door to open it, and waves his hand to coax him in. The men stare at each other, almost in a trance; finally, Mario pats the seat to indicate for him to sit down. The Aboriginal man continues walking without acknowledging him. Mario shrugs his shoulders, shuts the door and drives off. He watches the man walk in his rearview mirror, noticing his dark, curly hair and how his skin shimmers in the sun. He thinks about his life in comparison to that of the mysterious man he has just encountered. *A people that live on the land, and not in houses, where money and ambition isn't valued—I can't understand it, but I can admire it. The first Australians, the true Australians. To live free like that, and not be a slave to the dollar, would be nice—but you can't buy land or a house with fresh air and red dust.*

Mario's thoughts turn to the present as he stops the truck in front of the Tailem Bend Post Office. He pulls out an envelope and then his wallet. He takes out a wad of money and wraps it inside of a letter, then stuffs the letter into the envelope, seals it, and slips it carefully into the slit of a box of Lipton tea. He enters the post office.

"Another parcel to send home, Mario?"

"Yes, thank you."

Mario sends a box of tea each time he writes home, as he knows his mother loves tea. Tea is so hard to get and very expensive in Italy, but in Australia, it is abundant. The post master boxes up the package for him. Mario writes down the address, and then it is stamped ready to go.

"That will be five pence."

Mario hands over the money. "Thank you very much, Jim."

He is on a first-name basis with the postmaster, as every time he is sent on an errand, he posts a package, a perk that he likes, and he also buys cigarettes for the boys, which they like. On one occasion, he nearly drove off without actually picking up the goods for his supervisor. He returns to the tent city, where he is eagerly greeted by the men, all wanting their cigarettes, just in time to listen to the football match on the radio. Everyone is allocated two beers each, compliments of the railways, and Gazza mans a barbeque full of fried onions and sausages, or "snags" as they are called at the campsite. Everyone lines up for their snag sandwich with onions, which all of the immigrant workers enjoy, but the Italians still can't stomach the sweet tomato sauce that most workers pour on top, so they eat theirs without it. Everyone gathers around the radio as the football match commences. None of the Europeans really know what is going on, but they all cheer when a goal is kicked, regardless of which team has scored it. There is a lot of fun and laughter, and the half-time entertainment is Pietro singing his fantastic rendition of "Finiculi Finicula". The match ends with Geelong as the 1952 premiers, and everyone is happy except Willy, a Collingwood supporter. He decides to go and sleep off his disappointment along with his slight tipsiness, the result of sneaking in a few extra beers for himself.

The work on the line has been completed in the camp's current location. The group now needs to shift thirty kilometres up to the Coonalpyn area. It is quite a big logistical operation, so when Willy asks Mario to pick up supplies from Tailem Bend again, he is very happy to avoid all the dismantling of the camp, as he considers driving a much more enjoyable and relaxing activity than disassembling tents and the infrastructure of the campsite and listening to a bunch of co-workers bitch about it.

On his way back from the pickup and posting another letter and money-stuffed package to his mother and father, Mario comes across the same Aboriginal man he previously encountered. Mario stops again to offer him a ride, and this time the man accepts. The Aboriginal man plops what looks to be some sort of lizard onto the seat.

"No, no, no, no, no...in the back. In the back!" Mario says, pointing to the truck tray. The man frowns but obliges just the same. Mario is not going to drive with a lizard next to him, alive or dead—he actually doesn't know which, and he doesn't want to find out. The lizard is flung from the truck and put in the back tray along with the man's spear.

The Aboriginal man takes his place in the passenger seat. He has a strange smell about him, but Mario thinks his own body odour can't be much better, so he just opens the window while he drives.

"Where you going, mate?" says Mario in his best Aussie accent. The man just stares, then waves his arm in a forward direction.

Mario points to himself. "Maarrio. Maarrio." Then he points to the man. "You, what's your name?" There is no response. "I could give you a nickname...like Lizard Man. Yes, I can call you Lizard Man, is that OK?"

Still no response from Lizard Man. Mario has been driving for about ten minutes, essentially talking to himself, when suddenly the man says something in his own language and points to the other side of the road. Mario slows down.

"You want me to go that way?" he asks. Finally, some interaction. Lizard Man nods. Mario turns the truck in the direction requested, driving off-road on quite rough terrain, wondering if the Henry is going to manage it. Eventually, they reach an Aboriginal community, and the man instructs Mario to stop. The man exits the truck, retrieves his lizard and spear from the back, walks over to Mario's side of the truck and just stares at him.

"Ciao, Lizard Man," says Mario.

The man points to himself and says, "Macumba. Macumba." He turns and walks towards a pit of burning coals and throws the lizard onto them.

"Ciao, Macumba!" calls Mario.

CHAPTER 9: MARIA

Euplio enters the house after another normal day. He sits at the new kitchen table that he has just purchased with some of the money Mario has been sending. A parcel from Australia sits on the table, unopened, ready for Euplio. Antonietta serves him his dinner and is excited as Euplio grabs the parcel. She has been waiting since the parcel arrived. She didn't dare open it without Euplio, as she knew he would get angry if she did. Euplio carefully opens the tea box and removes the envelope; he passes the tea to Antonietta. She beams lovingly at it, and places it in the cupboard with the ten other boxes of tea Mario has sent over the past year. She misses him, and loves the tea he sends her so much that she uses it sparingly, as it comforts her knowing that the tea came from him. She preserves it in his honour; a piece of Mario sits in her cupboard, in the form of several boxes of tea. Euplio opens the envelope; the first thing he does is pull out the money, count it, and place it in the top pocket of his shirt. He pats his pocket and says, "Bravo, Mario."

He takes a mouthful of minestrone, and reads his son's letter out loud to Antonietta in between each slurp of food. The letter tells them that Mario is missing home but is still happy working for the railway company. He often goes to Adelaide, the capital of South Australia, and he likes it very much. It is where he would like to settle after his contract with the government ends. He also says that he is ready to get married, and asks if his parents could choose a good wife for him from the village, as he knows, this way, there will be no resistance when he returns home. Antonietta is very happy hearing this news and suggests a few local girls that she thinks would be suitable for Mario. Lucia Puopolo, or maybe her younger sister Gina, even Pasqualina Merola, but definitely not Marisa Vento—she is as tempestuous as the wind, and even though she has liked Mario since she was very young, she would never do. Euplio listens and ponders for a while. He scoops up the last drop of minestrone with a piece of bread and devours it.

"Tomorrow I will go to the Rossini house and ask about their daughter Maria," announces Euplio.

Antonietta is taken aback as she reminds him that Maria is destined for the convent and would not be interested in being married.

"Maria is too beautiful to be a nun," Euplio says.

"You won't convince her—all her life, she has wanted to be a nun."

"I won't convince Maria, I'll convince her father."

Antonietta says nothing as she replaces the empty mine-strone bowl with a plate of cut-up fruit. There is no thanks from Euplio, just a nod towards his empty glass of wine, which Antonietta obligingly refills.

* * *

Signore Rossini and Eupilo sit at the table enjoying some peaches soaked in wine, and they discuss the union of their children Mario and Maria. It is finally agreed that they will be married within six months, and then Maria will travel to Australia when Mario calls for her and, of course, pays her fare. Euplio shakes Signore Rossini's hand and graciously leaves. Signora Rossini sits with her husband, questioning the agreement and voicing her concerns, and arguing that Maria will never agree to the marriage. He tries to assure her that it is what is best for Maria, and that Mario is a fine boy who will give her a future that neither her father nor the church could give her; he tells Signora Rossini that she must convince Maria to accept the proposal.

Euplio whistles as he rushes to tell Antonietta the good news. "The deal is done!" he tells her, very proud of himself.

Antonietta's head turns in disbelief. "How did you manage that?"

"I told him about Sister Rosaria, who left suddenly because she got pregnant by the priest."

Antonietta is shocked. "Is that why she left?"

Euplio shrugs his shoulders. "How do I know?"

Antonietta is speechless, but she knows better than to argue about the morality of his actions. Despite her qualms, she absolutely supports the match, and thinks that, for once in his life, Euplio has made a good decision, even if it eventuated from unscrupulous means.

Maria pleads with her father not to force her to marry. She tells him that she desperately wants to enter the convent, that it is her calling and has been ever since she can remember. She is truly beautiful on the outside, but her inside beauty far surpasses that. She is a genuine soul, and in her heart, she always knew she would become a nun and marry her God and her church. To take this away is unfathomable to her; she cannot bear it, cannot understand how her father could do this to her. She has nothing against Mario Lanzani—or any man, for that matter—but right now, her father, the most important male figure in her life, is tearing her dream apart. She continues to implore him, but no amount of crying and begging is going to change her father's mind. Finally, he has had enough. He bangs his fist on the table and demands that she comply with his wishes. She runs out of the house towards the church as fast as she can. When she finally reaches the church entrance, she composes herself; it would never do to enter this most sacred place in such a state. She enters calmly, but her eyes are still watery. She kneels in front of the altar, praying.

The prioress approaches Maria to comfort her. Maria speaks of her predicament with great stress. The prioress puts her at ease when Maria asks how this could happen by answering: How could it not? She tells her to look upon this as her calling. It is not what she has envisaged it to be but what God has envisaged for her. There is much that can be done and many people to be saved as a child of God instead of a servant of God. These words make Maria feel better, although she is still not totally convinced.

CHAPTER 10: BIRTH DEATH & MARRIAGE

Macumba lingers on the side of the road with his fresh kill by his feet. He waits for Mario. The position of the sun tells Macumba that it is the time that Mario drives his truck past this spot. Today, the sun does not lie. Mario stops the truck in front of Macumba. He throws the dead kangaroo, along with his spear, into the back of the truck. Mario looks through the back window at the dead kangaroo and feels sorry for it, but he understands that it's a staple for Macumba's family, and he tries not to judge. He, too, is a meat eater, but he's not a hunter and doesn't want to be; it's much easier getting a pay packet each week. The two men are different in every way, and they say barely two words to one another, but there is a mutual respect and empathy between them, with each trip strengthening an enduring, silent friendship. They reach the settlement, where the cooking coals have been prepared by the Aboriginal women in anticipation of the spoils of a good hunt.

Mario stops the truck. Macumba takes a bit longer than usual to collect his goods from the back. Finally, he approaches the driver's side. Mario rolls down the window; Macumba hands over a kangaroo tail with a smile and says, "You good white fella."

Mario smiles awkwardly, surprised by the bleeding kangaroo tail on the seat and also by the fact that this is the most words that Macumba has ever said to him at one time. Macumba throws the rest of the kangaroo carcass on the coals as Mario waves and drives off.

Mario looks at the kangaroo tail. He really appreciates the gesture, but it almost makes him vomit—or "liquid laugh" as Willy would say. He arrives at the tent city and takes the tail to Gazza.

His eyes light up, "Where did you get the roo tail?" Gazza asks with delight.

"Macumba gave it to me."

"Ha, ya Black fella friend? He must really like you."

"Yes. Can you do anything with it?"

"Yu eva heard of kangaroo-tail soup?"

"No."

"I'll make some and you can try it, mate."

"No, thanks, you enjoy it, my friend."

Nearly two years into the railway contract, the upgrade has been completed. The powers that be are impressed by the work that Willy and his crew have done, so they offer another contract to upgrade the Port Augusta line. Mario, Pietro and some of the others accept contracts to work on this new project. Many others accept different jobs in major cities, and some go back to their homelands. Mario is happy about the new contract. He is offered a promotion, which means more money, something that will bring him closer to his goals.

One fine day Mario is driving from Tailem Bend. Willy sits in the passenger seat, napping. They have just picked up the last of the supplies for the tent city, which is to be dismantled within the week. Mario is expecting Macumba to be at his usual spot to be picked up, and thinks he will need to snuggle up to Willy or else sit at the back with his kill—he usually chooses to sit in the back when Willy is there. This particular day, he is nowhere to be seen. *Perhaps he didn't hunt today,* Mario thinks to himself. Then slams on the brakes, which wakes Willy up in a fright.

"What the fuck, Mario?" Willy shouts.

When the dust settles, Mario looks closer at what made him stop. He jumps out of the truck without answering and goes to the figure lying on the side of the road. Willy catches up with him.

"Strewth...He looks as happy as a can of worms going fishing."

Mario drops to his knees and shakes Macumba softly. "Oh no, Willy...I think he's gone."

"Yep, I reckon he's carked it." Willy stands with his hands on his hips as Mario performs the sign of the cross.

"No use doing that crossing shit, mate, that ain't going to help him any."

"It's never helped me either, but I need to do something—maybe pray to the Australian God?"

"Nah, mate, they don't have a god. The Black fellas have sprits or some shit like that."

Mario just stares at the lifeless Macumba.

"Let's put him in the truck and bring him back to his people."

"No, we can't, Mario."

"Why not?"

"Firstly, I'm not sure if a white man is supposed to touch him—they need their own people to do some sort of ceremony to connect to the land or somethin'—and secondly, we need to get back to the camp."

"We can't just leave him here like a dog."

"Jeezus, Mario."

"Come on, Willy."

"No, no...jeezus! Look at that."

Willy points to a group of Aboriginal men who seem to have come from nowhere, walking towards them from the distance. Mario stands and steps aside as they approach. The men surround Macumba, chanting as they pick up the lifeless body and disappear into the landscape just as enigmatically as they appeared. Mario and Willy look on in astonishment.

Willy rubs his eyes and runs his hand through his dusty hair, "Fuck me," he says.

"No, Willy, I no fuck you," says Mario.

"Err, no...no, Mario, just a figure of speech, mate."

"I know, Willy...I just want to laugh now because I'm so sad."

They both chuckle and get back into the Henry to drive back to the camp. Mario is relieved that Macumba is with his family.

Willy decides to nap again; Mario takes a detour towards Macumba's camp, just to see how his tribe is doing. He plans to look from a distance to see what is happening. But as he reaches the camp, he sees cars and vans that are usually not there. He hears a lot of commotion. Mario speeds up, then brakes as he reaches the site. It wakes Willy up again.

"What now, Mario?" Willy complains.

"What's happening there?"

Willy looks at the scene. There are men dressed in suits and official uniforms forcibly removing babies and children from their mothers. They scream and cry to no avail as the children are shoved into the police vans. Willy knows about the child removal policy, which is part of the government's assimilation program for the Indigenous community, but how is he going to explain it to Mario?

Mario rushes to the aid of the children. Willy calls for him to get back in the truck, but Mario doesn't listen. He gets into a scuffle with one of the men, not realising he is on the wrong side of the law.

"What are you doing?" Mario screams.

"Walk away, this doesn't concern you," the man in the grey suit says as they push and pull the frightened child. "Fuck off, you bloody dago!"

Mario, in his anger, curses and swears in his native tongue. Another government man, in a dark grey suit, comes to intervene; he hits Mario, but Willy intercepts before any real damage is done. Willy defuses the situation and tells the government men that he will sort Mario out, and that he is a New Australian and doesn't understand what he is doing. He pulls Mario away.

"Come on, mate, this is not our business."

Mario grudgingly retreats as the government man with whom Mario had the initial altercation shouts, "You'd better get him out of my sight or I'll deport him quicker than you can blink!"

"Why you take the children? What have they done?" Mario shouts back.

"I said fuck off, dago!"

Willy grabs Mario's arm. "Come on, Mario, that's enough. Ya need to pick yer battles, and this isn't one of them."

Willy guides Mario back into the passenger seat of the truck, and they drive off, leaving the children and mothers screaming. Mario momentarily covers his ears, as the sound is so disturbing.

"Willy, what's happening? Why are they taking the children?"

"They do it for their own good, Mario, they get food and education. They will be alright."

"They didn't look alright to me. Children should not be taken away from their mothers!"

"They will be OK, Mario, don't worry."

"They must be so scared. I was twenty when I left my mother to come here, and I miss her every day."

"I told you, it's for their own good, and more importantly, it's none of our business. And, I can't afford to have my best EY-TY worker deported. Tell me, why did you come to Australia?"

"To better myself, make money, go back home, and restart the family business."

"So you had to make a sacrifice to better yourself, right? Yes, so that's what's happening to the Aboriginal children."

"But that was my choice. They didn't choose, they are being forced."

"Well, keep doing what you came here for. Head down, bum up, and don't worry about something you can't change."

Mario nods but is still saddened by Macumba's death and the events he witnessed at his people's settlement. He has a sense of ineptitude and guilt at not being able to do anything about what has transpired, and is suspicious about the cause of Macumba's death. He knows that Willy's advice is right, but it doesn't make him feel any better. Not even Willy's jokes can cheer him up.

Willy teases him: "Come on, mate, I've got some fresh bum nuts at the back, I'll get Gazza to make you those omelettes that you like. What ya call 'em? Frryaters."

"Frittatas," Mario corrects him.

"Yeah. That will make you feel better."

Mario smiles at him, gives him a thumbs-up and says, "Bonza, mate," somewhat unconvincingly.

Willy tousles Mario's hair. "That's it. We'll make an Aussie out of you yet!"

There is quietness between them as they head back to the camp—much later than expected. Mario suddenly breaks the silence.

"Today is my wedding day."

"What?"

"Today I marry Maria Rossini in Italy."

Willy is gobsmacked. "Ya mean you just married someone thousands of mile away? Do you even know her?"

"Yes, she comes from the same village as me. Last time I saw her, she was about ten years old."

"Is she jailbait, mate?" Willy asks, laughing at his unintentional rhyme.

Mario gives him a questioning look.

"Is she underage?"

"Oh! No, no, no...she would be about nineteen now."

"Why don't you marry a local?"

"No, I can't do that... It wouldn't be fair to take someone from here back to Italy."

"Does she have a good rack?"

"A what?" asks Mario.

"You know, a good set of..." Willy takes one hand off the wheel and uses it to illustrate the shape of a woman's breast.

Mario isn't very responsive.

"Don't worry, mate, that was a just a bad sorry joke."

"A sorry joke?" asks Mario.

"Yeah...a sorry joke, you know, when you say something before your brain filters it and it usually ends up needing an apology after it. A sorry joke."

Mario takes a photo of Maria out of his wallet and shows Willy.

"She's a looker, mate."

Mario agrees. "I'll call her over as soon as I'm settled in Adelaide."

"So you won't be using the wedding tackle anytime soon!"

"Is that another sorry joke?"

They both laugh, Mario understanding the context but not the contents of Willy's statement.

* * *

Maria looks angelic in her simple floral lace wedding dress, borrowed from the convent. She will be married in her church, but not to it, as she would have liked. The dress is fitted to her slim waist and flares to her ankles, exposing the new shoes given to her by her future mother-in-law and paid for by Mario. Maria eventually agreed to marry Mario, on the basis that she could study theology while she was waiting to be called to Australia to live a life with a man she hardly knows. Most of her prayers selfishly ask for divine help to cope with it all, and occasionally she asks for forgiveness for being so selfish.

Mario's eighteen-year-old brother, Stefano, stands in as a proxy while the priest performs the ceremony, witnessed by both families. There are tears of joy from the congregation, and tears of sorrow from Maria; she is thankful that she does not need to lift her veil. Everyone claps when the priest announces the union of Maria to Mario.

Antonietta kisses her new daughter-in-law and presents her with a gold chain bearing a simple elegant cross, also paid for by Mario. Maria is elated by this offering, and her tears are genuinely ones of joy. Stefano asks his mother if he can bring the bride home. She gives him a swift slap on the head, disgusted by his tasteless joke. Euplio asks why Stefano was hit, and she explains, comparing Stefano's impropriety to his own. All he can say is that anyone would love to be married to Maria and that Mario is a lucky man. Antonietta responds that it is indeed Maria who is lucky, and that Mario is a good person for making such a sacrifice, from so far away, for the sake of his family. Euplio just grunts, then suggests to everyone that they need to celebrate the union with food and drink, also paid for by Mario.

CHAPTER 11: ADELAIDE

After four years working for the railways, Mario says goodbye to Willy and the rest of the workers, most of whom are now new immigrants. Pietro and many of the other lads left a year earlier to find work in the city. Mario secured a job at the General Motors Holden Woodville plant, and Pietro, who works at Penfolds Winery, has also procured seasonal work for Mario. Mario feels excited about working at the winery, as it is what he knows best. He will be juggling two jobs, but he doesn't mind. Working and living in the nomadic tent city took its toll, and he is happy to have some stability. The only reason he stayed was because Willy asked him to and the pay was good, but he will be making almost the same amount of money working two jobs. Mario keeps sending money home, building a nest egg for when he returns. He also saved enough money for a deposit on a modest house in leafy Rosemont Street, in the Norwood suburb of Adelaide, which is strategically positioned right in the middle of his two job locations.

When he told Willy that he had bought a house in Adelaide, Willy was baffled and asked Mario why he would buy a house if he intended to go back to Italy. Mario's rationale, as he explained, was that nobody would be able to kick him out that way. Willy told him he was "bonkers" to blow his dough like that; Mario didn't agree. There is something about paying rent to another person that didn't sit right with him. The house is a 1920s federation bungalow, a one-storey cottage with a sweeping low-pitched roof, low chimney, and a prominent brick veranda. It is a renovator's delight, as described in the sales advertisement, which means it is hardly liveable. The toilet and laundry are outside, away from the main house, and the shed needs a lot of work; it is a shack, so the price was right, and it is his.

Mario looks at the sold sticker proudly, placed across the "For Sale" sign. He walks through the four simple rooms, going through renovation plans in his head; he plans to bring Maria to Australia as soon as it is habitable. He doesn't mind camping out in the shed while he renovates—he's used to it—but that will never do for Maria.

General Motors Holden dominates the Australian car market. Increase in production capacity allows the company to meet the growing post-war demand for cars, as well as providing jobs for many New Australians. Mario works as a paint conveyer on the state-of-the-art assembly body painting line. It is good work, but labour intensive. He aspires to be a floor checker/timekeeper, since they seem to have it easy. They wear grey dustcoats with a red band, and walk the floor of each department every shift, checking on the workers to make sure they are where they are supposed to be. They are also involved in the payroll. Every Thursday is payday, or the "day the eagle shits" in Aussie slang. Two hundred pay packets need to be distributed each week from the pay office. At the end of their shift, each employee queues up at the sliding windows, shows their numbered badge, and says their name, then gets their name checked off and receives their pay packet. But, many of the checkers have trouble with the spelling and pronunciation of the ethnic names; this causes some issues with the wrong pay packets being issued. Mario believes he could do that job quite easily—after all, he is bilingual, and can understand Aussie slang as well.

Yes, I could do the job...one day, he thinks to himself. He graciously takes his pay and says, "Thank you."

"What you doing after work, Mario?" the checker asks.

"Working."

"Whacha mean 'working'?"

"Working. I have two jobs."

"When do you rest, then?"

"I rest when I die."

"You EY-TYs are funny buggers." The checker laughs, probably thinking he was joking, not knowing that, in fact, Mario does have two jobs and is renovating a house as well.

Mario's life is busy. Five days a week, Monday to Friday, he rides his bike to Penfolds Winery to start the workday at six in the morning. He finishes at 1 p.m., rides home, fixes himself some lunch, then rides to Holden to start the afternoon shift at 4 p.m. He rides back home at midnight, and starts all over again the next morning. That leaves the weekend to renovate the house. Even though the buses have replaced the electric tram systems, and are deemed to be faster and more efficient, Mario chooses to ride his bike instead, as this way, he will save that little extra bit of money for a car.

The Adelaide winter has revealed itself, and riding in the rain and wind is not pleasant. Some of the cold fronts actually ice up his hair and eyelashes, and he realises the time has come to buy a car. The FJ Holden is the car of choice in 1956, and the company gives its employees good deals on any car purchase. He does consider the newly produced Holden FE station sedan, because of the large rear compartment, but he opts for a secondhand 1951 black standard Vanguard Phase l saloon, at a fraction of the price of a new Holden, even with the employee discount. For Mario, it is never about acquiring boastful possessions but rather a definite, objective process, working towards repatriation to Italy. The Vanguard, which is imported from England, looks more like a hearse than a utility vehicle, but Mario makes good use of it, and he doesn't care that his friends and fellow colleagues call him "the undertaker with no hat".

General Motors Holden builds cars, and they are also constantly expanding their production plants, so any excess building materials are available to the employees at extremely good prices, and some materials can be obtained for free. Their best customer in this area is Mario Lanzani. Much of his house renovations are supplemented by Holden's excess supply, and the Vanguard proves invaluable for transporting it all. Some of the supplies are used to build an auxiliary outhouse and a chicken coop, and there is enough material left over to fix the existing shed and build another, as one can never have enough sheds.

Fred and Irene Brackenridge live next door to Mario. The front yards of the houses are separated by a low, cream-coloured picket fence, which leads up to another weathered wooden fence approximately six feet high, and reaches the end of the backyard boundary. Irene would often be at the front of her yard gardening and pruning her roses. Fred hardly left the house except to watch his beloved Redlegs playing football at the Norwood oval, or to have a frothy at the pub. Fred is a WWI veteran, and Irene—or Reenie—is his "domestic engineer" as he would call her, as she hates the word 'housewife.' They are both in their late fifties and have lived in the same house since they were married thirty years ago. Fred walks with a slight limp, which gets worse when it is about to rain. He calls the leg his "weathervane", but in spite of this, he looks younger than his years. Irene also keeps herself well groomed, with a weekly visit to the hairdresser. She loves gardening and can often be found in her front yard caring for her various rosebushes. She protects her pale skin from the sun by wearing a wide-brimmed hat and sunglasses as she putters around in her garden. These are also very useful when ignoring Mario's attempts to be friendly.

"Hello," he would say, and give her a wave.

Each time she saw him, her head would drop suddenly to her chest, and she'd continue whatever activity she was performing and then slide away inside the house as swiftly as she could, totally avoiding any interaction whatsoever. Mario gave up after a while, and ignored her as well.

The day Irene first encountered her new neighbour, she ran into the house to find Fred. She found him sitting in his favourite chair, sipping his sparkling ale and listening to the Redlegs and Tigers game on the radio.

"Fred...Fred!"

"Wait...wait, Reenie. Marriott's going for a goal," he said, alarmed.

The radio blared out the tense moment as the football player set up his shot. He kicked, the crowd was silent, and so were Irene and Fred.

"Oh bugger, another point...bloody hell!"

"Fred, I need to talk to you."

He turned down the radio. "What is it now?"

"I just saw the new owner next door, and I think he's an ethnic. He waved at me."

"Well, how dare he!" Fred said sarcastically.

"Fred, this is serious, and it's not good. You get one in the neighbourhood, and they'll just take over."

"He won't bother you if you don't bother him."

"Well, I'm not happy, Fred."

"You rarely are, love!"

Fred turned up the radio and took another sip of his ale as Irene stormed out to the kitchen and through the back door. She tiptoed to the weathered wooden fence separating her from the ethnic next door. There was a peephole in one of the panels, which, at one stage, had been a knot in the wood that had conveniently fallen out to provide Irene a view of the next-door neighbour's backyard. Her eyes cautiously approached the peephole. She saw a half-built chicken coop and different types of building materials stacked neatly around the property. She wasn't quite sure what to make of it yet, but you could bet your bottom dollar she was going to keep an eye on everything. She went back into the house to report what she had seen to an uninterested Fred, who was disappointed at the football results and sulking.

"You should see what's in the backyard, Fred, all this building material, and he's building something, but I can't quite make out what it is yet—it looks like a chicken coop. Ohhh, I hope it's not. Chickens bring rats!"

"They also lay eggs," replied Fred.

"And looks like he's going to build more, with all those materials around the place."

"Reenie, if he has bought the property, he can do what he likes."

Irene didn't take Fred's words under consideration at all. "I'll be keeping an eye on him, you can be sure of that!"

"Now, my love, can I ask you something very important?"

"Yes," she said with a smile, thinking that he was finally engaging in her concerns.

"What's for dinner?"

She bristled at his question, but headed into the kitchen to prepare dinner anyway.

Mario has now completed enough of the renovations that he can move into one of the main rooms inside. He has finished the chicken coop and started on the outhouse, all under the watchful peeping eye of Irene, unbeknownst to Mario; he has been way too occupied to notice. He is taking in boarders, usually migrants who he worked with on the railways. They would stay in the two sheds, and in return for lodging, they would help Mario with his renovations. The first major project was to build an indoor bathroom and refurbish the kitchen. His first boarders were fellow Italians. Alessio happened to have plumbing skills, and Pietro, his good friend, apart from having a beautiful singing voice was also quite a handy bricklayer.

It's a beautiful Sunday morning, a day of rest for most people, but not for Mario and company—and not for Irene, as she hears the loud banging coming from next door. She plates up Fred's Sunday treat of fried eggs and bacon and rushes outside to her spyhole. It's just as Irene suspected.

"EYE-TALIANS!" she mutters to herself. Though she can't understand what the busy men are saying, she can recognise the language. Fred enjoys his special Sunday breakfast, as every other day it's just porridge, but today he feels it's going to have a bad aftertaste. He sits at the table eating as fast as he can, as he can sense trouble. He isn't fast enough, and just as he's rising to leave the table, Irene storms in.

"Just as I thought! EYE. TALIANS. Fred! EYE. TALIANS!" she fumes.

"Reenie, let it go. They won't bother you if you don't bother them."

"Oh, Fred! They're EYE-TALIANS! They breed like rabbits. Before you know it, we'll be overrun by them."

"You didn't like the previous owners either."

"I know, but at least they were Australian!"

"You're making way too much of this."

"Why don't you support me, Fred?" Irene replies angrily.

"If and when they do something wrong, I will. Until then, let's live in peace." He puts on his hat and walks out.

"Where are you going?"

There is no answer.

"The pub, I suppose!" she shouts.

Fred shouts back, "Yeah, the only whining there comes from a bottle!"

Irene stomps her foot, flares her nostrils, and then sits at the table to eat her cold bacon and eggs.

CHAPTER 12: MR MAX, MRS MARIA

The year passes quickly, but not quickly enough for Mario. He is anxious for Maria to come from Italy, and in September of 1957 she finally boards the ship to destination "unfamiliar". In twenty-eight days, he will be united with his wife of nearly three years, who he has only met once or twice when she was very young.

Maria's family waves to her on the dock, tears in their eyes, but surprisingly Maria is resilient against emotional outbursts. Her stay at the convent has given her time to accept her fate, and she is resolved to leave it all in God's hands. Armed with three Bibles and five sets of rosary beads, she is ready for anything—or so she keeps telling herself.

Throughout the year, Mario worked very hard to make as much money as he could while restoring the house in preparation for Maria's arrival. He sent less money back home than usual, as he needed it to finish the renovations. Mario is convinced that the house is a shrewd investment and not a waste of money, as many have told him. A letter from his father scolds him for the reduction in money being sent, and then congratulates him on his marriage and Maria's pending arrival. Mario is slightly put out by this, but his mother's words of encouragement and her reassurance of her undying love for him lift his spirits, so he just dismisses his father as being as harsh as he remembers. The time and distance between them has not softened him at all.

Mario continues to work at General Motors Holden, as well at the Penfolds Winery. Holden pays better than Penfolds, but he prefers working at the winery. It is familiar to him, he feels at home, and his inherent skills are well suited to the day-to-day operations of the vineyard and cellars. He is involved in the Shiraz plantation of the estate, preparing the land with a horse-drawn plough, planting new seedlings and erecting the structure needed for the vines to grow. He is part of the team that ensures the vines will be optimal when it comes time to harvest, and keeps the vines pruned, clean and disease-free throughout the year. He is also involved in the cellars and relishes any task he is given there, from turning the sparkling wine bottles to separating the sediment, washing barrels, stacking bottles and even bringing samples to Max Shubert, the chief winemaker.

Mario likes Mr Max, who is of German decent, and Mr Max is well liked by everyone. Mr Max has a very large nose, and when he puts it into a glass to smell the wine, it is a joke between the workers that it will get stuck and not come out. He is very approachable, and if he sees you as a reliable worker, he is very complimentary. Mario is a hard worker, and they often have conversations together. One particular day, Mario complains that his neighbour doesn't like him, and that he thinks it is because he is Italian. In response, Mr Max tells him that he was born in Australia, and fought in the war for Australia against Germany, but because of his name, people judge him, and he says they will judge Mario as well. He advises him to be strong and proud and let it flow like water off a duck's back. Mario doesn't understand what he means until Mr Max explains the analogy to him. When he says, "Put your head down and bum up," Mario knows what that means and that he can do it, no problem at all. Mario finds comfort in the advice, and tells him so, and when Mr Max answers by saying he appreciates Mario's hard work, from that day on, Mr Max can do no wrong in Mario's eyes, and whatever he asks Mario to do, it is done with continuous respect. When Mr Max asks Mario to help him with a particular project that needs to be kept secret, Mario has no problem with being discreet and performing any task he is asked to do.

Penfolds Winery was founded in 1844 by Christopher and Mary Penfold, who brought French vines from England, initially for the production of fortified wines for medicinal purposes. The winery grew to include many other varieties of grape, producing both sweet and dry, red and white table wines, following the principal blending methods pioneered by Mary Penfold. Descendants of the Penfold family still own the company, and in 1948, Max Shubert became its first chief winemaker. Shubert spent time in Bordeaux, which led him to experiment with long-lasting wine production. His experiments started in 1951, and he named them Grange after the homestead of the founders. The Grange experiment was universally disliked, with negative reviews and poor commercial prospects, and in 1957, the board ordered Shubert to shut down his project. Shubert continued his project in secret, simply calling it Bin, and Mario did whatever Mr Max asked him to do, with absolute judiciousness.

The day Mr Max told Mario that the board stopped him from continuing with Grange, Mario tries to cheer him up with a joke, saying the board must be bored. After a chuckle, Mr Max responds by saying that they have nothing to do but break his balls, but he believes in what he is doing and he is going to continue without them knowing.

Mario buys himself a new suit for Maria's arrival. He looks very sharp, but Pietro reminds him that he is only half dressed without a hat. Mario doesn't care; he is keeping a promise to himself, and will not wear any dress hat except for the one he left back in Bovino. Finally the day arrives for Mario to pick up Maria from the station.

He stands on the platform waiting for the train from Melbourne, due in forty minutes. He is early, but he wanted to make sure he was not late. He paces the platform, switching between looking at his watch and Maria's photo. He glances at the schedule, then at his watch, then at the large station clock, synchronises his watch, and repeats the routine, which does not make the time go any faster. The clock strikes four as the train arrives at the station, and passengers stream out of the carriages. Mario paces up the platform with Maria's photo in hand, inspecting any young woman who might be her, bumping into people who tell him to watch it. He apologises profusely to each one. He looks a bit crazy as he runs up and down the platform, peering into the windows of the carriages in pursuit of Maria. Many questions go through his head: *Did she miss the train? Did she think Melbourne was Adelaide? Did she change her mind? Did she come at all?*

Most of the passengers have now disembarked, and Maria is nowhere to be found.

Maria sits in her carriage chair with her eyes closed, rosary beads in hand, praying. The conductor approaches Maria.

"This is the end of the line, miss."

Maria looks up at him, slightly confused.

"You need to get off," he says, pointing at the exit.

She nods, smiles politely, and stands up. The porter helps her with her luggage. Mario spies the porter unloading a suitcase and nervously watches as he pulls the suitcase off the train. Maria appears, framed by the doorway of the train carriage. She wears the shoes and the gold chain with the cross that Mario's mother gave to her on his behalf. Mario's strained look turns into a huge, grateful, relieved smile. She is even more beautiful than her photo. He approaches her, helps her down, takes the suitcase from the porter and thanks him with a tip. His full attention now turns to Maria.

"Signora Lanzani!" he says.

She smiles at him. Mario leans in for a kiss on the lips, but Maria turns her head, and it lands safely on her cheek. She smiles awkwardly. Mario is just happy to see her.

"Let's go," he says. *"Andiamo,"* he corrects himself.

Maria wears a double-breasted light-blue rayon suit that shows off her dark blue eyes and silky complexion. Her hair falls softly around her face, which has a constant soft, calming aura, regardless of whether she is smiling or frowning. Mario thinks to himself that she is much too beautiful to be a nun and that he is a very lucky man indeed.

Mario asks the usual questions about her trip and their families back home, and then reports what he has been doing in Australia for the past five years. He escorts her to the Vanguard, parked in the station's car park. Maria stares at the hearse-like car, impressed and unimpressed at the same time: impressed because Mario actually has a car, and unimpressed because it looks like a funeral van. It's five in the afternoon on an unusually cold November Saturday. Mario puts Maria's suitcase in the boot and opens the door on the passenger side for her. She shivers and says in Italian, "I thought Australia was hot?"

Maria laughs as he explains to her that Australia has cold days every now and then, but summer is coming and she will feel the heat. They drive off towards their new life as husband and wife. Maria fiddles with her rosary beads, too nervous to really notice the new Australian background passing her by. Mario gives her a gentle tap on the leg and asks in Italian, "Have you learnt any English?"

"A little," she says.

"You will need to speak English here, Maria. The Australians don't give you a lot of respect if you don't speak their language."

Maria starts to cry.

"Don't cry, Maria!"

"If I only cry once a day, it has been a good day," she replies.

"Maria, I promise you we will return home."

They pull into the driveway of the restored bungalow. As they stand together, Mario is proud of his achievement.

"Is this your house?" Maria asks.

"It's our house!"

"Why did you buy a house if you're going to return home?"

"Because if it's your house, no one can kick you out. You can't trust the Australian government."

Maria is silent for a minute. *Dove si trova la Chesia?* she asks.

"Speak English...Let me hear you."

"Wher isa de church?"

"Brava! The church can wait, we have things to do!"

Mario grabs her hand and drags her to the front door. Once inside, Mario kisses her on the lips with a mischievous look in his eyes. She trembles nervously, and the rosary beads fall to the ground. Much to her surprise, Mario drags her away from the bedroom, down the corridor, through the kitchen, and out the back door. Almost immediately, the piano accordionists play the "Wedding March". Maria is delighted.

The guests number around forty people, made up of Mario's New Australian friends — all Italian in origin, except Willy, who wasn't going to miss any piss up. Wine and song is flowing over, even beer making an appearance, compliments of Willy. Mario and Pietro have been given cartons of Max Shubert's secret stash as a gift for Mario's wedding celebrations, and also as a thank you for the extra unpaid hours worked to help Mr Max with his clandestine project. Although they appreciate the gesture of dozens of bottles of 1955 Grange Hermitage, they are put away in the back of the shed, as they much prefer the wine that Mario and Pietro made; it is lighter and sweeter, and more to their liking.

Maria is now relaxed as all the guests come forward to congratulate the married couple. She laughs and joins in on the festivities as Pietro sings his own version of the Italian hit song "Marina", replacing the lyrics with his own and changing the chorus from "Marina Marina" to "Maria Maria". Maria enjoys the serenade, commenting on Pietro's wonderful singing voice. The celebrations continue, getting louder as the night progresses, and not going unnoticed by the neighbours. Irene's ever-watchful eyes spy on the group as they dance the tarantella.

"How disgraceful, they have no regard for anyone, making all that racket!" Irene says to herself. She gets angrier as the wedding guests get happier, and marches back inside to a snoring Fred.

"Wake up! Wake up, by God, you can sleep through a hurricane."

Fred wakes up in a stupor.

"Come have a look what's happening next door!" she sneers.

"Do I have to, Reenie?"

"Yes, Fred, you need to see what's going on in your own neighbourhood."

Fred rises from his comfortable chair, bowing to the pressure, and walks outside, following Irene. He looks through the hole in the fence and smiles at the scene—it looks like fun, and he hasn't had much of that for a while; a sharp dig in the ribs reminds him of the fact.

"What a disgusting fracas, we shouldn't have to put up with this debauchery!"

"What would you like me to do? There's forty or fifty of them and only one of me."

"You need to make them stop. They should be respectful of the people that live around them! You tell them to stop or we will call the police. Well? Go on!"

"Quit the noise!" Fred shouts, and Irene gives him a nod of approval.

The wedding guests stop their dancing, and the music slowly winds down as they look at each other questioningly. Irene and Fred walk inside as he says, "And keep it down!"

The wedding guests, still looking at each other, laugh out loud, and then continue the festivities, unperturbed and rowdier than before. Irene stands with her arms crossed at the back door, incensed at such insolence.

"Fred...call the police!"

Constable Peterson draws the short straw when he is picked to inspect the disturbance in Rosemount Street, Norwood. He parks his bike in front of the Lanzani house, takes out his notepad and pen to scribble a few notes, and listens to the singing and cheering that he now needs to stop. Why? He doesn't know, but he does need to do his job. He knocks on the door and realises that nobody can hear him, so he finds a side entrance and follows the noise towards its source. Constable Peterson finds a happy group of people enjoying themselves, which almost convinces him to turn back and leave them alone, but he knows that they will only get another phone call about the disturbance. He blows his whistle. Nobody stops, so he blows it again, louder. This time, the crowd hears him and stops immediately, surprised at the sight of a police officer in the backyard.

"Who is the owner here?" asks Constable Peterson.

Mario comes forward to shake his hand. The constable does not take it; instead, he pulls out his notepad and pen.

"Name?"

Mario stands frozen.

"Name?" repeats the constable.

"But, mister, we are just celebrating my marriage." He grabs Maria. "This is my wife."

"You got married today, did ya?"

"No, we married three years ago."

"You trying to be funny?"

"Oh, no, no, it's true."

Willy interrupts. "Listen, mate, Mario and his missus were married by proxy three years ago. She arrived today from Italy, so this is their wedding night."

"Well, Mario, it's best you wrap this all up. I would think you have better things to do tonight." He winks.

Mario offers him a glass of wine and a piece of wedding

cake. The constable hesitates for a moment, licks his lips, and decides to take it; this starts up the musicians again. "Oi! Are your ears painted on? You all need to go home," he says as he takes a sip of wine and then a bite of the nicest cake he has ever tasted.

This is all being watched by Fred through Irene's peephole, with her behind him, prodding him for information. He pushes her away. The crowd starts to disperse, congratulating Mario and Maria as they leave, and also acknowledging the constable, who is now more approachable, plied as he is with cake and wine. The backyard wedding venue is now empty—only the newlyweds, Willy and Constable Peterson remain. Willy pats the constable on the back.

"OK, mate, it's time for Mario's pay in the hay. Let's go."

Constable Peterson, Mario and Willy all laugh at the comment. Maria laughs as well, but if she understood what he had said, she would not be laughing.

Everyone has left, and Mario and Maria are finally alone. She smiles at him as he kisses her hand, and he looks into her deep blue eyes and asks if she had a good time. She nods her head, then whispers, "Promise me you will take me home."

Mario nods. "Promise me you will not cry more than once a day."

"I can't promise that."

He leads her to the bedroom, where her suitcase awaits her. She opens it up to retrieve a wooden crucifix and neatly places it on the dresser next to her rosary beads, then returns to the suitcase to fetch a night bag. She leaves the room. Mario undresses down to his underwear and lies on the bed, waiting for Maria to return. After what seems to be half an hour, but is in fact only ten minutes, he calls for her. She responds that she will be there soon. Finally, Maria walks in wearing a beautiful white nightdress. Unfortunately for Mario, it's not see-through, but she looks like an angel. He blinks and looks again, just to make sure the scene is real. It is. Mario follows Maria with his eyes; she gives him an uneasy smile as she takes her rosary beads and turns to kneel before the wooden crucifix to pray in silence. She finally rises and leaves the room again to go to the bathroom.

Maria has been dreading this moment. The nuns at the convent prepared her for the consummation of her marriage, but she is so nervous and she feels too dirty to even pray to God to give her guidance, so she just sits in silence remembering what the nuns told her. *What would they know?* she suddenly thinks. *They're celibate.* She would just need to put her faith in Mario and let him guide her.

Mario looks towards the Jesus on the wooden cross who seems to be staring back at him. Mario holds up his hand and says, "How am I going to compete with you?"

* * *

Maria's days are mostly filled with domestic duties—cooking, cleaning and gardening—however, the day never started until her circadian 7 a.m. church service ended. She is particularly happy that Saint Ignatius Church is only a ten-minute walk from where she lives, and she attends the Latin Mass every day without fail. Sometimes if she has a spare morning, she will take the bus to Saint Francis Xavier Cathedral, in the Adelaide city centre, and attend the Latin Mass and then stay for the English one as well. This gives her a chance to worship and get an English lesson at the same time. She loves the cathedral; it reminds her of the one back home that she would frequent with the nuns. It sooths her, and for a short while, she feels as if she is back home.

Mario neither approves nor disapproves of her daily church practice; as long as his dinner is ready, there are no complaints. Mario comes home from work each night to find his meal on the table waiting for him. His routine is to kiss Maria on the cheek and ask her how many times she cried during the day. The usual answer would be four to five, but as each week passed, the crying sessions were reduced to an average of two, which they both agree is good progress. She waits for Mario before she eats, even if he arrives late, and Pietro, who still lives in the outhouse, often joins them. The three-course meal always includes some kind of homemade pasta, meat with vegetables, and a dessert.

Food and drink is in abundance at the Lanzani residence, and Maria often cooks much more than is needed, most probably a psychological reaction to food deprivation throughout the hard periods experienced in Italy. It doesn't matter much, as Mario and Pietro take the leftovers for lunch the next day, so nothing is wasted—another carryover from the hard times. The chickens provide enough eggs to make breakfast omelettes, pasta, cakes and biscuits. The yard has an abundance of fruit trees, as well as a vegetable garden, and any extra food needed is either bought in bulk by Mario and Pietro or at the corner store by Maria. Mario taught her about the Australian monetary system, so she knows exactly what amount she needs to buy her goods from the corner store, to avoid any sort of swindle. Maria now understands a lot of English, but she is not confident and is reluctant to converse in it with anyone other than Mario, who constantly reminds her that she needs to be fluent in the language. Maria is intelligent and she knows he is right, but she reminds him that they shouldn't need to speak English if they intend to return home.

"It is the language spoken in the country we live in at the moment, and it is to our advantage to use it, and not anyone else's," Mario would reply.

Each morning, Maria would return from her church service to find Irene and occasionally Fred in the front yard, attending to the garden.

"'Ello," she would say, and Irene would turn her back and snub her. This did not deter Maria, who would just say, "God bless you."

If Fred happened to be there, he would give Maria a slight wave behind Irene's back, and she would return the gesture with a gracious smile.

Maria has been in Australia for several months when Mario, on an unusual Tuesday off work, hugs her as tears of joy run down her face. The doctor has just informed them of Maria's pregnancy. They arrive home from the doctor's, and not even the sight of Irene can tarnish Mario's day. He would normally not acknowledge her at all, but today he and Maria look straight at her, smiling and waving. Irene stares at them for a moment, and Maria thinks she will reciprocate the greeting. She does not. Instead, she grunts louder and gives them a more disdainful look than she has ever given before. Mario turns to Maria.

"Have you taken a photo of her?" he asks her in Italian.

Maria smiles, knowing that he means metaphorically, to remember what she is like and that things are not going to change.

Irene now turns towards Mario. "Don't speak your lingo in front of me. Go back to your own country and speak it."

"Vaffunculo, stronza," Mario says.

"What did you say to me? Don't talk to me that way, speak English!"

Mario does not answer, but leaves, fearing that he may lose his cool. Irene now directs her anger at Maria.

"What did he say to me?"

Maria, with her usual gentle smile, replies, "God bless you."

CHAPTER 13: VINTAGE

Pietro continues to live in the Lanzani outhouse. He works as hard as Mario and makes the same amount of money, but he is not good at managing his finances, and regularly squanders his earnings on the latest newfangled items and the odd flutter or two on the horses. He also has a weakness for women and often sneaks a lady of the night in for the night, but he is very careful that Maria does not find out, as he knows she would never approve. Avoiding Maria isn't difficult, as one can set their watch to the minute she left the house to go to church every day, and Mario would always knock on the door to signal that she had gone, just in case. It is not that Mario totally approves, but he is more liberal about what a person chooses to do with his life, as long as it doesn't hurt anyone and is within the elastic boundaries of the law. His moral compass in regards to other people has a wide range; plus, Pietro pays them rent, and he figures that Pietro is entitled to do what he wants in his own space. Nevertheless, they keep it from Maria, out of respect.

Pietro has just purchased a new radio, and has it set to the station that plays all the new rock and roll songs. He loves all the songs of American singers such as Chuck Berry, Little Richard, Ricky Nelson and Jerry Lee Lewis, but he is particularly partial to Elvis Presley, and even sounds like him when he sings. Pietro sets up his new radio, and fiddles with the dial until he can get the best reception for the rock and roll station. He has invited three other musical friends over to listen to the music and see if they can copy the new style. One is a guitarist, one a piano accordionist and the other a drummer. Pietro wants to form a band, as singing and music are his real passion. He has stars in his eyes, and does not want to work at the vineyard for the rest of his life.

It is an overcast Sunday morning, and as Maria prays at her usual weekend service, Mario takes the beer bottles filled with preserved tomato sauce that they made the day before out of the now cooled copper boiler. He carefully stacks them in their designated area in the shed, to be used throughout the year. The preserved tomatoes are a staple used in many Italian dishes. Enough tomato sauce is made annually to last throughout the year—it is a tradition in many Italian households in the homeland, and it became a tradition in Australia due to the increasing Italo-Australian population.

Pietro and his friends listen to the rock and roll songs that come on, trying to get an ear for the sound. The radio volume dial keeps getting turned up so that the beat and rhythm can be clearly comprehended. Mario doesn't mind, but the next-door neighbour does. Irene continues to be disgusted at the disregard these Italians have for common decency. Today, she decides not to call the police—she will fight fire with fire. Out comes her portable phonograph, which she places on her back veranda, and she puts her favourite operatic record on the turntable. She positions the needle and turns the volume up as loud as she can. "Un bel dì, vedremo" from *Madam Butterfly* blares out into the neighbourhood and completely messes up the band's trial of rock tempo, which is exactly Irene's intention. Pietro turns up the radio's volume to full blast, but it still fails to make any impact, so the band members do what they do best and start to play the tarantella and various other upbeat Italian folk songs. Pietro's voice together with the instruments easily drown out Irene's libretto musical score; the competition is over, and she is livid. Mario choses to ignore the musical tête-à-tête, instead concentrating on his tomato sauce bottle stacking. He has had enough run-ins with Irene; today is Pietro's turn.

From over the fence, Irene shouts, "Stop that terrible Eye-Talian music, it's Sunday morning!"

Pietro stops and signals the band to do the same; the *Madame Butterfly* record continues as Pietro shouts back without any stuttering, but still with an accent, "What you think you're listening to? That's Puccini, and he's Italian!"

Everyone roars with laughter, including Mario, and suddenly, the music stops.

Maria is now four months into her pregnancy, and the bump is starting to show on her small frame. Mario is very protective of her, and it is agreed that they will return to Italy after the baby is born. The money that Mario has sent home should now be substantial enough, and with the profits he will make from selling the house, he'll have enough to restart the family cantina. Maria is happy about the plan, as she misses her homeland, but her pregnancy has given her a new perspective; she doesn't seem to mind the interim life in Australia. Mario provides a comfortable living, and he never stops her from worshiping her faith; as long as his needs are met, and she meets them constantly.

* * *

It is vintage in Australia: grapes are ready to be harvested, and it is time for Mario and Pietro to meet their annual wine quota, another tradition bought to Australia from the homeland. The McLaren Vale grapes are sorted and ready to be crushed. Mario loves to experiment each year with different grape varieties, and this year, it has been decided that grenache would be the grape of choice, as it is much lighter than the Shiraz that they normally use. They have also decided to try out the sparkling wine process they saw Mr Max do, and he has kindly given them some of the sparkling wine yeast for their experimentation.

It is a beautiful, sunny April afternoon, the barrels are ready and topped full of ripe grapes. Maria has made lunch for three, which is enough for six, and a delicious liqueur-soaked sponge with custard and fruit pieces. The men have eaten more than they would usually eat, as they need the energy to crush the grapes. Mario and Pietro take their shoes and socks off and exchange their pants for shorts. They hop into the half barrels with a tap leading to empty vessels, and begin the crushing process. This is by far one of their favourite parts of the wine-making process, second only to the tasting, but it is not Maria's, as they always get splashed with the grape juice, and she is the one who has to get all the difficult stains off the clothes after it's all done. It isn't long until the vessels are filled. It is Maria's job to replace the full ones with unfilled ones and empty the contents into the fermentation vats. The men sing as they move their legs up and down to the beat, and it becomes very noisy and garbled as they continue the wine crushing, probably as a result of too much liqueur in the sponge cake.

There is a wonderful honey-and-fruit smell wafting from

the grape juice, and, of course, this alerts the neighbours. Mario has identified the spy hole, and he is certain it is being used. At that moment, it is—not by Irene, as usual, but by Fred. The wonderful smell has lured him to take a look at what is going on; not in annoyance, but out of a genuine interest in the wine-making process. It isn't long before Fred has gotten a closer look at Mario's wine-making ability, as a full glass of grape juice has purposefully/accidentally splashed the voyeur. He is taken aback for a minute, but composes himself as he rubs his eye, ridding it of the wine; a bit of wine trickles down into his mouth, and a long tongue mops it up.

"Mmm, delicious," he says to himself.

Irene watches from the porch, "What is that on your shirt?"

"They're making wine," he answers.

She can't help but take a look; what confronts her nearly gives her a heart attack. Both Mario and Pietro are bent over with their shorts pulled down and backsides—plus extra—exposed, pointed directly into the spy hole whilst they continue to crush the grapes. It is all too much for Irene and she screams so loudly that the whole neighbourhood can hear her. Maria is also shocked, but she laughs anyway, as it's the funniest thing she has seen in years. The grape crushers nearly collapse with laughter. Within ten minutes, there is a knock on the door. Maria shows Constable Peterson to the backyard, where Mario and Pietro are washing their feet. Maria offers him a piece of her sponge cake, which he graciously accepts. With a full mouth, he asks, "Did you expose yourselves to the neighbours?"

"No," answers Mario innocently.

Constable Peterson looks sternly at Mario as he puts another forkful of cake into his mouth.

"We were just crushing the grapes...without any pants on," says Mario, trying desperately not to laugh, but Pietro can't help himself and doubles over with hilarity.

"How we make the wine in our own backyard is our business, isn't it?"

"Yes, I suppose it is...but I have to do something about this, Mario."

Mario and Pietro are now not so jovial, and Maria is looking to the constable with fear.

"Get me a piece of flat wood, a hammer and nails."

Mario responds quickly to the constable's request and scampers around the shed to find the requested items. The constable finishes the last bite of cake, compliments Maria as he hands back the plate, and takes the items from Mario's hand. He then walks up to the spy hole, holds up the piece of wood and hammers the nails in securely so the hole is well and truly covered.

"OK, that should do it." He hands the hammer back to an appreciative Mario.

"You owe me a bottle of wine, Mario, the next time I'm here... and I'm sure there will be a next time."

"I'll give you two bottles," replies Mario with a smile.

Constable Peterson nods his head as Maria escorts him back to the front door.

* * *

Maria returns from her usual church service, the first step in her daily routine—the second being lunch preparation for Mario in between job shifts. She is tiring now as she enters her third trimester, and the morning sickness has not let up.

She battles through, knowing very well that she will need to miss her daily ritual for a short while. Usually, she would be lucky and not encounter the neighbours, but today her luck has run out. Ever gracious, although she does not currently feel it, she smiles and waves to Fred and Irene. Fred waves back, and Irene ignores her as usual.

"God bless you," Maria says as she walks into her house.

"God bless you? God bless you, is that all she can say?" rebuffs Irene.

"She could say worse," replies Fred.

"And I told you they breed like rabbits... She hasn't been here five minutes, and she's ready to pop one out. Jesus Christ, we are going to be overrun."

Fred stares at her.

"Well?" she says to him.

"Irene, you need to let this go," he replies calmly, then he walks away.

"Where are you going?"

Fred doesn't answer, he just keeps walking, and she decides not to pursue it, as she knows that when he calls her Irene instead of Reenie, he is angry and things are best left alone.

Maria sets the table before Mario returns form work. The pasta sauce simmers away, the preprepared antipasto plate is positioned next to his favourite glass, ready to be filled with homemade wine. She places the knife and fork neatly on the folded woven cotton napkin.

BANG! BANG!

Maria freezes; it sounds like gunshots.

BANG!

She holds her stomach as she cautiously looks out the back window; she sees nothing.

BANG! BANG!

The sound is close, but she can't determine where it is coming from. There is a knock on the door. *It must be the police,* she thinks. She has never been so happy to have a visit from the constable as she is now. Maria opens the door and is surprised to see Fred standing there.

"Are you alright? What's going on?"

Maria shrugs her shoulders.

"Where are those gunshots coming from?"

Maria shrugs her shoulders again.

BANG! BANG! BANG!

Fred moves into defensive mode and stealthily advances in the general direction of the sound. The bangs seem to be coming from the backyard. He looks around; everything seems to be in order.

BANG! Both Fred and Maria jump in fright.

"It's inside your shed...Go inside, I'll have a look."

Maria says a teary, "Thank you."

Fred enters the shed; he is now out of Maria's sight.

BANG! BANG!

Maria breaths heavily, tears flowing down her fearful face; suddenly, she hears an enormous roar of laughter. Fred comes out and waves her into the shed. She enters, and what she sees is a pool of wine on the floor mixed with broken glass, and light-coloured splatters all over the wall.

"It's the wine bottles...they're exploding!" declares Fred.

Fred gives another belly full of laughter, and Maria joins in with relief. Another *BANG!* sends them both running for cover outside the shed, laughing hysterically as they encounter a frantic Mario.

"Your wine bottles are cactus, mate!"

Mario looks inside the shed to see the liquid mess on the floor and all over the walls. He wonders what went wrong. He is to find out later from Mr Max that you can't use beer bottles for sparkling wine; you have to use specific bottles that can handle the pressure.

Another bang also sends Mario darting out of the shed. Maria's relieved laughter now turns to annoyance as she says to Mario in her best English, "I no clean. You clean, not me."

"*Va bene,*" Mario says as he scratches his head.

Maria turns to Fred. "Thank you very much, Mr..." She stops as she realises that she doesn't know his name.

"Fred," he tells her.

Mario shakes his hand and introduces himself and Maria. Fred removes a package from his pocket and gives it to Maria. She pulls out a pacifier and looks to Fred questioningly.

"It's a dummy, for the baby...You put it in its mouth when it cries." Maria understood what it was even before Fred mimicked the motion of putting it in the mouth, and she is touched but also confused by the gesture.

"Thank you," she says again.

"Well, I bought it for you so you can keep the baby quiet, or else I will have to put up with my wife complaining about it."

Maria nods with a smile, while Mario just rolls his eyes, but even he is appreciative of the gesture.

CHAPTER 14: THE NEW AUSTRALIAN

Mario drives his Vanguard into the driveway, turns off the ignition and collects the package of lamb chops and pork ribs from the passenger side. Today is Sunday, and Mario is hosting a barbeque for the compatriots he worked with on the railways. He sits in his car thinking about the events that have led him to where he is. The lamb chops are significant to them all, as they are reminiscent of their time in the camp sites whilst working for the railways. Young Australian lamb chops on the barbie, as the Australians say, can't be beaten—they are delicious, and a far cry from the sloppy, smelly mutton they served up at Bonegilla. The pork ribs are an added bonus, as they, too, are delicious on the barbie—combined with homemade bread, wine and Maria's liquored sponge cake, life, as far as food went, is almost perfect. He often thinks about the day he will finally return home, and bring to his homeland the parts of Australia that he loves. Can he combine the two worlds? He is sure that he has changed and that he certainly is not the same man who left his mother crying with a broken heart. That is the memory that haunts Mario the most, and he is determined to see a smile on her face when he returns. He is about to become a father in a distant land, and though he is relatively happy, Australia isn't his place to be. He would also think about Macumba at times, and his tribe, and the harrowing events that he witnessed, the many unanswered questions that still remained in his thoughts. How did he die? Why did they take the children away? Was there anything he could have done to help?

Willy often told him that it was all out of his control, and that there was nothing he could have done to change things, and of course he knows Willy was right, but it doesn't stop the constant questioning in his mind.

He thinks about Alesky, and wonders what he is doing, before he tells himself it would be best if he didn't know.

Mario is startled by a knock on his car window.

"Are you alright, mate?" asks Fred. "You've been sitting in your car for a while."

"Oh yes, good, just thinking about things," replies Mario.

"Well, I'm thinking, why do you drive around in this piece of shit? Don't you work at Holden? You can buy a new car there, can't you?"

"Yes, but this car was cheap, does the job, and I'm going back to Italy after the baby is born, so I don't need a new car."

"Ahh, my missus will be happy."

Mario laughs. "Not as happy as me. I'm having a barbeque this afternoon, you want to come?"

"You're not going to serve any of that exploding wine, are you?"

"No, the wine will be safe, I promise."

"OK. Reenie's going to the bridge club, so I'll need to make sure I'm home before she comes in...It will be our secret."

"OK, see you this afternoon."

Back at the Brackenridge house, Irene puts on her best

hat and readies herself for the big bridge tournament at her women's club; Fred sits on his chair on the back porch, and she comes out to greet him.

"You look nice, dear," he says.

"Thank you. Are you sure you wouldn't like to join me, Fred?"

"No, no, I'll be OK. I might make my way down to the pub."

"OK, that's a good idea, especially if those rowdy Eye-Talians get too much."

Irene keeps talking, but all Fred is thinking about is the freshly barbequed meat aroma wafting from next door.

"You had better be going, love, or you'll be late," he says.

"Yes. Yes, OK. There are pasties for you in the oven. Bye-bye."

"Bye, have a good day."

The minute the coast is clear, Fred scurries to the Lanzani household, and is greeted by the rowdy Italians. A plate of freshly cooked meat with homemade bread is thrust into his hand along with a glass of wine. As he sips his wine, he thinks to himself that this is going to be a good day. The wine and beer flows, and the conversations get less comprehensible. Most of Mario's friends understand English, though none of them speak as well as Mario, but between the broken English and the drunken Italian sign language, Fred understands the general substance of the day's conversational exchanges. Generally, they speak of their experiences in Australia, and at times, some of the more uncouth guests make insulting remarks about Fred and his kind, disguised in friendly amicable banter. Fred assumes it is just cultural discourse in good fun, and it is certainly taken that way. The afternoon progresses to a sing-along with Pietro at the helm, while Maria, after serving her famous sponge cake, rests inside. None of Mario's friends are married yet, so no other women are present for Maria to entertain, and there is no one to voice her anxiety and concerns about her impending birth to. It doesn't really matter, as her church group supports her. One of her friends, who is on her fifth child, has given Maria many pieces of valuable advice, the most important being that your life will never be the same again!

Mario checks in on her every now and then to make sure she's all right, as she is due to give birth any day now. Maria tells him to go outside and stop worrying, and that God is watching over her. He agrees that the Australian God is good and will take care of her. Maria tells him that there is only one God, and to go outside and join his friends, dismissing his blasphemy as drunken stupor. He does as she asks and joins in the gaieties with Fred, who has not been this happy or drunk in a long time.

Irene calls out for Fred as she enters the house, and there is no reply. She puts the kettle on; a nice cup of tea is needed after the long walk home from the bridge club. The Eye-Talians are at it again, she thinks, listening to the muffled merriment. She decides to have a look, despite her better judgment. The singing and laughing annoys her, but she can't call the police, as she was explicitly told that she was only to ring if she witnesses any illegal activity. Constable Peterson said being an immigrant is not illegal, but being a public nuisance is, and she is teetering on the edge of that herself. She is angry, to say the least, but she understands clearly that the police do not want any more calls about the neighbours unless something is legitimately unlawful. She will be on the lookout.

"OK, chaps, how about a good Aussie song now?"

Irene hears a familiar voice from over the fence. She ignores it, as there is no possible way that Fred would be there. The voice sings his song.

"*Click go the shears, boys, click-click-click, wide is his blow, and his hands move quick...*"

The spy hole is covered, but some gaps between the fence panels allow Irene to investigate to whom the voice belongs. Time and alcohol have thwarted Fred, and his secret is discovered. Through the gap, Irene has glimpses of Fred, who stands a foot taller than most of his fellow partygoers, dancing around all arms and legs, looking like a huge praying mantis with no coordination whatsoever.

"Fred! Fred Brackenridge, you get yourself back here now!"

Everyone hears Irene as she screams louder than a banshee. Fred stops dancing.

"I think I'm in trouble, boys," says Fred.

This is followed by protests for him not to leave.

"I need to go. She's scarier than Hitler's ghost," Fred says with a hint of regret.

He scurries away, then comes back for one more swig of wine and cradles the bottle to his chest. "I'm going to need this."

The atmosphere is dampened after Fred leaves, and everyone goes home, much to Maria's delight, as now she can rest in peace and Mario can rest his throbbing head.

* * *

Late September 1958, Maria is bundled into the Vanguard and driven towards the beginning of her life as a mother. Maria is calm, as usual, always putting her trust in almighty divinity, but Mario is a wreck, making the situation so much less exciting than it should have been. Maria wishes that someone else could have driven her to the hospital, as a couple of times she screamed, not from contractions but rather from near misses with other cars. Luckily the hospital is only a short drive from where the Lanzanis live, and Maria doesn't have to endure the ride for very long, although it feels a lot longer. Maria is greeted at the reception by a midwife and a wheelchair. Mario kisses her, and she is wheeled away, crying out in pain. Mario is just crying. He stands at the reception desk wiping his eyes, trying to fill in the hospital documents as best he can. The receptionist assures him that his wife will be fine and he can go home and come back later, as these things usually take a while. Mario asks if he can stay at the hospital. The receptionist does not recommend it but says if he wants to, he can sit in the waiting room. He decides to go to work instead, as there is really nothing he can do sitting in a waiting room chair, and his employers need to be told about the birth, as it's nearly two weeks earlier than anticipated.

Going to work is a waste of time—Mario's mind is not on the job, so his supervisor sends him back to the hospital. Mario paces the floor. It has been hours, and no one has let him know what is happening. The other men in the waiting room can't help him, as they are in the same position, but there is a certain amount of solidarity between them until the nurse appears, and then it's every man for himself. Finally the head nurse enters and calls out for Mr Lanzani. Mario leaps towards her. Her solemn look confuses Mario, and she asks him to follow her into the nurse's station area.

"Please take a seat, Mr Lanzani."

"Where is my wife? What about the baby?" Mario asks in agitation.

She pushes some paperwork and a pen towards him. "Your

baby is fine, you have a beautiful boy."

It's just what he wanted to hear, but the look on her face does not match his short-lived joy.

"Mr Lanzani, there were complications with the birth, and your wife—"

"Maria," interrupts Mario.

"Yes, Maria has experienced a postpartum haemorrhage."

"What is that...? Is she alright?"

"She is losing a lot of blood, and the doctor needs to operate. It's quite serious, and we require you to sign the permission form."

Mario's mind is racing. He dare not even fathom the notion, but he must ask the question anyway.

"Is she going to die?"

"Not if we can help it. Do we have your permission?" the nurse asks bluntly.

"Yes...yes! Please don't let Maria die."

Mario signs the papers and looks to the nurse for any sort of assurance; an uneasy smile is all he gets.

"Try not to worry, we have very good doctors here," she finally says.

Worry is all he can do. How can such joy and utter despair share the same moment on the spectrum of life? Worrying is the only thing that can neutralise the conundrum. Mario is in a state of polarisation.

"Do you have a church here?" he asks.

"There is a chapel on the first floor," replies the nurse.

"I need to speak to the Australian God, he is good to me."

The nurse finally smiles. "Well, I'm sure whichever god is there today, he will listen."

Mario kneels in front of a familiar image of Jesus in the small chapel. He has watery eyes; his demeanour is awkward, as he doesn't know exactly what to do. The last time he was in a church was for his own Communion at the age of nine. Mario inherited his agnostic attitude from his father, long before his encounter with Padre Domenico, but accepts that religion and faith have their place in people's lives. Now he is kneeling, asking for help. Not for himself, but for Maria—after all, she has said enough prayers for the both of them, and God should not turn his back on her now. He is desperate enough to try anything. He did not bring Maria to Australia to kill her. He really doesn't know any contrition or petition prayers, or any type of prayers, for that matter, but he can do the sign of the cross, which he does, and then he thinks about what he can ask of the Australian God.

What will he do if Maria dies? This is not part of his plan, and Alesky's words come back to him: *You shouldn't be so stubborn in your ideas, you don't know what destiny has in store for you.* How was he going to look after a child on his own? How could he go back to Italy and face her family? These are all very confronting and selfish questions, but valid in Mario's mind. Is this a test? If it is, he is failing miserably. It takes all the strength he has not to fall apart. Was he tarnished by the same curse as his father, who lost his first wife? He looks for a sign, any sign, that could give him hope; nothing is forthcoming. Mario is angry now, and the silent prayers stop. He resigns himself to the fact that he is on his own; he rises from the small dais and shouts to the statue of Jesus, "Just take me instead!"

As Mario steps down from the dais, he tumbles to the hard floor with a thump. He collects himself, and starts to laugh. He notices a sharp pain in his shoulder and laughs even louder, lucky he is already in a hospital.

Mario looks at Maria's bed through the window of the intensive care unit, nursing his dislocated shoulder. She is still unconscious, and has been for hours, but she is alive at least. He keeps a close eye on the sister as she checks her vitals every half hour. The doctor comes in to check on Maria, and then speaks to the nurse. She points to Mario. Finally, the doctor approaches Mario.

"Hello, Mr Lanzani," he says politely.

"Hello...how is Maria?"

"Your wife is going to be fine, but unfortunately, we had to remove her uterus to stop the bleeding."

Mario looks dumbfounded. "What does that mean, Doctor?"

"It means she won't be able to have any more children."

"Oh, but she will live?"

"Yes."

Mario breathes a big sigh of relief and shakes the doctor's hand.

"Thank you! It's good, it's alright," says a very pleased Mario.

"Have you seen your son yet?"

"No."

"The nursery is two wards down, if you would like to see him."

Mario thanks the doctor again, and rushes to the nursery. He hadn't been able to look at the baby until he knew what Maria's outcome would be. He looks through the nursery window, scanning the cribs for his son. The nursery sister pops her head out.

"Name?" she enquires.

"Mario Lanzani," replies Mario.

She hands him a pen and paper. "Can you write that down

for me, please?"

He does so. She enters the nursery and matches the name to a placard, and wheels the crib with a little white bundle in it towards the glass front. He looks hard for any sign of life as the nurse lifts the bundle to the glass. Mario hasn't really seen any newborns before—he never took notice each time his mother gave birth—and he wonders if they all look like skinned rabbits, because this one does. The nurse puts the baby back into the crib, and then smiles at Mario. She approaches him.

"Congratulations, Mr...L..." She hesitates, and then mispronounces his name to the point that he almost doesn't recognise it. "What do you think of your new son?"

Mario pauses, then says, "I think he's been hit with the ugly stick."

The nurse is taken aback at first, but then sees the humour of the comment.

"They all look that way when they're first born. When they fill out, they're adorable."

Mario certainly hopes so.

Maria begins to wake; she is totally disorientated. She speaks to the nurse in Italian, and the nurse responds, "Sorry, I don't understand you."

Maria gasps, suddenly realising where she is, and starts to scream.

"*Mio bambino...mio bambino?*" Maria demands. The nurse tries to calm her down. Maria points to herself. "Me baby...me baby?"

Mario hears the screams as he returns from the nursery, and runs into the ward, directly to Maria, who is still screaming and crying.

"Maria, *che c'e?*"

"Mario, *dov'e' il bambino...dov'e' il bambino*?"

"Everything is good, I've seen the baby...He's beautiful," Mario lies in Italian. He turns to the nurse.

"She's just asking for the baby."

"Yes, she woke up in shock. Tell her to keep still, and I'll go and get her baby. She can have a cuddle for a while."

She smiles at Maria. Mario doesn't need to interpret, as Maria understands what the nurse says, and she calms down and nods her head. Mario cups Maria's hand with his free one.

"I thought I was going to lose you."

Maria notices his sling. "What happened?"

"A sign from the Australian God." He laughs. "I fell in the chapel."

Maria grimaces. "Mario, there is only one God."

"You worship your way, I'll worship mine."

Maria's sermon is interrupted by the nurse placing a white-blanketed bundle into her arms. She starts to cry as she looks at her infant's contented sleeping face. Mario wonders if she is crying because he's so ugly.

"He's beautiful. Mario, he's beautiful."

"Yes, he is, congratulations to both of you," says the nurse. "I'll leave you alone for a few minutes, then I'll need to bring him back to the nursery. You will need to rest, Maria, you've had a very big operation."

"OK, thank you," responds Maria.

Maria now looks up at Mario. "I forgive you."

"What for?"

Maria gives him a "you know what I mean" look. "For your blasphemy...and I thank you."

"What for?"

"For giving me this wonderful gift."

"I didn't do much, Maria, you did all the hard work."

"Mmm, it was worth it."

"Pop this in your mouth, Maria," the nurse says. She places the thermometer under Maria's tongue and looks at her stopwatch.

"Your little man needs a name."

For Mario, it is an easy choice; one that he's made without consulting Maria.

"Yes, his name is Euplio."

"I beg your pardon?" says the perplexed nurse.

"E-U-PLIO, after my father."

Maria says nothing, not because she has a thermometer in her mouth but because she would never change tradition.

The nurse takes the thermometer out of Maria's mouth. "Your temperature is good, Maria. Mr Lanzani, you can't call him that—nobody will be able to pronounce it. You live in Australia now, he needs to have an English name."

"He is Italian, and his name is Euplio, just like my father!"

"I don't mean to offend you, but if you name him E... E...?"

"E-UP-LI-O," Mario spells the name out in syllables.

"Yes, umm...*that* will make things difficult for him. Why don't you put your father's name on the birth certificate, and call him, um...maybe...Elliot? It will make life easier for him, and for us!"

Mario is not impressed.

"Just a suggestion," says the nurse as she turns to Maria and beckons for the baby, which Maria kisses and gives to her half-heartedly.

"I'll bring him back tomorrow. You get some sleep now, and I'm afraid you will need to leave as well, Mr Lanzani."

Mario frowns but does as she says, and has the last say in

Italian, so the nurse doesn't understand.

"His name will be Euplio. I'm not listening to these bloody people!"

The Vanguard splatters into the driveway. Mario waves to Fred, who puts down his hand-push lawn mower to approach the dividing fence.

"Are you a father yet, Mario?" shouts Fred as Mario closes his door.

"Yes, I am, Fred," Mario says proudly.

Fred reaches out to shake Mario's hand and congratulate him. "Well done, a boy or a girl?"

"A boy."

"Fantastic! What's his name?"

"Euplio."

Fred wrings his ear with his pointer finger. "What was that?"

Mario hesitates, then says, "Elliot."

"Ohhh, Elliot, that's a fine name. A fine name. So when's the next one, then?"

"There won't be any more. Maria had some complications, so no more children."

"Oh. Sorry. Well, never mind, it's quality, not quantity, as they say."

Mario has a little chuckle with Fred. A loud whistle is heard, followed by a shout.

"Hey, overprivileged Italian!"

Mario can hardly believe what he's seeing as Alesky jogs up the driveway towards him.

"Hello, old friend!"

Alesky shakes Fred's hand. He introduces himself as Denis May with an excellent Australian accent. Mario looks dubiously at Alesky as he puts one arm around Mario and waves goodbye to Fred with the other one.

"So, what's been happening, mate?" Alesky asks.

CHAPTER 15: WHO ARE YOU?

Belogorsk, Ukraine, April 1944. Denys Maykaporvic awakes to feel pain in his shoulder and a heaviness on top of him. The pain is the result of a gunshot wound from a German bullet when he was lined up with Jews, political commissars and any partisan sympathisers that the German army saw fit—or rather unfit—to be executed. The heaviness comes from the executed bodies that were piled on top of him as he lay buried in the pit. The last thing Denys remembers is the ray of sunlight warming his face before the screams and the gunshots fell silent. Only a claustrophobic blackness surrounds him. An urge to find that last evocation of sunlight propelled him to climb his way out of the darkened, slimy pit. It was a long, arduous crawl between the corpses, and up towards the edge of the ditch, until he finally climbed out into more darkness, dimly lit by a quarter moon.

He was very careful to be quiet as he inhaled a long-awaited breath of fresh air so as not to alert any soldiers who might still be lurking around. Denys walked slowly and silently towards a candlelit window, hoping to God that the inhabitants were sympathetic. He encountered a dog that luckily did not bark, and instead was content just to sniff him and be on his way. Denys tapped lightly on the window to alert the occupants, and dragged himself towards the door. The Kushnirenkos, fortunately for Denys, were very much humble and good-natured local Ukrainians who looked at the blood-soaked teenage boy in disbelief, but unfortunately not in surprise, as they had witnessed many human brutalities over the past few years: first from the Russians and now from the Germans. Denys stared beseechingly at the Kushnirenkos, and then fainted.

Simferopol 1941, the German army were welcomed by the local Ukrainians, as this would end the tyranny of the NKVD—the People's Commissariat for Internal Affairs, the interior ministry of the Soviet Union—which orchestrated the famine responsible for the starvation of numerous Ukrainians. As Einsatzgruppen D pushed into the capital, the retreating NKVD police shot many captives and nationalist leaders in the city's prisons. Denys's father was one of them.

His father was an academic and a Ukrainian national. His mother was a linguist, and Jewish. The marriage was a happy one, not condemned by either side. A ten-year-old Denys was well aware of the political climate, but neither he nor his mother could have ever imagined the demise of their family so quickly. Within four months, his father was dead along with his maternal Jewish grandparents, as well as many other much-loved family members.

The horrific scenes of public killings became a daily occurrence, provoked by the Germans and performed in local pogroms. Male partisans, communists and Jews were the primary targets; however, eventually women and children also started to be executed. Denys's Aryan descent gave him a certain amount of protection, but his mother was constantly in danger because of the anti-Jewish sentiment of the local

Ukrainians, fuelled by German propaganda; eventually, she was rescued and hidden by a sympathetic local priest. Denys lived with his paternal grandparents, but would visit his mother every chance he could. She would hold him in her arms for hours as they conversed in English, her favourite foreign language. No one else could understand them, and they told each other private jokes—laughter would always override the fear. She was proud of how he could grasp the complexities of any language at such a young age, even better than she could. He would also report on what he saw every day. What he told her was very disturbing: the German liberators were Russian oppressors speaking a different language, and the local inhabitants couldn't see it.

There were things that he told her, and some things he did not. Particularly, he did not tell her that some days he played the piano accordion to entertain the Germans soldiers while gathering information. The Germans did not know that Denys could understand their language, and he didn't let them know, usually playing the foolish, innocent child. In return for his playing, they would give him gifts, like candy, or items taken from a victim. The soldiers were usually drunk, and the information flowed freely as they conversed amongst themselves. *Knowledge is power,* he thought. The education he received on the streets of Simferopol was more significant than any education he could have received at school. He would often pass this intelligence on to the priest, or the small band of Jewish escapees hiding in the swamps.

Two years of intensified ethnic cleansing had passed, and Denys had hardened, but it was very difficult for him to understand why this was all happening. His mother was still alive, thanks to the priest, but he was ever more careful not to provoke any suspicion when he visited her. Two or three times a week, Denys left his grandparents' house and walked towards the church unassumingly. One day was different. He saw a large crowd of people gathered outside the church. His heart sank; he did not have a good feeling inside. His intuition was proven right when he saw the priest hanging dead in the front of his church for all to see. Some were horrified, some were damning the dead priest, but Denys's attentions were directed towards the cartful of people crammed in like sardines and carefully guarded by Ukrainian and German military.

He summoned all the strength he had not to shout and cry when he saw his mother in the cart. She spotted him and discreetly put her finger to her mouth and blinked twice, very slowly. He understood not to react. Denys was approached by one of the uniformed soldiers and asked to identify himself. He showed his certificate of Aryan descent; he was safe. His mother smiled and put her hand to her heart as the cart pulled away. He knew he would never see her again. He ran back to his grandparents' house, an empty shell of his former self. The second he entered the house, all his built-up emotion released, and all his grandparents could do was watch. They knew then of their daughter-in-law's fate.

A year on, Denys was a week away from his fourteenth birthday; he had grown, but still had his wiry, muscular build. The only thing that would comfort him was the memory of his mother and the time they had spent together, speaking and singing in different languages. On the odd occasion, he would witness the resistance group overthrowing and most times killing a German; this also made him happy. The German occupation was coming to an end, and they knew it, but this did not quell the violence—in fact, it escalated the urgency to rid as many 'Untermensch' as possible. In the last days of the occupation, Denys was denounced by a neighbour; not even his certificate of Aryan descent could save him—he was the son of a Jew, a half-breed, and needed to be exterminated. He did not resist when the Gestapo came to detain him, so that his grandparents would not be harmed. He was tired; the last four years had taken a toll on him. He allowed himself to shed tears as the crammed cart travelled to Belogorsk, its final destination.

* * *

Denys wakes up in a warm bed in the Kushnirenkos's house, momentarily shrouded in the safety of his dreams, but it isn't long before the horrors of his experience are resurrected in his mind. His arm throbs underneath his bandaged shoulder, but his blood-stained body has been washed and cleansed, which makes him relax a little. There are various rustling sounds and a sense of urgency in the atmosphere. He listens intently, not really knowing if he should move. Ultimately, Olek and his wife, Nina, approach him to assess his situation. They explain that they are leaving the city, as they fear the Germans will burn down the town and kill any witnesses to the genocide; he is welcome to come with them if he likes. Denys thinks about his grandparents, but decides against trying to find them and takes up the Kushnirenkos's offer. The family gives Denys a much-appreciated meal, and they talk well into the night about the past, the present and, most importantly, the future.

Nina prepares all the food and incidentals needed, as well as carefully concealing anything of value within the folds of their clothes. Olek and Denys ensure the cart is roadworthy; there is no donkey to pull it, as the Germans took that a while ago, but the two men modify the cart so that they can pull it instead. In the very early hours, and within the safety of darkness, they depart for the Port of Sevastopol. There, they will catch a boat and sail to Kosovo, where Nina has family. Five hours in, the sun exposes the small convoy to their surroundings. They do not travel on the open road, instead choosing the less used but longer path.

They stop for a while to rest and eat. Denys needs to urinate, so he walks into the dense scrub to do his business. He hears shouting from the direction the Kushnirenkos are resting. From where Denys stands, he can see a German officer intimidating Olek and pointing his gun towards Nina. He looks around to see if there are any other officers, as it is unusual to see only one—they typically come in pairs. *He must be a deserter,* Denys thinks.

When Nina gives the officer some of their food, he scarfs it down with one hand while still holding his gun in the other. This gives Denys an advantage. With all his rage and a large rock in the hand of his unwounded arm, he blindsides the German and disarms him. Not content to just hit him once, Denys uses the rock to bash the German's head repeatedly until he is dead and unrecognisable. Denys has killed his first German, and it felt good. Olek and Nina stare at Denys with a combination of fear and admiration.

Denys rummages through the pockets of the dead man, and as expected, finds several bags of valuables stolen from exterminated victims. He takes all of the officer's personal documents before rolling him into the scrub and covering him with forest debris. They continue their journey, saying very little, and finally reaching the Port of Sevastopol. There they find a line of expatriates waiting to board boats for mainland Eastern Europe. Denys feels uneasy about the situation; he wants to leave the port as soon as possible. He looks inside one of the bags he took from the German man he just killed; it contains various rings, gold teeth and other stolen valuables. He decides against the teeth, for obvious reasons, but there is a ring with no markings. That is enough to get him and the Kushnirenko family on the next departing boat. They cross the Black Sea to the mainland, towards their new future, but it takes another week before they safely reach Nina's family.

Nina's sister and her husband own a small tavern attached to a farmhouse near the Albanian border. They have plenty of room for their new guests and welcome them warmly; they also welcome the manual labour provided by two extra men. As the weeks go on, Denys discovers that the tavern, although a legitimate business, is a front for the People's Liberation of Albania, and when asked if he wants to drive the Germans out of Kosovo, he says only if he can kill them as well. By the end of 1944, the German army is driven out of Kosovo, but this does not bring immediate peace and order, as now there is much anti-communist sentiment and a push against the Yugoslav Partisans, with constant armed uprisings that aim to resist the incorporation of Kosovo into communist Yugoslavia.

By the end of 1945, the Kushnirenkos are planning to travel to Ally-occupied Italy, to a displaced-persons camp, and eventually emigrate to America. This has been Denys's plan as well, but he has found a reason to stay. That reason is the tavern owner's daughter, Ljubica. She has captured his heart with her sweet face and caring manner.

Three years on, Denys continues to fight for the anti-communist movement, but he becomes seriously wounded in a particularly bloody skirmish. He was the only one to survive, helped by a quick-thinking farmer who hid him buried in pig mud, breathing through a reed, as the enemy came looking for him. Denys was in a serious state by the time he reached the tavern after that, but Ljubica nursed him back to health. With the blessing of her parents, Denys and Ljubica are married in 1949. At first Ljubica's father, Jorik, was against it—he liked Denys and admired his bravery and intelligence, and had seen firsthand his fighting skills as they banded together against the Yugoslav Partisans—but now, he was a wanted man, and this would put Jorik's daughter in danger. Still, Ljubica insisted that she and Denys marry. In the end, Jorik had no choice but to agree.

The time comes when Denys has had enough of all the political ideology, interracial tension and unnecessary bloodshed. He is about to become a father, and his ideals have shifted. He and his wife are to follow in the footsteps of the Kushnirenkos, travel to Italy and emigrate to America, or anywhere as far away as possible from Europe. There is only one problem; he is wanted by the Yugoslav security agency for treason. He looks through the various identity documents he has, deciding who he will become—one, in particular, is perfect. Yes, he is now a Polish national. His name is Alesky Gulan.

CHAPTER 16: HE'S A PIG

Mario and Alesky, who now calls himself Denis, stand in the driveway looking at a flat tyre on the Vanguard. They assess it, but nothing is actually going to happen until they've smoked at least two cigarettes. It is necessary to fix it, as Maria and the baby need to be picked up the next morning. Denis now resides in the outhouse. Pietro moved out as soon as he heard of Alesky's arrival and now lives as far away as he can from the man he knew as Alesky. Mario would miss Pietro, as apart from being a good singer, he could also cook and proved to be invaluable while Maria was in hospital. Mario would especially miss Pietro's gnocchi with ragu sauce, which is a specialty dish from his region. The day Pietro left, he packed the last of his possessions and gave Mario a hearty farewell—and Alesky a lukewarm one. Pietro was always wary of Alesky, even more so when he changed his name. He let Mario know of his concerns. This plays on Mario's mind. Maria is coming home in the morning, and he needs to clarify Alesky's situation.

"Alesky?" Mario says nervously.

"Denis," corrects Alesky.

"OK, Denis, you're here and I now have a family. I need to ask you...are we in any danger?"

"No, you're not in any danger. But I might be!"

This does not comfort Mario, but Denis's smile makes him laugh a little. "So, can you tell me what's happened?"

"All I'm going to say is that not all the Ustasa and Chetniks stayed in Yugoslavia. And I might have said and done some things I shouldn't have...The open wounds of Europe have found their way here, and it might be a while before they heal."

"I thought you were Polish?"

"I never said I was Polish, I just had a Polish passport."

"So, you're Yugoslavian?"

"No!"

"What are you?"

"I'm Australian, mate. Naturalised a few months ago! You should become one as well."

"I could never become an Australian. We will be going back home to Italy next year."

"The difference between you and me is that you look forward to the future; I'm trying to escape to it."

Mario says nothing. He takes a drag of his cigarette and flicks the ash on Irene's roses. Irene comes out of her house to inspect the situation, and she is not happy, as usual.

"Stop flicking your ash over my roses!"

"Ash is good for roses," responds Mario sarcastically.

She lashes out. "Why don't you go home?"

"I am home, this is my house."

"Go back to your own country!"

"You go back to your own country."

"This is my country!"

"You don't look Aboriginal to me."

"What are you talking about?"

"If you're not Aboriginal, then you're an immigrant like me. Go back to your country."

"I'm third generation, and my ancestors made this country better."

"And we will make it even better."

Irene scoffs.

"Anyway, I am going back to my own country, and you're paying for it."

"What are you talking about? I'm not paying for anything, although I would consider it if it would get rid of you."

"I work here in Australia, I make the money and I take your money back to Italy," Mario says.

Irene stares in disbelief. "You're working for it, you damn fool; I'm not giving it to you. You truly are an ignoramus."

"No, I am Italian!"

Irene's flared nostrils now point towards Denis, who speaks with a German accent—he has been told about the bigot next door and knows this will infuriate her.

"He's right, you know, we are all migrants."

Irene's anger turns into terror as she runs off. *"Guten tag, Fräulein!"* he shouts as she runs away.

Mario and Alesky are in stiches as Alesky says, "She is right, you know."

"How?" says Mario.

"You're working for your money, no one is giving it to you."

"Ahh, just details," sneers Mario.

Irene once again is in a panic, but this time she is shaking. She frantically looks for Fred. He is in his usual spot, listening to the radio with a beer in his hand.

"Fred, we have Italians and Germans living next door now!"

"What are you talking about?"

"That bloody Italian has a German friend. Oh my God, it's the Axis alliance right next door."

"Who, you mean Denis? He's not German."

"Yes, he is! He probably changed his name, but he is German...How can they let these people into our country, what is the government thinking? It wasn't long ago that we were fighting against them!"

"Irene...the war is over."

Irene can't take any more of his attitude and runs off crying. Fred takes a deep breath, and then another sip of his beer.

Maria and the baby have settled in, and Fred's dummy has come in handy quite a few times. Mario is warming up to the ugly slug, and Denis adores baby Euplio from the beginning. He thinks Maria is a gem, way too good for Mario, which he tells Mario often.

Mario and Irene are often at each other's throats, which causes stress for Maria—she always suggests that Mario be the better person, and stop baiting Irene, purposely giving her reasons to be angry. Irene has ramped up her attacks on Mario and Denis. Any dishonourable behaviour that she thinks should be investigated by the local police is reported. Most times, because of the rotating shifts, there is a policeman knocking at the Lanzani's door. This makes Denis nervous, even though they haven't done anything wrong aside from being very loud when drunk. Denis should let it go, as Maria suggested, but he can't let it rest, it isn't in his nature—when he sees what he thinks is an injustice, he always reacts in some way. Irene doesn't know who she is dealing with—if she is frightened of Germans, she does not know what a Ukrainian half-Jew could do.

A quick visit to the hardware store to buy some sulphuric acid-based drain cleaner, and his plan is set. He doesn't tell Mario or Maria what he is doing, just in case it backfires and they are questioned. If they honestly don't know, they can't be implicated. He carefully dilutes the drain cleaner with the correct amount of water; he doesn't want to kill her, just cause some discomfort. He waits for a day she has her washing hanging on the clothesline. Her big cotton underwear are flapping in the breeze; it is the perfect time to strike. Armed with his solution, he executes his mission with covert precision. Dennis is very careful not to make any noise as he approaches the flapping white cotton underwear and then proceeds to paint the solution all over the material. He covers four pairs of female underwear, but he leaves the male ones, as he quite likes Fred. Sulphuric acid dries clear and odourless, and doesn't eat through cotton, but it does burn human skin. Now, he just needs to wait and let the acid do its work, without leaving a scrap of evidence to incriminate him.

* * *

The dawn sky is full of eerie blue-black clouds ready to burst into rain. Irene hears some rummaging sounds coming from next door. She put her ear to the fence to listen; whatever it is, it is out of the sight line of the slight opening in the fence.

"Bloody hell, he's heavy," says Denis.

"Yes, he is a big one."

Irene's ears prick up. Although she can't see who it is, she knows it is Mario and his German friend. *What are they up to?* she wonders.

"I feel sorry that we had to kill him."

"He's a pig!"

Irene is frozen; she keeps listening to the conversation.

"We need to hang him in the shed, let the blood run out, and

159

then we can cut him up tomorrow."

Through the small slit in the wooden fence, Irene glimpses a body wrapped up in a blood-soaked sheet as the two shadowy figures walk past. She stays still and silent until the men have entered the shed, and then she rushes inside. She doesn't even bother to tell Fred, she just directs herself straight to the phone to call the police. Fred overhears the conversation.

"Yes, that's exactly what I said, I saw two men carrying a dead body covered with a sheet into the shed next door. I heard their voices, and I'm certain it's the Eye-Talian who lives next door, and another man who is a German, or at least he speaks German...Yes, please hurry. I'm very frightened." She hangs up the receiver.

"Reenie, are you serious?"

"Yes, very, very serious!"

"Are sure you saw a body?"

"I saw what I saw, Fred, and now you see the trouble we have living next door. I've been expecting this...Oh, my nerves! And I've got this persistent rash to deal with as well."

Fred is stunned, not really knowing what to believe. He knows Irene is neurotic, but she isn't a liar. Through the front window, he sees two police cars arrive with four armed policemen. He decides to go to the backyard to see what he can find out.

The policemen storm the household. Maria is frightened and confused, and Mario tells her in Italian to take the baby into the bedroom and lock herself in. He is thinking of the government men taking the children away from the Aboriginal camp. He soon finds out the policemen are not there for the baby but for the dead body he has hidden in the shed. Denis stays put in the outhouse; he does not want to get involved with any type of law enforcement. *Mario can take care of whatever they are here for*, he says to himself. Mario is perplexed, but cooperates with the police and leads them to the shed; he didn't know it was illegal to slaughter a pig. He soon finds out that it is not.

"You have a pig carcass hanging in your shed," states the policeman.

"Yes," answers Mario.

All the police put away their weapons. "What are you going to do with the pig?"

"Oh...well, I make sausages, and prosciutto, small goods and other things like soap from the fat. Lots of things," explains Mario.

"Are you a butcher?"

"No, no, we just used to do this back home, so I thought we can do it here. You can't get this sort of food here in Australia, the way we do it...Is this wrong?"

"Um, no, it's perfectly alright. Sorry for any inconvenience, but we always need to investigate a suspected murder."

Mario launches into the biggest laugh as he connects the dots, and the police laugh along, very relieved with the outcome, as is Denis. Fred, not so much.

"Irene? Irene, where are you?" he shouts.

Irene comes out of her safe place and rushes to him. "What happened?"

"They found the pig!"

"Yes, yes, that's what they called the poor soul."

"Irene, they found a pig. A real pig, the animal kind!"

Irene's mouth is wide open as she ferociously scratches her buttocks. "Well, how was I supposed to know? And what are they doing with a dead pig?"

Fred reaches for another beer from the fridge. Even though

it's only midmorning, he definitely needs one.

"They're making small goods with it, which is perfectly legal, isn't it?"

Irene has a sheepish look on her face as she scratches herself intensely.

"Yes, I suppose it is. I really need to see the doctor about this rash, it's just not going away."

* * *

Mario and his friends, including Pietro, gather to make sausages from the pork meat, which is carefully cut and prepared for processing.

Denis packs his bags in preparation to leave. He isn't really sure where he will go, but he knows it will be somewhere near the ocean. He loves the sea; he finds it extremely calming and it gives him a sense of equanimity. He doesn't want to stay at Mario's anymore, as police visits to the house are becoming way too regular for his liking, and he doesn't see Irene's zealous appetite for harassing foreigners waning any time soon. Fred told them that he gave her a very stern warning and the police had put her on notice again. The harassment would stop now, Fred said, but Denis doesn't quite believe it. He has seen far too much prejudice and hatred to have confidence in any immediate change of human nature. Irene is no match for what he experienced, but it is time for him to move on, or else he might not be able to stop at just the one act of sulphuric acid warfare.

Denis is all packed ready to go. The work Mario secured for him at Penfolds has given him enough money to move on. He stays for a few more hours to help Mario and the team process the pork meat, which also ensures he will get a good feed before he leaves. Denis stands with Maria and little Euplio, watching the loud and animated discussions about how much salt and spice should be added, and how the way each person makes their sausage is the best. After much deliberation, Mario puts his foot down and takes charge so that the sausages finally start being made. The large, continental, homemade sausages are delectable; everyone takes credit for them being so. Denis helps himself to more sausage before he waves goodbye to all the wannabe master butchers. He gives Maria a thankful kiss on the cheek. He will miss her cooking and tells her that if she ever wants to leave Mario, she should seek him out. She laughs, but Mario just reminds him that it's time for him to go.

The birth of Euplio Jr did not deter Maria from her daily religious ritual; she just pops him in the pram and walks to the church as usual. Her path always takes her past Fred and Irene's front yard, and if they happen to be there, she stops to bid her friendly greetings.

"'Ello," she says.

"Hello, Maria. How are you, and how's my little mate?" says Fred with a friendly wave. Irene ignores her.

"Very good, thank you, and how are you, Irene dear? I am told you are better from your rash?"

Irene stares, and gives a slight grunt to acknowledge her.

"God bless you, Irene darling," Maria says with a beautiful and sincere smile.

"Off to church, are we?" Fred asks, trying to counteract Irene's rudeness.

"Yes, bye-bye." Irene's eyes follow Maria as she wheels the pram up the street.

"She is so annoying," Irene says through gritted teeth.

"Who, Maria?"

"Yes. She's very hard to hate, that's very annoying!"

"Very annoying!" Fred says sarcastically.

The 1960 vintage sees Mario and Fred making a batch of cabernet sauvignon together, another experiment for Mario, as he has not used this type of grape before. It's also a master class for Fred, as he has pestered Mario to teach him. Irene, of course, is not happy about it, but Fred is determined to learn how to make wine; he has resorted to sleeping in the spare room just to stop the nagging. Fred is growing very fond of Mario, Maria and adorable little Elliot. It eventually goes so far that Irene no longer talks to him at all, which suits him just fine. Mario gladly agrees to show Fred the wine-making process, as Fred has agreed to buy all the wine-making equipment from Mario when they leave. This will be the last vintage in Australia for Mario; the plan is to move the family back to Italy by the end of the year. With the money that Mario has been sending back to his father, and the tidy profit that will be made from the sale of the house, Mario is in a good position to realise his aspiration of resurrecting the family business. Maria is also happy about going home, and writes to her family about how excited she is to see them again. This includes her immediate family as well as her family at the convent, who she also misses, although not as much since Euplio Jr was born.

Mario and Fred are up to their knees in crushed grapes, in two adjacent half barrels, their legs moving up and down to upbeat Italian songs. Maria watches through the window in amusement as eighteen-month-old Euplio escapes outside.

"Euplio, my son!" Mario says, holding out his hands. He has turned into an adorable little boy and not the skinned rabbit Mario saw him as when he was first born.

"Hello, little Elliot," says Fred as the infant runs to them in sheer delight.

Fred doesn't really understand why Mario and Maria call him another name; he thinks it must be some sort of Italian nickname, and a strange one at that. Mario pulls him up to the barrel, and screams of laughter come from the toddler, mixed with bad singing from both Mario and Fred. Maria, watching the comical grape crush from the window, is not laughing.

"Mario, I just gave him a bath!" she shouts.

"Good, that means he won't contaminate the grapes!" he shouts back.

Maria stands at the door with a stern look. "Now I have to give him another bath. You make so much work for me!"

"Ah, blah-blah-blah!" answers Mario as he lifts the toddler out of the barrel.

He immediately runs to Fred. "Play...play?" Elliot gabbles.

"Not now, my little mate, I need to help your dad make the wine. Later I will help him drink it. You need to go to Mama Bear because she looks angry!"

Elliot laughs at Uncle Fred's funny face.

"Vieni amore mio," Maria coaxes Euplio Jr with open arms.

"When will lunch be ready?" Mario asks.

"After I bathe the baby," retorts Maria.

Fred and Mario continue their crushing with even louder and more out-of-tune singing.

Irene peers over through the crack in the fence. "Damn fools," she says to herself, and then shouts from behind the fence: "Fred Brackenridge, you'd better not step into the house with those dirty wine legs of yours!"

Fred picks up a glass, fills it with the contents of a bottle from last year's vintage, and toasts her whilst continuing to crush the grapes. Mario laughs hysterically; they are both becoming increasingly intoxicated from the wine they drink throughout the process. The men finish the crushing, wash their legs, and transfer the must—the freshly pressed grape juice—into the fermentation tank; now it's just a matter of waiting. Maria has prepared lunch, and Fred politely accepts the invitation to stay and eat. He knows Irene will have prepared some sausage rolls for him, but he can eat them for dinner if she doesn't throw them out. He hopes that Maria's lunch will be as tasty as Irene's famous sausage rolls.

The table is set while the baby sleeps soundly. Maria takes the focaccia bread she has just made out of the oven. The two men stumble in, clean but tipsy and happy and in definite need of some food to counteract the alcohol. Fred sits at a beautifully arranged place setting, with a folded cloth napkin beneath precisely arranged cutlery on the left side, an empty plate in the middle and a large, bohemian crystal drinking glass on the right. In the centre of the table stands a jug of wine with cut-up pieces of peach soaking in the contents, next to another, smaller jug, which is filled with fresh water and ice. Mario sits in his customary chair; waiting, as always, to be served by Maria. Fred rises from the table, feeling uncomfortable, and asks Maria if she would like any help. Both Maria and Mario give him an odd look. Maria politely says no and tells him to make himself comfortable at the table, although she is inwardly impressed by his politeness. She pours both the men a glass of water, then returns to the kitchen. Fred takes a sip of his water as he stares at the jug of wine, thinking he would much prefer that, but wondering what the deal is with the peaches. Maria presents a platter of antipasto, which consists of olives, two types of cheese, pickled vegetables and three types of cured pork product, then she returns with a tray of freshly baked focaccia and sits down to eat with the men. Mario begins to select his preferred salumi and encourages Fred to do the same. Fred, not knowing how to eat this fare, looks for guidance from Mario. He is soon munching away like a true Italian.

"This is delicious," says Fred.

"That came from the dead pig your wife nearly had me arrested for." Mario laughs.

"You made this yourself?"

"Mmmm," responds Mario with his mouth full.

"Wow! I've seen something like this in France, but I never ate it. If I knew it was this good, I would have."

"You were in France?"

"Yeah, during the Great War."

"You fought in the war?"

"Yeah, I did. Wow, I'm as full as a doctor's wallet, thank you so much, Maria."

Sensing that Fred doesn't want to talk about his experience in the war, Mario changes the subject.

"Leave some room for the pasta, Fred."

"What, there's more?"

"Yes, I made lasagne," responds Maria.

Fred doesn't think he can eat any more, but doesn't want to be rude, so when Maria serves him his plate he accepts it. Strangely enough, he finishes it, even mopping up the leftover sauce on the plate with a piece of bread, as Mario does. It is the most delicious thing he has ever eaten; with its layers of pasta sheets filled with bolognaise sauce and melted mozzarella, it is heavenly. It no longer matters if Irene has thrown away the sausage rolls, as his belly is about to explode; he can't fit another thing in, except for the nice glass of wine Maria has just poured. Then she forks the peaches, soaked with wine, onto a small plate and offers them to Fred as dessert. He manages to eat all of them as well. Not wanting to overstay his welcome, Fred rises from the table with his hands patting his very full stomach and says, "Maria, that was absolutely marvellous, thank you very much. Can I help you with the dishes?"

Maria, wide-eyed with a smile, says, "No, no, no, no! You are my guest, you don't wash the dishes."

With that, he kisses her hand, then turns to Mario to shake his. "Mario, my friend, you've got yourself a keeper! Let me know when you need help with the rest of the wine making, especially the drinking part."

Both Mario and Maria laugh along with him as he leaves on his wobbly wine legs to face the domestic storm he knows is ahead.

CHAPTER 17: CONFESSIONS

Mario returns from a day of double shifts: one at Holden, one at Penfolds. He is dog tired and very much looking forward to the day he can ease his workload. He sits at his daily place of worship—his favourite chair at the kitchen table, set out by Maria with the wine glass positioned right next to the jug full of last year's vintage. Maria has placed a letter from Mario's family at the side of the placemat, ready for him to read once he eats his dinner.

Little Euplio babbles his way through some buttered pastina, most of it ending up in his hair or on the floor. Maria laughs as she continuously cleans up after him—he can do no wrong in her eyes, even if he does make a mess of her spotless floor; he fills her days with constant joy and constant activity. Mario finishes his second bowl of minestrone and waits for Maria to fill the third glass of wine for him. A piece of fruit for dessert—and dinner is done. Contented, he licks his lips, then wipes his saucy mouth on the now wine-stained napkin. *Maria really is a great cook, and there is nothing better than a wholesome home-cooked meal*, he thinks to himself.

He opens the envelope; it has been a while since he wrote to his family letting them know of his plans to return, so he welcomes the response from home. He is excited about seeing his mother again—their exchanged letters are always emotional, her ending words invariably: *Your hat is here waiting for you. All my love, Mamma.*

This time, there is no letter from his mother, just one from his father. As he reads it, Mario's face becomes pale and there is an unusual silence.

"What's wrong?" asks Maria.

"My father is telling me off for not sending any more money, and wants me to keep sending more because he needs it. What does he need it for? I've sent him so much money over the years, why does he need more? Is Mamma sick, or maybe one of my brothers or sisters? It's strange, he sounds desperate. I'm worried."

"I will write to my father to find out what is happening; he will know," reassures Maria.

Mario nods his head in agreement and then turns his attention to little Euplio.

"Oh, my beautiful boy, Nonno Euplio and Nonna Antonietta are going to love you!" He puts his face up to little Euplio's nose, and the boy responds by giving Mario a face full of cold, gluggy, buttered pastina.

* * *

Mario tinkers around in the shed, checking the fermentation progress of the crushed grapes. He is particular about his wine—he wants it neither too dry nor too sweet, so he constantly monitors the sugar levels. He hopes this will be as good a batch as it was last year: light and fresh, with a smooth, subtle sweetness. He may even experiment with blending, as he has seen Mr Max do. Fred hears Mario's rustlings, and from behind the fence, he shouts, "Is that you, Mario?"

"Yes, Fred, come over!"

Within a split second, Fred is in the shed with his snout over the fermentation tank, inhaling the floral fumes of the fermenting must. It is blissful.

"Wow, you're as quick as a fly, Fred!"

"Yeah, and just as hard to kill."

Mario laughs. "Unless the fly falls into the fermentation tank," he says as he pulls out a dead fly out from the must.

"Ahh, what a way to go, in a vat full of wine, oh yes!"

"The wine will be ready to be put into the barrels soon, probably in a couple of days. Would you like a drink?" Mario says, combining important information with just as important a question.

"Thought you'd never ask."

Fred walks over to the wall of wine stored in beer bottles stacked against the wall. In a few boxes in the corner are actual wine bottles, which seems odd, as Mario always uses recycled long necks to bottle his wine.

"What are these, Mario?"

"Oh, don't drink those. They are the bottles Mr Max gave to me, the Grange Hermitage he made. They're really horrible. I think I will throw them out one day."

"Don't throw them out, that will be a waste. Maybe you could mix them with a bit of lemonade?"

"Good idea, I could also make a sangria."

"A san...what?"

"Sangria, it's Spanish."

"Oh, OK, well, I'll grab one of your bottles, then."

"Yes, get one from the right, that's last year's vintage, there aren't many left."

171

"Just as well that we've made some more, then," Fred says, taking the top off a bottle and settling himself down on one of the two chairs next to the fermentation tank. He places two glasses on the wooden crate that doubles up as a table, and pours the wine. They toast each other and take a large gulp of last year's vintage.

"Maria! Maria, bring us something to eat!" Mario shouts.

Within ten minutes, a platter of cold cuts, cheese and bread is placed in front of them, and within ten seconds, the men begin devouring the contents. Maria returns to the house to attend to little Euplio. The men carry on enjoying their food and drink. The wine flows, as does the conversation, their filters lowering with each sip of alcohol.

"Tell me, Fred, why does your wife hate me so much?" Mario asks.

"Ahh, don't worry about it. I come from Scottish stock, she hates me as well."

"She's always angry, but you are always happy; how do you put up with it?"

"She lives in the past, it's not easy for her to forgive and forget."

"You love her?"

Fred thinks for a while. "'Love' is a strange word, what does it actually mean? If it means convenience, obligation and complacency, then I suppose I do. We're not all as lucky as you, Mario, to have an angel like Maria."

"My father chose Maria for me."

"Your father?"

"Yes. I needed a wife, and I couldn't marry anyone here. I needed someone who would be willing to go back to Italy."

"Did you even know her?"

"Yes, I knew who she was, but the last time I saw her she was very young. I never thought she would agree to marry me, she was supposed to be a nun."

"Oh, that would have been a waste!"

"Yes, indeed. I love her, but I'm not sure she loves me, at least not as much as her God."

"So, you're a convenience for her?"

"Probably not even that."

"Well, you gave her a beautiful child, she seems happy enough."

"Mmm. Fred, what do you mean your wife lives in the past?"

"Her first husband died in World War I, and her son died in World War II, so I suppose she kind of blames the Germans and their allies for her loss."

Mario sits silently for a minute or two, almost feeling sorry for Irene. Then he says, "But I didn't kill them, and neither did anyone else here."

"That's logical, but when someone experiences great losses, they don't always exercise reason."

"Why didn't you have any more children?"

"Problem with the plumbing, mate. I can syphon the python, but I can't whack the crack, if you know what I mean!"

Mario knew what he meant, but made no comment; instead, he plucked up the courage to ask the question he really wanted to ask.

"You said you fought in the Great War, so how come you don't feel the same as your wife?"

Fred took in a big gulp of air and refilled his glass with more wine. Mario just stared at him, wondering if he had overstepped the mark. Fred took a long swig of the wine, and his story began. Once he started, he didn't stop. Mario was engrossed.

"It was war, and all we wanted to do was go over to France and kill Germans. We were kids, Mikey and me, he was my best friend, but more like a brother. We were very tight, and it was just a great big game for us. We watched this movie from Britain about all the heroic combat and fighting, it all seemed so exciting. Everyone thought it wouldn't last longer than a year. Me and Mikey went to the recruitment office; there was a queue of hundreds waiting to enlist. You were supposed to be nineteen, but Mikey had just turned eighteen and I was seventeen. We were scared that they would reject us because we weren't old enough. When Mikey told the recruitment officer he was eighteen and two months, the officer said, 'Do you mean nineteen and two months?' Mikey said, 'Yes,' and the recruitment officer said, 'Sign here please.'

"So he did. My turn came around, and when I said I was seventeen, the officer told me to go outside, have a couple more birthdays, and come back in. So I did, and we went off to have a go at Jerry. I didn't have a sweetheart, but Mikey and Irene were keen on each other—she was quite a looker in her younger days.

"We were shipped to England late in 1916 for our training. It was brutal. I always struggled, all arms and legs, no coordination whatsoever, but Mikey was a natural, especially with a gun. He would get bull's-eyes every time; they made him a first-class rifleman. The sergeant kept telling us a man's best friend is his rifle, so I thought, *Excellent—I have a rifle and a best friend who's a crack shot with one, it's all good for me.*

"Training was hard. They were preparing us for war, but they didn't prepare us for the reality of warfare. Plunging a bayonet into a sack and plunging one into a human being are two entirely different things. Then we boarded a ship. We had a great time on the way to France; we were full of euphoria, and no one was worried. They marched us for miles through the French countryside. It was beautiful. The farmers would give us bottles of wine, French bread, flowers; we loved it. They never told us where we were going, just to keep marching, so we did as we were told. I had a lot of trouble with the army boots—to get them pliable, I had to urinate in them, so I smelt like piss all the time, but at least I could march. We marched and marched for ages. We knew we were getting closer, as it was becoming noisier. We were in Belgium at this point, marching past derelict villages and gravesites. The devastation was eerie. Finally, we ended up in a village about eight kilometres from the front line. For the first few months, we were behind the line, mostly involved in manual labour—making duck boards, carrying supplies, stacking and organising shells. The only action we saw was in the local brothel, which we didn't mind at all. The pecker worked back then, and Mikey forgot about Irene for a while. When we were finally called up for trench duty, we passed the other divisions coming back, and we asked how it was up there. They answered, 'It's bloody awful mate, it's deadly warfare. Good luck, lads, give our love to the Jerries and mind yourselves.'

"We didn't really understand what they meant, but we soon found out. When we reached the sentries, I knew we had arrived, and there was a smell—a nasty, suffocating smell. I couldn't place it at first, but then you realise it's the odour of decaying corpses, and it clings to everything. When you ate, you could taste it, the stench of bits of human body parts lying around. You never forget it, the smell of death.

"All my romantic notions of war vanished at that point.

You're a small piece of the churning wheel, and as long as it churns, you just have to go along with it. You have a job to do, so you just do it. Each duty shift in the trenches was for four days—two hours on, four hours off, and then they gave you a week's rest. The captain directs you to the front trenches and tells you to get in single file. No smoking, no talking, keep your head down and always have your rifle prepared. You took the trenches as you found them—leftover mess tins with tea, pieces of blankets, old biscuits with mould, beds made of sandbags and big fat rats as roommates. There were funny times, though; I remember one time—there were no toilets, it wasn't the Ritz, you had to dig a trench, stick a pole across it, and eight or nine chaps would have their bums hanging over do their business with flies buzzing all around, there was no such thing as toilet paper, you just had to use your hands. This particular day, we heard a terrific crack and then huge shouts at the back of the line, so we all went to see what had happened. The men who had been sitting on the bar were now swimming in all that shitty muck. They came out like slimy ferrets. You only got one uniform, so they had to stay like that until their changeover. Oh boy, did we laugh that day."

The serious mood turned to hilarity as Mario and Fred enjoyed a moment of reprieve from Fred's story. It soon turned back to a solemn atmosphere.

"They shifted Mikey up the line, because he was a sharp-shooter, looking out for German snipers who would hide in no-man's land. He got his fair share of them. I had my first look at no-man's land through the periscope—you could see hundreds of shell holes, our barbed wire and the Germans', dead bodies hanging on them. No sign of life, and yet you knew that within shouting range, there were hundreds of men ready to kill you. I gave the periscope to the boy next to me, and then I heard a *pop*—his head exploded like an egg. I had never been that close to a dead man. How? Why? He must have put his head up a little too far where a sniper could aim at him. I didn't even know his name. At that point, everything changed. I went numb at first. Then, the captain came around, removed the body like it was nothing, looked at my shocked face and said, 'Welcome to the war lad...carry on.'

"And I did. After your first kill, it became easy and instinctive. You were a soldier and your job was to kill the enemy. The acceptance you developed of continuous shelling, gassing and the danger we faced each time we were in the trenches came from the fact that you were incapable of thought. You had no feeling of fear, you did what you had to do, and you didn't let your mates down. Each time we survived a stint of trench warfare, we would live it up, clean ourselves up from living in such conditions, collect our mail and pay, and either gamble it away at two-up, or spend it at the brothels. The officers all turned a blind eye, and most times would also indulge in a little impropriety.

"I was always anxious until I saw Mikey come back from a mission to join me for some fun. He was cheerful under the circumstances, making the best of everything, until he got a letter from Irene. She was pregnant with his baby. He said he had spent the last night before he was shipped out with Irene; it was a going-away present for him. What a present, right? We found out from later letters that she had a boy, and she named him Michael after his father.

"There were no real provisions for a legal will going into battle—we never bothered with it, because we had nothing. But now that Mikey had a family, he made me promise to look

177

after them if anything happened to him. Nothing was going to happen to him. He was a crack shot, and quick as a whip. He had been on a raid where they captured three German prisoners, he was that good.

"They were the first Germans I had ever seen—alive, anyway. They were shaking like scared rabbits; they were boys, even younger than me, so they were glad to be captured and out of it. At that moment, I realised they weren't the enemy, they were us in a different uniform. These chaps were Bavarian, and cursed the Prussians for getting them into this mess, the same way we cursed the Brits. We were in France again now—conditions weren't much better, but the brothels were. I fell in love with little French Emilie—so did a lot of others apparently; she gave the clap out so many times, it turned into a round of applause. Mikey was quite blunt; he used to say, 'Enjoy the day, mate, it may be your last,' so I did. I learnt more about life there than I would ever have done in civilian life."

Mario gave a little chuckle to say that he knew what Fred meant, then refilled both their glasses. Mario had been in the military in peacetime, but had absolutely no idea what actual warfare was like. His gun had been an accessory rather than a necessity. He was totally captivated by Fred's story, and he toasted him again and encouraged him to continue.

"Behind the line, they put us through intense training, getting us ready to break through the German lines. We got ready for the offensive—we knew the Germans were outnumbered, and they knew it too, but they were tough. The German retaliation came, and for hours we had to sit there and take everything they gave us. The ground shook. The tanks went in, joined by the planes, and we just waited and waited. The noise rose to a crescendo, the air was ablaze. In your mind there was another inferno, and the veneer of civilisation had gone. You knew you were going to be killed or wounded. I wasn't worried about being killed, but I was terrified of losing an arm or a leg. The bombardment created a contained hysteria; I remember one man screaming and crying, and the officer in charge ordering the sergeant, 'Find that man and shoot him, he's no good to us!'

"I'm not sure if he got shot, but the crying stopped. The officer stood behind the trench with a revolver in his hand and said, 'Anyone turns back and I'll shoot them.' So you didn't have much of a choice. Mikey was with me, we were going to look out for each other. We got the order to fix bayonets; I took a long swig of rum and fumbled my way through getting the damn thing on. Mikey laughed at me. In the midst of all the horror around us and before us, he had something to laugh about. I will never forget that last laugh; I was so glad it was because of me. I don't remember the actual moment we ran onto the battlefield, but one minute we were laughing and the next we were running over the bodies of our mates; it was absolute carnage, all I could hear was the cries and screams of the wounded, legs and arms everywhere. Even the tanks just ploughed over the dead, there was no way the bodies could be cleared. Then you were in the world of noise, shrapnel, bullets everywhere, shells exploding, people dropping all around you—they faded away on either side of you, but you just carried on. I followed Mikey—he was always in front of me, looking back to see if I was OK.

"Then it happened in front of my eyes, all in slow motion: Mikey got hit by a shell. I dropped down to help him. His whole left side was missing. He was still alive, just barely; he was trying to say something to me, but I couldn't understand him. They say your whole past comes up in your mind when you're about to die, but Mikey didn't have much of a past at twenty, and neither did I. He was gurgling, his left eye pulsing out of his head. I couldn't do anything for him, but I couldn't let him suffer either. I shot him. I shot him dead. I killed my best friend because I couldn't bear to see him suffer."

Fred breaks down in tears—huge, uncontrollable tears.

Mario doesn't know what to do. He has never seen such an outburst of justified emotion from a man. Instinctively, he approaches the sobbing Fred and hugs him. At first, Fred embraces the comfort, but then he collects himself and pushes Mario away.

"Oi, oi, oi, what are you? Some sort of poo puncher? Leave me alone!" he says, followed with a bellowing laugh, which is more like the old Fred, much to Mario's relief.

"You alright, Fred?"

Fred once again fills his glass with wine. "Yeah, mate. You're the first person I've ever told that to. Not even Reenie knows I killed her first husband—well, technically. He would have married her if he'd made it back."

"You don't have to talk about it any more if you don't want to."

"No, I want to. After all these years, I need to get it off my chest. It's like this constant pain you can't get rid of, so you just learn to live with it."

Three bottles of wine in, Fred continues. "After I shot him, I just knelt next to him, holding what was left of him, hoping to die, crying and praying to God to make it quick. After all, my chances were good—if I could have, I would have bet a quid or two on it. Suddenly my collar was yanked. 'What are you doing son?' a voice said, and I got thrown into a big shell hole. It was the sergeant; we took cover while the barrage continued.

"'What the fuck were you doing out there?' he asked. I told him I wanted to die next to my friend, then he said, 'You probably will die, but you're not dead yet, so you might as well give yourself a chance. If you're lucky, you'll survive, and if you're even luckier, you'll get shot in the head and get your wish. But right now, I need you to grow some balls and kill some of those bastards out there.'

"Others joined us, and we managed to infiltrate the German side. We went like hell into the Germans. The killing became automatic—if they ran, we shot them, if they had their hands up, we would wave them on. The only Germans we were fighting now were the machine gunners—they fought to the death. They were killed even if they put their hands up. It was just slaughter. Until we got some sort of order, everyone was screaming, moaning and groaning, but eventually there was silence, the battle was over. Then the cleanup; those that could walked to the medic stations—I had a leg full of shrapnel so they stretchered me. All the officers and sergeants, even the one who saved me, and three-quarters of my division were killed. The medics looked after me pretty well; I didn't lose my leg, but a lot did. I thought as soon as I could walk I would see if I could find Mikey, to give him some sort of burial, or say a prayer or something, you know, but before that happened, they handed me his identity tags. He was buried in a mass grave, I didn't even know where. We had German prisoners with us; they were underfed and in really poor shape. We didn't have any deep feelings of anger against them—we actually respected them, and they didn't seem to bear any malice against us either. They had to do what they were told, just like us; we were all stuck in a uniform, fighting another man's war. Some of them spoke English, and some of us spoke German, so we got to know them and talked about family and how pointless the war was.

"Mr Rumour had told us that the German authorities were negotiating an armistice, and everyone was glad, especially the Germans—they didn't care who won, we were all fed up with the whole thing. Eleven o'clock, on the eleventh of November 1918, the noise of gunfire rolled away like a cloud of thunder in the distance. It was completely silent. That was strange. We cleaned our boots and our buttons, and the war was over. We all felt happy and relieved, but there was no celebration, everything just stopped. We were too exhausted to enjoy it, and I remember thinking, *What now?*

"When I returned home, I kept my promise, married Reenie and looked after her son like he was my own. It was the least I could do for Mikey. Mikey's mother never spoke to me—she was angry that I came back and he didn't, which was hard for me. No one ever spoke about the war, no one was interested—every soldier I spoke to said the same thing, that the civilians didn't understand, how could they? The magnitude of the suffering was just way beyond their comprehension; they couldn't understand that people were being killed all around you, the way you lived like animals and behaved like animals. A soldier's life was worth nothing at the end of the war—none of us were heroes, we didn't like being in the business of killing, not one bit.

"The war ended, but the battle in my head kept going... Jesus Christ, it was so bad, I thought for sure it could never happen again. But it did, we had another world war! Why didn't anyone learn from the past, and now what's bubbling up in

Vietnam? Don't ask me what that's about. I just...I just don't get it. Eventually, I got a job at a hardware store, and that's where I stayed until I got an early disability pension. Mikey Jr worked with me for a while. He was a smart kid, Mario; he had been accepted into university, Mikey Senior would have been so proud. The day he told me he had enlisted in the army, and was going to join the war effort, I went crazy. I begged him not to go. He said he wasn't going to wear a white feather in his hat. I told him better a white feather in your hat than a bunch of them on your back...but he didn't listen, even Reenie didn't take me seriously, until the day she received that bloody telegram. Mikey Jr was killed in the Mediterranean somewhere. Reenie never told me where, and I never asked. She's very angry, still, but she did help me through my darkest days, I will always appreciate that. The trouble with the pendulum of grief is that, at times, it gets wedged on the wrong side, so it can blind you until something releases it, if ever."

Mario is in awe of Fred. He has complete empathy for his story. "OK, Fred, I won't be so nasty to your wife. For you, I will behave myself."

"Oh no, no, no. You give it to her, mate, it's fun to watch. Plus, it may unwedge the pendulum and make all our lives a little more peaceful."

Laughter returns to the conversation. Fred's story has bonded the two men even more than before, along with their love of drinking. They have, unbelievably, drunk all the bottles of last year's vintage, but they are far from finished. Fred doesn't know that the wine bottles and the tomato sauce bottles are separated by an empty row, so when he goes to get another bottle of what he thinks is wine, he mistakenly opens the wrong bottle; after all, they are all in the same long-neck beer bottles, how is he to know? When Fred empties the tomato sauce into his glass and drinks it without looking, he quickly spits it out.

"I think this wine is off."

Mario laughs as he explains to him he has picked up the wrong bottle. More alcohol is needed, so they decide to buy some beer, just to change things up a bit.

Mario and Fred stumble to the Vanguard in the driveway, laughing and joking around, as the combination of wine and the sudden hit of fresh air stuns them into a different level of drunkenness. Mario turns the key. *Rrrrrrr...rrrrrrrrrrr...rrrrr.*

"Oh bugger," complains Fred. "No beer for us!"

Mario turns the key again and again, but the Vanguard refuses to start. Maria and Irene, hearing the noisy revs of the car, emerge from their houses to stand in their respective front yards, staring at the absurd scene. Mario is determined not to let the Vanguard beat him.

"Come on, Fred, help me push."

Fred can hardly hold his head up, but he does as Mario asks. Irene can't believe her eyes as these two fools push the Vanguard out onto the road.

"Are you serious, Fred? Get yourself inside!" Irene barks.

With the courage of wine, he shouts, "Mind your business, woman!"

"OK, kill yourself, then." Irene has to have the last word as she stomps back into the house.

Maria, who is also concerned, shouts to Mario, who is now in the driver's seat, steering the car with the door open, while his one leg pushes against the ground.

"Mario, what the fuck are you doing?" she yells out in Italian.

Mario is momentarily taken aback, not by the realisation

that what he is trying to do whist intoxicated is truly ludicrous, but by the fact that Maria has sworn at him.

"Shut up!" he shouts back.

Maria shakes her head, knowing better than to say anything more, then she, too, goes back inside, leaving Fred and Mario to fate.

The Vanguard is now on the road in preparation for a push start and a beer stop, but the car is not cooperating. Fred is at the back, pushing with all his might, Mario is steering with his foot depressed on the clutch, coordinating the petrol pedal with the other. They manage to rotate the engine several times without any success. Finally, the engine turns over and the car is on its way. The only problem is that Fred has collapsed with exhaustion, and Mario has fallen out of the car onto the road. Fred catches up to Mario, huffing and puffing as they both watch the shiny black Vanguard make its own way down the street, narrowly missing a parked car but not missing the trunk of a large fig tree.

Fred helps Mario up, and they run to the car to inspect the damage.

"She's had herself a right big kiss there, Mario." Fred states the obvious, putting his arm around Mario's shoulders. "Don't worry, mate, you work at Holden, you can get yourself another one."

Mario's frown turns into a smile, as does Fred's when he sees what Mario sees. Fifty yards down the street is the local pub—the golden path to the beer they were chasing. The Vanguard is left to rest at the base of the tree as they set off in pursuit of the magic amber liquid.

Three hours later, the two buddies carelessly walk home, passing the Vanguard. They salute it, laughing hysterically as they do. Eventually, they reach Mario's front yard, singing loudly and joking about the unfortunate car. Their volume coaxes both Irene and Maria outside again. From the distance of their respective front yards, the women give each other questioning looks, which turn to disgust as they stare down their husbands. The inebriated display comes to an abrupt end as Fred and Mario fall to the ground, luckily onto the soft lawn, curled up next to each other under the increasing darkness of the skyline. Irene makes her debut on Lanzani property, but only to kick Fred into consciousness. Fred snorts out a small whimper, but his position does not change. Irene gives him one final kick and then leaves, turning back to give Mario a good kick as well. She then heads back to her own home, appalled; she doesn't even look at Maria, and she has no remorse for kicking Mario. Maria has no animosity towards Irene, who has just done what she herself would like to. Maria, being Maria, goes back inside and then comes out with two blankets to cover the unconscious men; they will be sleeping under the million-star hotel tonight.

CHAPTER 18: THE CONTINENTAL STORE

A week later, Mario sits at the table as usual, waiting for Maria to serve him, still feeling the effects of his bender. The wine jug is not present; it has been replaced with a jug of lemonade. Little Euplio sits in his high chair, smashing his toy car against the edge of the tray and into his plate of food, hurtling most of the plate's contents onto the floor. Mario smiles at him but does not discipline him, nor does he lift a finger to clean up the mess Euplio has made—after all, that is a woman's job. Maria serves the second course, a beautifully cooked steak with a baccalà fish salad. Mario is so happy, as it reminds him of home—not so much the steak, as they couldn't afford to eat meat back home, but the baccalà fish was what his mother used to cook on Good Friday every year.

"Where did you get the baccalà?" Mario asks.

"A friend from my church group has opened a new continental store, and they have a lot of things that I couldn't get before."

Mario is impressed and voices his approval. Maria is happy that the fish salad has put Mario in a good mood, as she is about to drop a bombshell. She hopes he will take the news well. Maria serves the fruit and coffee and then slips the letter from her father into Mario's hand. He looks up to her as she gives him a nervous smile. He drinks his coffee and begins to read the contents of the letter. Maria watches his facial expression change from one of calm resolve to surprise, then to utter disbelief and finally to anger; her hopes of Mario taking the news well are dashed.

"*Bastardo!* Bloody fuckin' *bastardo!*"

Little Euplio is startled by his father's outcry; Maria covers his ears to shield him from the verbal bombardment that is to come.

"*Bastardo!* He gave it to me right up the *cullo*. I am a *cuccio*, too trusting...right up the bum like this."

Mario rises, shows a fist and knocks his elbow to describe his feelings, as if Maria needs an explanation.

"You know you can't trust the government, you know the Australians don't like you, you know, so you are aware, you prepare yourself, you protect yourself against them...but when your family...your own family!"

He puts his head into his hands and sways in disbelief, then he points to little Euplio.

"And your name is not Euplio, no, not anymore—it's Elliot! You are Elliot!"

Elliot begins to cry, and Maria lifts him from the high chair to comfort him.

"He has spent all my money—over eight years of work, gone! On lawyers! My father, that *bastardo*, has spent all the money I sent him for us, on greedy fuckin' lawyers, and he wants more! More to fight his neighbour over water rights! It's a losing battle, why doesn't he understand that the fountain is on his land, but the water belongs to everyone? The lawyers are just sucking *him* dry! No, not him, sucking me dry, *me!*"

"It's alright, Mario, forgive him. God will provide."

"No, Maria, God doesn't provide, I provide. My backbreaking sweat and tears provide!"

"I will help you. I will find a job, and we can go back a little bit later."

"No, you don't work, you look after the baby. I will work even harder, and when we go back, if he's not dead, I will kill him!"

Maria resists saying anything more as Mario storms out, slamming the door on the way to the shed and prompting another burst of tears from Elliot.

Sounds of smashing glass and wood hitting corrugated iron walls can be heard from the kitchen, where Maria stands crying, unsure of what to do. Elliot, with the changeable mood of his age, is totally oblivious and squeals with delight as he plays with his mother's earring. Mario, meanwhile, is in his shed, hunched over the wine barrel, with a jug that replaces the glasses that have been smashed. He fills his jug to the brim, guzzles the contents, then speaks to the barrel.

"Ahhh, you are my best friend, my only friend! I come to this country, and the only friend I have is you, Mr Barrel. Why did my father do this to me? What is this world coming to when you can't even trust your own family? My own papa robbed me, why? Answer me, Mr Barrel, answer me!"

The barrel answers Mario with splashing sounds as he opens the tap and refills the jug for the third time.

There is a frantic knock on the front door of the Brackenridge household; Fred opens the door, and Irene peers out from behind him.

"Hello, Maria," says Fred.

Maria stands with Elliot in her arms and stares at Fred with a tear-tracked face. "Please, Fred, come with me. Mario has gone crazy. Please help me."

Fred takes Elliot from Maria's arms and gives him to Irene. She is about to protest, but is stopped by Fred's demand: "Look after him."

Maria and Fred leave, and Irene is left holding the toddler uncomfortably. It has been quite a while since she has held a child in her arms. Elliot gives her a drowsy look and flops his head onto her shoulder. He looks like a sleeping angel, which softens her.

"What has your stupid father done now?" she whispers in his ear.

Fred arrives to see Mario still hunched over the barrel. He is slightly annoyed that Mario has spilt nearly a quarter of its contents and is drinking without him, but he comforts himself that there are still two more barrels. Mario manages to raise his eyes to Fred's concerned face.

"Hello, Fred..." Mario says tipsily. "Oh yes, you're my friend, Fred, but not as good a friend as Mr Barrel here. My money is gone, Fred, gone, my *bastardo* papa took all my money."

He bangs on the barrel, then falls over in bevvied limpness. He starts to cry. Fred picks him and directs him outside to a soft patch of lawn, followed by Maria.

"Come on, mate, sleep it off... He'll be alright, Maria, don't worry."

"He so upset about losing the money. I tell him, don't worry, but he not listen."

"He's lost more than money. He's lost trust! That can change a man."

"I'll pray for him."

"You do that, Maria. If anyone can help him, you can."

"Not me. God will save him."

Fred smiles and nods.

As hard as Maria prays, God does not curb Mario's anger, or his new drinking habits. He trusts no one, not even Maria, who continues to support him in every way she can. Maria does not like this new Mario; he has turned into a self-absorbed, unreasonable monster, which puts a great strain on their relationship. Mario stops working at Holden, even though they have offered him a position as a floor checker; the money isn't attractive enough for him. He finds work at the brickyards that pay double the amount of money than Holden and Penfolds did combined. It is extremely hard work, but there is plenty of it, as the demand for bricks in the growing Australian economic environment is high. The booming housing market demands more bricks than can be made, so it provides a great opportunity for Mario to make good money in a short amount of time. He is like a well-oiled machine. For six days a week, he works from 6 a.m. to 6 p.m., comes home to a prepared meal, eats, gets drunk and goes to bed, then repeats it all again the next day. On his one day off a week, he sometimes takes Maria and Elliot to the beach or shopping, but most times, he drinks with Fred or Pietro.

One particular day off, when it is raining, Maria convinces him to drive her to the new continental store, owned by her church group friend, for a bulk shop of goods that she needs. He complains all the way there, as he does not like food shopping—that is a woman's job. He doesn't ask her to make bricks, so he shouldn't have to shop for food, although the old Mario would gladly have done it. Maria says nothing, she just thanks him for taking her and says he shouldn't have to do it again for a long time once they get all the bulk food they need.

The owner of the continental store's wife is in Maria's church group, and they have developed a unique friendship. She is very different from Maria, loud and boisterous. Many people do not like her, but Maria thinks she is delightful—she makes Maria laugh.

As soon as Mario walks in, a voice comes from behind the counter, one that sounds familiar to him.

"Mario *sensa capello!*"

Mario looks around to find out to whom that familiar voice belongs, and there he is, Genaro the Napolitano. The very next minute, a large bosomed woman charges at Mario, giving him a big, suffocating hug. It is Stella—nine years older, eighty pounds heavier and five children later.

"Mario! What a surprise!"

No one is more surprised than Maria to find out that her church friend, Stella, knows Mario, and Mario is surprised to see both Genaro and Stella. It seems that they have built themselves up a healthy business, and it also looks as if they are eating a lot of the profits: they both are double the size of when he last saw them at Bonegilla.

Stella releases her hold, and Genaro replaces her, wrapping his large arm around Mario's shoulder.

"So, you're Signora Maria's husband? You lucky man, she's an angel, too good for you, my friend!"

Before Mario can answer, he continues with his questions.

"I was sure you would have gone back to Italy, but here you are. And Pietro Pistola, Trippa Nera, Calze Caggata, Alesky...*ce ne saccio*, have you seen any of them?"

Mario doesn't get to answer any questions as Genaro continues. "Come, let me show you around my shop."

Mario follows him, suitably impressed by what he sees: an array of imported Italian groceries and bulk foods such as olive oil, cheese, cured meat and fish, legumes, speciality flours and spices, all catering to the growing Italian market. Most customers are of Italian origin, but more and more English-speaking customers are starting to frequent the store. Mario notices misspelt signage all around. He isn't sure if he should let Genaro know to correct them, but when he sees the signage for the toilets spelt "TO LET", he decides to say something.

"Genaro, that sign is spelt wrong, would you like me to fix it for you?"

"What you mean, is wrong?"

"The way it's written, it means you have something to rent like a room, or a house."

"Ahh, that is why."

"What is why?" asks Mario.

Genaro laughs as he explains: "An Australian lady, she come in, and she asks me, 'What is to let?' I say to her, it is 'TO LET', and then she say again, 'What is to let?' And I say, again, 'It is TO LET, you know, where you piss and you poo.' Then she walk out the door, and Stella got mad, saying, 'Stop scaring the customers,' but now I can tell her it's her fault the customer goes, because she spelt 'toilet' wrong. Can you fix for me?"

Genaro gave Mario a pot of black paint and a small brush, along with a ladder to reach the sign at the top of the door. He paints a thin *I* in the middle of the *O* and *L*, and suddenly it becomes a very clear sign to the *toilet*. Mario also corrects the 'SOLT' to 'SALT' and the 'PEPA' to 'PEPPER', and fixes various

193

other misspelt signs to cater to the English speakers. Mario explains to Genaro that English is very different from Italian, in that Italian words are spelt as they sound, but in English, this isn't always the case, because there are different rules for different words. Mario asks if he still has the Italian/English dictionary he gave him, and Genaro tells him he left it in Bonegilla. Mario offers to give him another dictionary and encourages him to read English newspapers. This is all just too much for Genaro to bother with; he dismisses the suggestions with a wave of his hand.

"Give it to Stella to do. I learn the English from the radio and television."

Apart from the misspelt signage, Mario thinks that Genaro has done very well for himself and congratulates him on his success. What Mario doesn't know is that the success of his continental store really could be attributed to Stella, who works like she has a never-ending supply of built-in battery power. Not only does she manage to take care of five children, she also runs the shop and performs all the administration, while Genaro spends most of his time not doing much, and the remainder of his time at the club two doors down, gambling away the profits. Stella still idolises him, however, and no matter what he does, she will love him until the day she dies and beyond. It is for this reason that Maria sees less of her at the church group, as her attention is focused on the business. It's also because Stella told a group of particular worshipers that they were nothing more than a bunch of fluttering blowflies shitting on everyone, and the sooner someone swatted them, the better. Maria inwardly agrees with her, but she is ever the peacemaker, and acts as the mediator. In the end, Stella decides it is far better to concentrate on her family and the shop. She can practise her faith from home rather than put up with any unnecessary aggravation. Stella does look forward to Maria's visits to the shop, however, and is always grateful when she tells Stella not to worry, as she prays for her well-being all the time, and God is in her heart.

As five rowdy children run through the shop, Genaro puffs up his chest, and instead of disciplining the children, he just says, "They're all mine."

Elliot squirms in Maria's arms, wanting to join the boisterous children, but Maria strengthens her grasp; she is not going to let him run around the shop. Stella quickly raises a firm voice, and they fall into line immediately. She introduces them to Mario and Maria.

"This is Lorenzo, my eldest, then we have Vincenzo, Immacolata, Concetta and Kevin."

"Kevin?" asks Mario.

"Yes, Kevin. We wanted to honour this beautiful country we live in, and call our son an Australian name, so we called him Kevin after Kevin Crease—every night he reads the news to us, and we can trust him, he is a good Australian, we want to be good Australians too," says Stella proudly.

"You are Italian, Stella, you will always be Italian," retorts Mario.

"My children are Australian, this is their homeland now. Wasn't it you who said we must learn to speak English?"

"Yes, but only so you have the advantage, so that you could live amongst them, not to become them!"

"So, why haven't you gone back, then?"

Mario hesitates before he carefully answers. "Just a couple more years, and then we go back."

Genaro interrupts: "Stella, you spelt all the English words wrong—see, it's your fault the Australian lady left, not mine."

Stella starts to protest, and the animated disagreement between them, which sees arms and hands flying to and fro, captures everyone's attention, including incoming customers. Genaro finishes the discussion, as always, by nibbling on her neck affectionately and telling her how much he loves her. Then he says, "Don't worry, Mario will give you another dictionary so you can spell the English."

"That's just something else I have to do around here!"

The vigorous discussion resumes until Maria diplomatically asks, "Where are your cannellini beans?"

"OK, Signora Maria, what do you need today? We will give you a good price on anything you want, won't we, Stella?"

"Of course."

"Mario, bring Maria and your son home, then come back and I'll take you to the club," says Genaro, more of a demand than an invitation. Before Mario can politely decline, Genaro continues. "You can meet new friends. Bring Pietro Pistola with you."

Mario doesn't really want to meet new people, but he thinks he might as well pick up Pietro and go to Genaro's club; it could be fun.

Genaro, Stella and Mario reminisce about the time they spent together at Bonegilla, both good and bad memories, and the somewhat exaggerated tales bring a lot of laughter and merriment. Maria hasn't seen Mario laugh this much in a long time; she is happy about this chance meeting with his past, although it gives Mario another excuse not to be at home with her, as now he has a new place to be: with Genaro at his club.

CHAPTER 19: THE CLUB

Many Italian migrant men frequent the club two doors down from Genaro's continental store. It is the place where they can share their cultural experiences, past and present, in a familiar and supportive environment, so far away from their homeland. They reminisce and try to solve the problems of the world as they play cards or bocce while drinking many small cups of coffee with shots of alcohol in them. The rooms are filled with cigarette smoke, and there are always delicious panini available, provided by Genaro's store, where they are made fresh every day by Stella. The club even has a chef who cooks large pots of spaghetti with meatballs every Sunday afternoon. It isn't entirely legal, however; there is gambling between the members which, at times, causes disputes and flares up into free-for-all fights. The larger-built fellows, of whom Pietro is one, usually break them up. Pietro still stutters—not as much as he used to, but it prevents him from speaking a lot. Instead, he lets his fists do the talking. He also has his little band that plays at all the ever-increasing weddings happening due to the growing immigration of Italian compatriots. Pietro loves the club—he feels comfortable and included, and spends a lot of his time there. Mario, not so much. He did enjoy the club in the beginning, but as the seedier side of society begins to infiltrate the association, he questions his involvement.

Pietro has befriended two strangers from Melbourne who also patronise the club, both of Italian origin and both untrustworthy according to Mario. Women are not allowed in the clubhouse, except for the women who accompany the two Melbourne men. Pietro calls them *zozze*—dirty girls—and Mario knows exactly what they are there for. The two men are procuring customers and exploiting the women as slaves; from what Mario witnesses, business is booming.

Both men speak English with an Australian accent and Italian with a Calabrese one. Mario has deduced that they must have been born in Australia to parents originally from Calabria. They are younger than him, one around seventeen or eighteen, and the other, more dominant one, around twenty-five or twenty-six. They call the younger one Bambino. He does look very young and almost innocent, but with a consequential attitude. Slight in stature, with well-groomed, curly hair, he follows in the shadow of the more dominant one called Bastone, meaning "the big stick". He is well-built, and constantly throws his weight around. Mario doesn't know their real names, nor does he want to. From his first encounter with them whilst playing a traditional Italian card game called scopa, which translates to "sweep", he sizes them up the Mario Lanzani way. Bastone is a big man and often brags about his heavy-handed tactics when dealing with people who upset him. He holds up his blood-stained knuckles.

"You know what these did today?" Bastone boasts.

The other three card players—Pietro, Mario and Genaro—wait for the answer.

"These fists smashed in a man's face."

"Why?" asks Mario.

"'Cause he called me a wog."

"But you call me a wog all the time," says Genaro.

"That's because you are one."

"So, why do you call a man a name that you take offense to?" asks Mario.

"'Cause another wog is allowed to call a wog a wog, but if you're not a wog, you can't call a wog a wog. These bloody Aussie slobs and whinging Poms need to learn respect."

"Do you realise that you have just called these other nation-alities offensive names?" asks Mario.

"Yeah, but they deserve it. They shouldn't be calling us wogs. I can call them what I want in private, and when I'm smashing their faces in...understand?"

Mario does understand exactly what he is dealing with. He just lets Bastone ramble on while he plays his turn. Mario clears the table with a clean sweep of the remaining cards to win the game, to the delight of his playing partner, Genaro. Bastone throws down his cards in disgust, then leaves the table to get himself another drink at the bar, where Bambino is procuring potential customers.

Mario is uneasy about Pietro's involvement with these men, so he pulls him aside and quietly sits him down to voice his concerns.

"What are you doing, Pietro? Why are you involving yourself with these men?"

"D-don't worry Mario, they're OK."

"No, Pietro, they are not OK. You know what they are, what they are part of!"

"Why you are such a h-hippop-potamus?"

"Hippopotamus?" Mario questions.

"Yes, I warned you about Alesky, and you no l-listen,

now you tell me about Bastone and Bambino, you h-hippopotamus!"

"You mean hypocrite?"

"Yes, y-you say one thing to me not to do, but you did the same when I warned you about Alesky."

"It's not the same, Pietro. Alesky is not Mafioso, he is not a part of organised crime, he has never killed anyone."

"H-how do you know what Alesky is, d-did he ever tell you about his past?"

"The only thing I know is that he is not Polish and not Yugoslav, he did have a wife...and now he's changed his name to Denis May."

"And t-that is not strange to you?"

"Well, um, yes, but he's a just a friend. I'm not involved with him."

"Well, Bastone and Bambino are m-my friends. I'm not involved, and I not judge them...Where is Alesky now?"

"I get postcards from him every now and then, from Port Augusta, from Coober Pedy, the last one I got was from Port Lincoln. He was working on a fishing boat, that's all I know."

"Don't worry about me, you w-worry about your family."

"My family is alright."

"If I had a wife like Maria, I w-would treat her better. D-don't be a hippopotamus, Mario!"

Mario is offended by Pietro's remark, but chooses not to retaliate or correct his English; rather he ends the conversation at that time, deciding to distance himself from the club and Pietro.

Mario has always known about the Mafia, but has never encountered them in Italy; he came all the way to Australia only to have the misfortune of meeting members of the organised crime syndicate so far away from Italy. Most of the Italian community knows of their existence in Australia, it is an open secret, but no one publicly speaks about it, and most have no affiliation whatsoever. There is a clandestine drive to recruit associates, and one either chooses to be part of it in some way, or not at all. In many cases, people do not choose; the decision is thrust upon them by family association, or simply by the occupation they have chosen.

Italy produces three of the world's most infamous criminal groups: the Cosa Nostra from Sicily, the Camorra from Campania, and the 'Ndrangheta from Calabria. These groups are collectively referred to as the Mafia; however, this term is exclusively Sicilian in origin and membership. The cell that has infiltrated Australia is wholly Calabrian and is derived from the ancient secret criminal society known as the L'Onorata Societa—the Honoured Society, or 'Ndrangheta, as it is called in the Calabrian dialect. It is rumoured to have started in the 1930s in Queensland in a reign of terror conducted to extort funds from sugar cane growers. Fellow Calabrians who resisted the standover tactics were subjected to the heavy-handed *mano nera*—or "black hand"—consequences, including homicides and bombings. The 'Ndrangheta came into Australia hidden amongst thousands of honest Italians through the migratory system, the same way Cosa Nostra permeated America. It is the ugly side of an otherwise great culture. Many Italians are honest and industrious, despite their lack of trust in the authorities.

By the early 1960s, the Calabrian mafia was well-established in Melbourne and the rural areas of Victoria and, to a lesser extent, in New South Wales and South Australia. The 'Ndrangheta is well schooled, as some immigrating

Calabrese, particularly from the town of Plati, are already members, or have ties to deep-rooted members in Calabria. The criminal society is entrenched in the illegal operations of extortion, prostitution, counterfeiting, sly grog, gambling, the smuggling of aliens and firearms—but the most lucrative operation of all is the control and domination of the fruit and vegetable produce business in the Queen Victoria Markets.

The produce industry is one in which any man can carve out a decent living for himself and his family, providing he is a hard worker and has access to land. Rural land can be purchased cheaply, and many migrants take the opportunity to farm the land, as it doesn't necessarily require knowledge of language and culture, and the skills needed for a mid-century farmer are inherently present. As the honest person sets up, so do the dishonest and parasitic. If one does not speak English, and is ignorant of the sale and distribution part of the industry, they become easy prey, and can be taken advantage of by a corrupt commission agent from the Victoria markets. The Mafiosi can exploit inexperienced farmers by offering services to help them sell their wares after gaining their trust. A criminal has avenues where he can pull cons and run scams by underpaying sellers and overcharging buyers, making himself rich on the sweat of his countrymen. The "black hand" method of labour racketeering and corruption tactics, brought over with them from the old country, are being perfected by the mysterious 'Ndrangheta, enabling them to monopolise the fruit and vegetable industry.

One of the major growing areas that plays a prime role for the Queen Victoria Market racket is the Sunraysia district, in particular the town of Mildura. Vineyard owners and fruiterers of Italian extraction are subjected to a system of controlled distribution, and the disruption of free and honest trade by a criminal organisation thriving under a very tight code of silence. Many victims endure the standover tactics, as resistance to demands for tribute and protection money are first met with threats, then water pollution, stock poisoning and crop burning—all ancient and traditional tactics in Calabria. Failing that, if the resistance continues, homes are bombed, and if necessary, this is followed up by assault or murder, even reaching as far as the family of the victim, who might still be residing in Calabria. The Honoured Society is protected behind a wall of absolute silence by victims who are too scared to complain to the authorities for fear of reprisal.

Mario laughs at various news articles and journals that understate the presence of the blackhanders and ridicule the notion of a Mafia presence in Australia. Mario may have become a drunken fool, but he is no idiot.

CHAPTER 20: THE WEDDING

Pietro checks his audio system to make sure it is ready for the evening's event. Serafino is a friend of Pietro's who has worked at Penfolds; he is from the same Abruzzese region as Pietro. Serafino is getting married to Angela, a local girl of Italian descent. Pietro agrees with the general consensus that Serafino has done very well for himself. He is an immigrant like the rest of them. He came to Australia as a young, naive eighteen-year-old, and within five years, he scored the ultimate prize—he is marrying a beautiful and educated Australian woman from a well-established Italian family. Serafino didn't come to Australia on the assisted government scheme, so he avoided the Bonegilla saga; instead, he was sponsored by a close family friend who had settled in Adelaide some years before. But he is still as poor as a church mouse. Pietro can't see what Angela sees in Serafino—the only thing he has going for him is his good looks and work ethic, which seem to be enough for Angela.

It is extremely advantageous to have a wife that can speak perfect English and understand the ways of both Australian and Italian cultures. Pietro has met a lot of girls, but none are of Angela's calibre. He wishes that he might marry as well as Serafino, inwardly admitting to being envious, even though he is happy for him. Pietro's wedding gift to them is for his band to play at the reception party. He is always excited when he is commissioned to play at an event, and this is quite the event; there are over five hundred guests due to arrive in the next hour, including Mario and Maria, and Bastone and Bambino. It seems that the whole Italian community is attending the ceremony.

Pietro is eager to see Mario. He hasn't seen him in a while, and he misses him terribly. Mario has stopped coming to the club, and each time Pietro goes around to see him at his house, he is either working or passed out from another wine session. Pietro often consoles a frustrated Maria, who constantly turns to an unresponsive God for help. Both Maria and Pietro know that Mario is a good man, but he just can't get past the fact that he has been cheated by his father, his rage seeming insatiable to the point of absurdity. Who is Pietro to talk? His lifestyle at the moment is not to be admired. The warnings he received from Mario about not getting involved with Bastone and Bambino are justified; however, it is his life and he will do as he pleases.

Mario and Maria look very dapper in their new attire, purchased especially for Serafino and Angela's wedding. Mario has worked with Serafino at Penfolds and genuinely believes he will thrive in Australia. He is a good worker, and he is about to marry very well; to marry someone like Angela is a very smart move. *Serafino is a fortunate man,* Mario thinks. Many people think that Mario is fortunate, as well, to have a wonderful partner such as Maria. Mario agrees at times, but he never really acknowledges her worth. She knows he loves her. He doesn't need to tell her—he just works hard to provide for the family, which is enough to show his love.

Fred has kindly offered to babysit Elliot, who is not a baby anymore. He has grown into a very intelligent four-and-a-half-year-old. It amazes Fred how Elliot can speak to his mother in Italian, then switch to speaking English with him within the same conversation. Elliot loves being with his Uncle Fred, as he calls him. They sit down to watch television together, something he can't do at home; as Mario refuses to buy a television, insisting it is a waste of money. Elliot loves watching *Mr Squiggle* and any cartoon shows. Fred loves watching shows like *Bonanza* and *Gunsmoke*. Elliot doesn't even mind watching the news, as long as he can fix his eyes on that square box with the moving images. Tonight, Elliot is particularly excited, as his favourite show, *The Wonderful World of Disney*, is screening.

Fred often says, "You know, Elliot, they call this the idiot box, but I think you're an idiot if you don't like it!"

Elliot totally agrees with him.

Maria gives Elliot a kiss, hands Fred a plate of homemade biscuits and thanks him for looking after Elliot. She says to give her regards to Irene. Fred comments on how nice she looks, tells her what a pleasure it is to spend time with her son, and says he will certainly relay her good wishes to Irene. The pleasantries over, Maria is off to her very first wedding in a hall. She is looking forward to it, as it's not often that Mario takes her out to any social event. Mario knows Pietro will be performing at the wedding with his band, and although he doesn't admit it, he is excited about seeing him again after such a long time. Maria is also happy about seeing Pietro, and listening to his wonderful singing voice again.

The happy couple greet all five hundred guests, each of

them receiving a satin-wrapped bomboniere of five sugared almonds, a traditional offering at most Italian weddings. The significance of there being five almonds is that the number five is indivisible, which symbolises a strong bond or union between the newlywed couple that will never be broken or divided. In addition, each sugared almond has its own meaning—health, happiness, wealth, fertility and long life. The guests pile into the large hall and find a table. As the seating is unreserved, many people scramble to find a place.

Mario and Maria sit at a table with Genaro and Stella, the women chatting on one end of the table, the men on the other, neither interested in what the other group is conversing about. Much to Mario's dismay, Bastone and Bambino sit at their table with two different *zozze* that he hasn't seen before. The two scantily dressed girls join Stella and Maria, and move only when Bastone nods his head. Mario is cordial but doesn't really engage in the conversation. Between the Calabrian and Neapolitan dialects, and the broken English, together with his lack of interest, he doesn't comprehend what they are actually talking about. Instead, he chooses to listen to Pietro sing, focusing on the chatty women who are well invested in each other's discussions. He compares Maria and Stella, who are polar opposites, then focuses on the two girls, who don't even get a ranking, yet they all find things to speak about and seem to be genuinely having a good time. The only similarities between the women is that when their men nod, they come running—except for Stella, since it is usually she who does the nodding, and Genaro who comes running.

Everyone is served a main meal of roast chicken with salad, and an oil panini bread roll, and they all enjoy the food along with the music. In between sets, Pietro joins them, and

Mario is sincerely happy to see him. Mario and Pietro enjoy a beer together, absorbed in a personal conversation. Bastone interrupts them.

"I can help you, Mario," says Bastone.

Mario looks at him, bewildered. *Why would I need his help?* he thinks to himself.

"The black hand extends to Italy, you know," Bastone continues.

"What are you talking about?" asks Mario.

"Well, I have heard you've had some trouble with your father, and I can help you."

Mario turns to Pietro. "What? You tell people all my business?"

Pietro says nothing, he just looks at Bastone to signal for him to stop the conversation. Bastone does not heed him.

"Don't get so upset, Mario. I'm just trying to help you."

Mario gets close to Bastone, staring him in the face menacingly.

"I don't need your help. If anyone is going to kill my father, it will be me. This is a family matter, why are you even...? I can't believe this!"

Bastone pushes him away and reaches for his knife. Pietro holds Bastone as Genaro holds back Mario. At this point, the women and a few onlookers notice the confrontation. Pietro calms Bastone, then makes a joke of it all.

"I'll let this go because you are a good friend of Pistola."

"He's no longer my friend," sneers Mario, not letting it go. Even though he knows who he is dealing with, he doesn't care. His anger overtakes his common sense until Genaro pulls him away and implores him not to ruin Serafino's wedding. This makes him grab Maria's hand to march her out of the hall and back home. Maria asks what is wrong, but Mario just grunts, and then says, "I took another photograph!"

Maria doesn't push for any extra explanation. Though they've left the wedding early, Maria did enjoy it, and later will learn the details of the altercation from Stella. The next day, Maria attends three church services and spends most of the day with rosary beads in her hands.

Genaro checks in on Mario to see if he's all right. He's spending time with his best friend, Mr Barrel. Genaro joins the duo in a deep and meaningful symposium. Mario learns from Genaro that Bambino is the son of a convicted murderer who is in jail for killing his wife, who was having an affair. Bastone is the illegitimate son of a high-ranking 'Ndrangheta enforcer called Mr Fluff. Obviously, this is not his real name. He's described by the two Melbourne men as cloudlike, just calmly floating around until he becomes mad, and then you feel his rain, thunder and lightning. Bastone and Bambino are low-ranking soldiers, wanting to prove their worth, to elevate their standing within the society by offering themselves as guns for hire. They are in Adelaide lying low after a contract in Mildura went wrong. They are dangerous, particularly Bastone, who has quite a bad temper. Mario says that Bastone is only dangerous because he's stupid; Pietro even more so for being involved with them, and Mario can't understand why he would associate with such men. Genaro agrees but advises Mario to lay low and not to aggravate any more tension. Mario assures Genaro that he will have nothing more to do with the wannabe Mafiosi, and Pietro is struck off his friendship list for good.

CHAPTER 21: VINO VERITAS

After Mario's brush with the Honoured Society underbelly, he really knuckles down, working even harder, if that was possible. He never goes to the club, and all attempts made by Pietro to contact him are snubbed. He is close to his financial goals again, which makes him very meticulous with the distribution of his money. Each payday, a third of the money goes into the bank, a third is kept in Mario's wallet for living expenses, and the other third is hidden in glass jars and buried in the chicken coop. Not one penny is sent to his father, no matter how many letters are received begging for help. Mario's insatiable lust to save money and his unrelenting distrust of everyone still exists. His bond with Fred has weakened over the years, but his disdain for Irene has not. Mario still respects Fred very much, but he no longer has time for unnecessary friendships, and he really wants to avoid Irene. Fred is not too bothered; he empathises with Mario, as he understands grief and its effect on people.

Mario becomes miserly with money and tightly controls every penny they spend. Maria does not complain; instead, she procures herself a part-time job as a cook at the local seminary, and Mario is none the wiser. He has no idea that she is working; he isn't around very much, and when he is, he is usually intoxicated, so he doesn't have a clue. His dinner is always prepared, the house is always in order, Elliot is growing up nicely, so nothing gives him any reason to suspect anything. Elliot has turned five, and he is a very bright and independent child. Now that he is attending school, Maria has a lot more time on her hands. She walks him to school, then takes the bus to the seminary, cooks lunch for the theology lecturers and students, picks Elliot up from school and is home in time to prepare dinner. She has her own money jar hidden in the condiment cupboard, somewhere she knows Mario would never look. A third of her pay goes into the jar, a third is sent to her father to give to Mario's mother, unbeknownst to Mario or his father, Euplio Sr, and the final third is donated to the church.

The first days of Elliot's school attendance are hard for Maria. She feels as if she has almost lost her purpose in life, and she is worried about how he will cope with other children, as he only really spends time with her or Fred.

Maria walks Elliot into the school grounds; she meets his new teacher, young Miss Shepard, who reassures all the mothers that everything is going to be fine, and tells them to go home. After several minutes of chitchat between the anxious mothers, they eventually disperse—everyone except Maria. She needs to make sure Elliot is OK.

Miss Shepard tries to quieten down the class, which consists of new five-year-old students, as well as English-as-a-second-language children in the range of six to twelve years old; it's quite chaotic. Miss Shepard thinks that she has definitely drawn the short straw of classes. Elliot is comforting the Italian-speaking students, some whom are crying and very stressed at not being able to understand the teacher. Elliot acts as the interpreter, and Miss Shepard is very grateful, as it makes her job a lot easier. Even something as simple as roll call is a nightmare. Most of the Italian given names are anglicised: Ignazio is Ian, Flavio is Flynn, Giuseppina becomes Josie and Massimo becomes Max. There are two Francescos, so one becomes Frank and the other Tim, for no particular reason. The teacher is very happy that Elliot presents himself as Elliot when she had seen that his real name was Euplio, which she doesn't even try to pronounce. Between the two of them, some order is established in the classroom, which is all witnessed by Maria from the far window. She is happy with what she sees, but this doesn't stop her from watching.

"Now, children, everyone look at the blackboard, get out your pad and pencils, and copy me," Miss Shepard instructs. Elliot dutifully translates her directive.

"Thank you so much for your help, Elliot."

Elliot's chest puffs up with pride as he waits for his next instruction.

"Now, Elliot, I need you to go to the far window and tell your mother to go home, and if she continues to stay after the bell, she will be in big trouble!"

Elliot marches angrily to the window to relay the message. Maria never spies on Elliot again; she gets a job instead.

* * *

The relationship between Fred and Mario has weakened, but the strong bond shared between Elliot and Fred has replaced it. Fred even walks Elliot to school on the mornings that Maria needs to start early. They always arrive slightly late, as along the way, Fred stops at the corner shop to buy Elliot a musk stick for recess, which he loves, as his mother would never buy him any lollies. Every day his lunch box is full of more food than he could ever eat, all homemade—usually an Italian panini, pickled vegetables, continental salumi and a homemade sweet biscuit or piece of cake. He comes home every night with his lunch box empty, which makes Maria happy. *But he's still very skinny*, she thinks. What Maria does not know is that Elliot will swap his continental lunches with the other kids, who have Vegemite-and-Cheese sandwiches with the crust cut off, carrot sticks and yo-yo biscuits. He doesn't really want the carrot sticks, but they usually come with the deal, and Elliot wants his fix of Vegemite. He has asked his mother many times to buy Vegemite, but she will not.

"What is this Vegemite? I don't know, you eat Mamma's food, it's much better," Maria always maintains.

Every Saturday is "Uncle Fred day" for Elliot. His father works while his mother either food shops or cleans the house; he doesn't have any siblings, so Fred is his best mate. He skips excitedly to the neighbour's house, rings the doorbell, but doesn't wait for it to be answered, he just walks straight in, and encounters Irene halfway up the corridor.

"Hello, Auntie Reenie, is Uncle Fred in?" asks Elliot.

"The whole purpose of ringing a doorbell is to wait for it to be answered," says Irene, fed up with his uncouth manners.

"Yes, I know, but you were taking too long, and I'm late for *Bonanza*."

Elliot runs into the lounge, and Irene follows him. "I'm not your aunt, you know!"

"I know."

Elliot finds Fred in his favourite armchair, positioned in front of the television set on the speaker side, as his hearing isn't as good as it used to be. Elliot sits down in the armchair that is Irene's usual spot; in between the two chairs, there is a small table. Irene isn't very impressed that Elliot just makes himself at home, or that he sits in her chair, but she knows how much Fred enjoys the boy's company, so she doesn't verbally protest, although her various scornful looks—totally ignored by Elliot—are frequent.

"G'day, little mate, you're just in time," says Fred as he pours him a glass of lemonade.

Irene is in an interrogative mood and questions Elliot. "So why do you call me 'aunt' when you know I'm not?"

"Because my mum says I should respect you."

"Well", claims Irene "That's very nice of her."

"But my dad says you don't deserve any respect."

"Your dad is an ignoramus."

Fred gives Irene a sharp look. "Don't listen to her, little mate, she doesn't mean that."

"It's OK, my dad calls her worse than that."

"Really?" she scoffs. "And what does he call me?"

"He calls you a *strega*."

"A what?"

"*Strega*...it means 'witch'. He says your broomstick is parked in the cupboard."

"Humph, if I were a witch, he would be the first one I would put a spell on."

"Reenie, are the sausage rolls ready?"

"I'll just fly into the kitchen and get them for you, shall I?"

As she leaves, Fred gives Elliot a wink.

"I think I need a beerstashe, Uncle Fred."

"Coming up."

Fred pours his beer, ensuring he gets a good head on it, then positions the glass near Elliot's mouth and tips it slightly to produce a stripe of beer froth across the top of his lip. Elliot looks at himself in the cabinet mirror, happy with what he sees. He sticks out his tongue, glides it across the top of his lip, gathering up all the froth and slurping it into his mouth, happy as a Cheshire cat. He looks over to Fred as the *Bonanza* theme song comes blaring out of the television speaker; Fred has his arms crossed with his feet comfortably positioned on the ottoman. Elliot mimics the same action. He tries to give Fred a wink, but only manages a blink.

The sweet-smelling waft of baking pastry comes into the lounge from the kitchen.

"Ohh, that smells so good, I wish my mum could cook sausage rolls."

"Reenie can teach her. She can make them blindfolded, that's about all she cooks. What's your mum cooking tonight?"

"Pasta...again!"

"Can you tell the time?"

"Sure, I can."

"You're a smart lad. How about you come to the back fence about six thirty tonight, and I'll swap whatever I have for dinner for your pasta?"

"How?"

"Never mind how, you just be there."

"OK."

"Don't tell your Mum or Auntie Reenie, they might not be too keen on the idea...Shhhhhh."

At that moment, Irene walks in with a plate of sausage rolls. Fred puts his finger up to his lips, and Elliot nods in agreement. Irene puts the plate on the accent table and looks at Elliot, sitting very contentedly in her chair, engrossed in the gunfight battle raging on the TV.

"When are you going to get your own television?" Irene asks.

Elliot answers without taking his eyes off the screen. "Well, I asked Father Christmas for one this year, but I'm not sure about him."

"What makes you say that?" asks Fred.

"Well, last year, I asked for a bike, but he gave me a Bible. I think he's confusing me with my mother. Yeah, not sure about him."

"I think he must have been on the piss," Fred says.

"Yeah, whatever that is? Can I have another beerstache?"

"Sure, little buddy."

Elliot happily slurps his new beerstache, takes a sip of his lemonade and helps himself to a sausage roll.

Later that evening, Elliot patiently sits on a wooden crate waiting for Fred. He brings his plate of spaghetti Bolognese up to his nose for a sniff. He is getting hungry now, as Fred has not shown up as yet. He fiddles with the fork as he hears a small scratching noise. A section of the fence comes away, and a plate of sausages and chips slides across from the other side.

"Thanks, Uncle Fred!" Elliot says excitedly. Elliot takes a couple of chips and chews away. "Yum," he says with his mouth full.

"Where's my part of the deal?" demands Fred from the other side of the fence.

Elliot quickly reaches for the plate of spaghetti he has placed next to his feet. He shoos away the other neighbour's annoying cat that has been sniffing the plate, then slides it under the fence to Fred. He then continues eating his sausages and chips.

"Delicious," comes the lip-smacking assessment from Fred.

He finishes the spaghetti in record time, then passes the empty plate back under the fence towards Elliot's feet.

"Can you get any more?" asks Fred.

"Sure."

"And can you put more of that smelly cheese on top?"

Elliot runs into the house with the empty plate in his hand. He helps himself to another serving of spaghetti and piles on the Parmesan cheese; Maria looks at him suspiciously.

"I'm really hungry, Mamma."

"Eat, grow, my darling," she replies.

Mario sits patiently, waiting to be served by Maria. She replaces his empty plate with a small plate of fruit.

Mario watches as Elliot runs out. "Good he's eating more... He eats like a pigeon, but shits like a lion." Mario laughs at his own joke, giving Maria a look indicating she should pour him another glass of wine, which she does.

Maria stands at the kitchen window, which has a view of the backyard, as she washes dishes. She witnesses Elliot passing the plate of spaghetti under the fence and finishing the last remaining chips. He passes his plate back when all the chips are gone. Maria is slightly put out by the exchanging of food, but decides not to say anything, as Elliot looks so happy. Nothing is more important to her than Elliot's happiness. As a surprise, Fred passes a green frog cake through the hole in the fence; Elliot's face lights up like a Christmas tree.

"Oh, thank you! I love you, Uncle Fred, I really do."

Fred responds with a full mouth. "Mmmm, me too."

He slides back the almost clean plate and replaces the missing fence portion. "Let me know when your mum makes pasta next."

"She makes pasta almost every day."

"Oh, OK, well, same time next week, then. Can you ask for some of that lasagne?"

"Sure. Can you ask for Vegemite-and-Cheese sandwiches, with the crusts cut off?"

"No problem, little buddy."

As Maria and Elliot walk back from school, they pass the Brackenbridge house and wave to Fred, who is edging the lawn. A large "For Sale" sign is planted in front of the Lanzani house. Elliot stares at the sign, and the cogs in his head try to compute what it means. He looks to his mother.

"We are selling the house, my darling."

"Are you buying another one?"

"No, we are going home."

"What do you mean, we are going home? This is our home."

"Well, we are going back to Italy to live."

"Why?"

"Because we are Italian."

"I'm Australian!"

"You were born in Australia, but you are Italian."

"No! I'm Australian!" Elliot turns and shouts to Fred. "I'm Australian, isn't that right, Uncle Fred?"

"You're as dinky-di as a merino sheep," says Fred as he walks up to Elliot and Maria, sensing he needs to defuse the situation. He ruffles Elliot's hair. "Yep, dinky-di as a sheep, but not as shaggy." He looks at Maria's face, which is full of doubt. "Come on, Little Joe, let's go to the ranch," Fred says in a Texan drawl. The ranch is what Fred calls the playground, where they often go to play out their *Bonanza* theatricals.

"OK, Horse, I'll go get my hat and guns."

When Elliot is out of sight, Maria takes a deep breath and confides in Fred. "I'm not sure I want to go back, Fred."

"Do you think you can convince Mario to stay?"

"No, he is very sure about going back."

Elliot runs from the house towards Fred, his straw cowboy hat on his head and two cap guns in his loose holster. Fred tightens up the holster for him. Elliot holds his cap guns in the air and shouts as he imitates Yosemite Sam from the *Looney Tunes*.

"I'm the hootiness, tootiness bobcat, wildcat in the West! I'm the fastest gun in the North, South, East and West. Come on, Horse, let's go catch us some varmints!"

Maria can't help but laugh, her whole face lighting up with an infectious laugh that brightens everyone's mood.

"I think he's got his *Looney Tunes* mixed up with his *Bonanza*," says Fred.

Elliot runs down the road towards the playground. It doubles as a Wild West scene, where Little Joe and Horse play out their imaginary *Bonanza* or *Looney Tunes* scenarios, depending on what Elliot has been watching. Fred is in tow behind Elliot, shouting in an American Western drawl, "Hey, Little Joe, wait up!"

Elliot loves going to the playground with Fred, where he can let his imagination go wild. There are a lot of trees and bushes that double up as the frontier landscape, a slippery dip attached to a wooden structure that serves as a mini fort, and many other pieces of play equipment, such as seesaws, roundabouts and swings, which are all handy props. Every bird is either a good or bad cowboy, or a good or bad Indian, the geckos and lizards are lonely strangers, and the ants are a wagon train—a very small one, always directed to safety by

Elliot aka Little Joe.

Little Joe turns into Sheriff Elliot, and Fred turns from Horse to a dirty cow-rustling outlaw. There's a lot of running around and whooping from Elliot, and Fred moves as fast as his age and bad leg will let him. Elliot is moving in on the outlaw; he surprises him as he lies resting under the tree. He points his cap gun at Fred, who scrambles away, but the caps don't fire, so, in frustration, Elliot throws his gun down, points his finger and shouts.

"BANG! You're dead."

Fred keeps running.

"Hey, you're dead!" shouts Elliot.

"No, I'm not, you missed," Fred shouts back.

"I couldn't have missed you from that distance."

"Your gun didn't work."

"I used my pretend gun, with my pretend bullets. I couldn't have missed you from that distance...You're dead!"

"I ducked!"

"No, you didn't, I got you!" Elliot insists.

Fred submits, giving the performance of his life, the dramatic death scene lasting longer than it should have. When Fred eventually dies, he lies still for a while, as the rule is that you have to "lie dead" for a period of at least five minutes. Elliot approaches his kill and says, "OK you dirty rustler, where did you hide the cows?"

"How can I answer you if I'm dead?" Fred whispers.

"I just wounded you badly, you can still talk."

With that, Fred pulls out his imaginary gun and shoots Elliot with his imaginary bullets.

"You can't shoot me," Elliot protests.

"Yes, I can, you just wounded me. My pretend gun works

just as well as yours, and there's no way that I missed you."

Elliot thinks for a moment. "OK, you shot me, you dirty cow rustler; there will be a place for you in hell". His death scene is even more dramatic and overacted than Fred's was, the boy crawling across the grass and eventually falling down on his back, arms and legs spread-eagled, eyes closed. Fred watches the exaggerated act, propped up on his elbows, making sure Elliot doesn't get too close to the running creek, which he's fallen into in the past. Elliot, as per the rules, lies still for a while. Fred approaches the grass-stained, dead sheriff.

"OK, little mate, time to go."

Elliot remains dead.

"Come on, Elliot, let's go."

Elliot still remains dead. Fred begins to worry slightly but knows what will wake the dead. He prepares his tickling fingers and goes in for the assault. Like Lazarus, Elliot is raised from the dead, laughing, screaming, trying to avoid Fred's enormous tickling digits.

"OK, OK, I'm alive! Can we go for a raspberry and a beer-stashe?"

"Sure we can. We need to replenish ourselves after such a long day of cow rustling and killing."

On the way home, Fred and Elliot walk into the corner pub, parched and ready for a pick-me-up. They sit at the front bar and are greeted by the barman.

"G'day, Fred, I see ya got your little wog boy with ya today."

Elliot is oblivious to the slur, but Fred turns to the barman with clenched teeth and says, "If you ever say that again, I will send your teeth and tongue on a holiday to the back of your head. Now get me a frothy and a raspberry."

The barman, somewhat surprised by Fred's threat, goes

about preparing the drink order. "There ya go, Fred, a frothy for you and a raspberry for…"

"Elliot," responds Fred.

"Elliot. The little wog boy," retorts the barman.

Elliot doesn't even flinch an eyelid at the insult, since all his needs are being met and he doesn't recognise the word as derogatory; this is what his school friends call him all the time. Fireworks go off in Fred's head, and with the accuracy of a flying arrow, his fist knocks the barman out with one single punch. Elliot doesn't even notice, as he's far too busy slurping his raspberry drink with his eyes fixated on the peanut jar. The two men at the end of the bar remain silent in shock. One of the men reaches over to the beer tap handle to pour himself a free pint of beer, then raises the glass to Fred and says, "Here's to racists pricks."

Fred places the edge of his beer to Elliot's lips to give him his customary beerstache. He then gulps down his frothy in record speed. Elliot finally notices the unconscious barman.

"What happened to him?" he asks.

"Oh, he just had a bit of a fainting spell," answers Fred.

"Oh…yeah, my dad has those sometimes."

Fred can't help himself from laughing, but as the barman stirs, he rises from his chair. "We need to go, your parents will be wondering where you are."

Walking back from their adventurous day, Elliot is not as chatty as he normally is. Fred notices his mood.

"What's up, Doc?"

Not even Fred's Bugs Bunny quip manages to produce a smile from Elliot. He finally speaks.

"I don't want to live in a shoe," Elliot says, almost crying.

"What are you talking about?"

"Italy. It's a shoe."

"Oh...well, technically, Italy is a boot."

"A boot is a shoe, Uncle Fred!"

"Mmm...yes, you got me there."

"If my mum and dad go back, can I stay here and live with you?"

"Your mum is not going to let you stay here, that's one thing I know for sure."

"You didn't answer my question, can I stay with you?"

"Sure you can, little buddy."

Elliot is more content now. He holds on to Fred's hand. Fred gives him a forced smile.

Maria and Mario sit at the table, eating. Maria has prepared one of Mario's favourite meals of tripe and beans, aiming to appease his mood and make the conversation less tense than she thinks it may be. Mario enjoys his meal. It's perfect, and he washes it down with a second glass of wine.

"Where's Elliot?" he asks.

"He's with Fred. Has there been any interest in the house?"

"A bit."

"What if I said you didn't need to keep your promise?"

"What promise?"

"The promise you made to me on our wedding night."

Mario looks perplexed.

"The promise to take me back to Italy. What if I said you don't have to take me back?"

"That promise was made to myself as well, we're going back!" Mario pushes the empty plate towards Maria. "Get me some more tripe and beans, and put more salt on it, you never use enough salt!"

Maria snatches the plate and stomps to the kitchen, where she says a quick prayer.

"And stop praying, it won't change my mind."

Maria keeps praying, but only in her mind. As she opens the cupboard to get the salt, she spies the rat poison at the back. *Please God, don't let me replace the salt with the rat poison...give me strength to put up with this man.*

She aggressively pushes the plate towards Mario. "I don't want to go back anymore, I want to stay here!"

"I don't. We are going back, and that's it!"

"Your son is Australian."

"My son is Italian."

"No! He was born here; his first language is English. He doesn't even eat my food. I see him swap his food with Fred all the time."

"Well, I think Fred is definitely getting the better deal."

"He is Australian, his future is in Australia."

"His future is where I say it is! We are going back, firstly because we are Italian and always will be, and secondly because I need to kill my father."

"You are impossible!"

"No, I'm Italian!"

Maria takes off her apron and grabs her bag.

"Where are you going?"

"To church, to pray for you."

"Make sure you pray to the Australian God, and tell the Italian God to send us back to Italy safely!"

"There is no Australian and Italian God, there's only one God, like the Italian sun and the Australian sun are the same sun!"

"There is a difference, Maria—the sun actually exists."

Maria is outraged. "God exists, he just doesn't exist in you!" She storms out and slams the door shut.

"You forgot to pour my wine!" Mario shouts at the door and then laughs sarcastically. He looks at the wine jug, picks it up, and doesn't bother to fill his glass; he just drinks straight from the jug.

Fred and Elliot finally reach home. The garage entrance is shut, so they go in through the front door.

"You coming in, Uncle Fred?"

"Yeah, just want to have a word with your dad."

They pass through the lounge room on their way to the kitchen. Fred stops at a wall full of framed black-and-white pictures of people, with lit candles positioned on the mantle directly underneath them.

"Who are all these people on the wall?" Fred asks.

"They're my mum's friends. They're all dead."

"So, is that your mum's wall of death?"

"Yeah."

"I'm not in any hurry to be up on that wall. Let's find your dad."

They enter the kitchen. Mario is nowhere to be seen, but from the kitchen window, Fred sees Mario downing a full jug of wine. He turns to Elliot, who is too small to see anything.

"Looks like your parents aren't home. How would you like to come over and watch a bit of telly?"

Of course, Elliot does not refuse.

Mario reenters the kitchen with another full jug of wine, and he is now very drunk. He sits at his usual spot at the table and swigs the wine, spilling half of it on his shirt. He looks to the crucifix hanging on the wall, points at it and speaks to the inanimate object with slurred words.

225

"You...you *bastardo*, I've never been able to compete with you. You win every time. If only Maria would look at me the way she looks at you. I love her, you don't, you give her false hope...and I...I give her reality! You *bastardo*!"

Mario rises from the table and smacks the crucifix off the wall; it smashes on the ground. He does the same with all the other religious statues and pictures he sees. After his act of desecration, Mario slumps on the table with his head to the side, staring at the broken artefacts. They seem to be rising from the floor and floating around his head. He swats them away, but they don't move. Finally, he stumbles out the door.

Elliot sits in Irene's chair, his usual television viewing spot—like father, like son, he likes his usual spot. Two glasses are positioned on the table. The television blares out the *Bonanza* theme tune. Fred walks in with one bottle of stout and one bottle of lemonade.

"How about a beerstache, Little Joe?"

"I won't argue with that, Horse."

Fred pours his stout into one glass, ensuring he gets a good head of froth, then pours lemonade into the other glass. He places the frothy beer head to Elliot's lips to give him his beerstache. Fred then gives him the glass of lemonade, and they swig their drinks in unison.

"Ahhhhhhhh," both Fred and Elliot verbalise their satisfaction, and the glasses are placed back onto the table.

Fred puts his feet comfortably onto the ottoman, and his action is mimicked by Elliot; they are two unlikely twins. Irene enters, not expecting Elliot to be in her chair. Although she wouldn't sit to watch *Bonanza*, she's annoyed at the unexpected occupation of her spot.

"Don't you have a home to go to?" she barks at Elliot.

"Reenie, that's enough!" interrupts Fred.

"I'll be glad when you go back to Italy," she says, totally ignoring Fred.

"I'm not going back to Italy, I'm not living in a shoe! Uncle Fred says I can stay here and live with him," Elliot barks back.

"Well, I'm sure your mother won't let that happen, and neither will I, for that matter!"

"I'm Australian."

"No, you're not, you are Italian, and you should go back to your own country."

"I was born here, I'm Australian," argues Elliot.

"But your parents are Italian!"

"Where are your parents from?"

"My parents were born here, I am third generation."

"And where are your grandparents from?"

"They were born in England. They were English."

"Then you should have gone back a long time ago!"

Irene is dumfounded at Elliot's response, but Fred's roars of laughter nearly shake the room.

"You are much too smart for your own good, and stop pinching my sausage rolls!" Irene says as she walks out.

Elliot shouts at her back as she disappears through the doorway: "I don't pinch your sausage rolls, it's a fair swap with Uncle Fred!"

Irene grunts from the other room.

Fred leans over to Elliot. "It's probably not really that much of a fair swap for you, little buddy."

"I'm not going to Italy, Uncle Fred. I'll run away, they won't find me."

"Don't worry, my little mate, these things have a way of sorting themselves out."

Fred picks up his glass. Elliot does the same, and they toast.

"Cheers, big ears!" they say to each other. They drink in harmony and position their feet on the ottoman, relaxing and watching what's left of the *Bonanza* episode.

* * *

Light streams through the stained-glass window of the church, the image reflected on the dais like a projector being operated by the divine. Maria kneels on the hassock of a pew, chanting along with the priest. He conducts his sermon in Latin; Maria knows every word by heart, saying them most times before Father Patrick Kavanagh does. His soothing voice gives Maria the calm she needs. There is a sudden bang from the side door of the church. The entire congregation sees the back of a man trying to silence the door. From the corner of her eye, Maria spies the jacket that the man is wearing—it looks familiar, like the one she bought Mario last week. It is.

Mario turns around, staggers to the water font, cups a handful of the holy water and sprays his whole face with it. He wipes his eyes and face with the lapel of his jacket and looks to the back of the priest, who continues his homily with his arms held up in holy ceremony. Mario moves as quietly as he can to position himself behind Father Kavanagh as he impersonates the priest's ceremonial actions, mocking him. All the eyes of the congregation are now locked on Mario, and not Father Kavanagh; some are disgusted, but most just try not to laugh. The children can't help but laugh, their parents finding it difficult to silence them. Maria is shocked, and she implores God, *Strike him down now, I beg you.*

Her prayers are not answered. Father Kavanagh turns to his

mimicker, slightly irritated but mostly amused, and tries to reason with him.

"Maria? Where is my Maria?" shouts Mario.

Most of the assembly turn to where Maria sits, as they know who she is, but Maria is no longer there: the seat is empty. The priest tries to convince Mario to sit down. Mario rambles on about finding Maria, and then concedes.

"OK, OK, I'll sit down, but you have to promise me you will tell your boss to stop interfering with my marriage."

"My boss?" asks Father Kavanagh.

"Yes, your boss...Jesus, tell him to stay out of my marriage!"

"Yes, OK, I will."

"You promise?"

"Yes, yes, of course. Now come with me, sit down."

Father Kavanagh directs Mario to an empty pew. He would have promised Mario anything just to get him to comply. Mario sits quietly for a moment, then slowly sways to the side to lie down. The priest continues his sermon as best he can, emphasising the need for absolution and tolerance. The children are still laughing at the snoring Mario.

Maria, full of tears and outrage, storms into the house; her rage is exacerbated by the sight of her religious artefacts in pieces all over the floor. She falls to her knees, not even having the will to pray. Eventually, she gathers enough strength to collect a broom and dustpan to clean up the broken fragments, still with tears in her eyes and an aching heart. The doorbell rings. Father Kavanagh holds up a slouching Mario. Maria and the priest look at each other. Mario hangs his head as he passes Maria to enter the house.

"I am so embarrassed, Father," says Maria self-consciously.

"Forgiveness, Maria. If anyone can do it, you can."

Father Kavanagh blesses Maria and leaves. Maria throws the contents of the dustpan in the bin. Mario sits at his favourite spot at the dinner table, just watching Maria, waiting for her to say something.

"Maria," he says.

Maria says nothing, she just continues to clean.

"Maria," he says again.

"Don't even say my name!"

"OK, then, I will sing it. *Maria, Maria, Maria!*" he sings, and then laughs at his own pathetic joke.

"This is not funny, you disgraced me and don't even have the decency to say sorry!"

"You won't even let me say your name!"

Maria's look is menacing.

"I know you want to kill me," Mario says.

"I don't have to kill you, you will kill yourself if you keep drinking the way you do—all I have to do is wait, but I'm not going to wait, I'm leaving you!"

"Where are you going to go?"

"Anywhere but here. Elliot will come with me, and you can drink yourself to death in peace."

Mario laughs loudly. "You're not leaving me, never! Only in a box you will leave me!"

Mario becomes increasingly agitated, and Maria runs from the kitchen, locking herself in the bathroom. Mario chases her and knocks forcefully on the door. He keeps knocking as Maria holds herself against the door, silently crying. Mario finally gives up and falls to the floor, sobbing. He picks himself up with a rush of fury.

"Maria, you won't leave me, I'll make sure of it!" he shouts as he stomps out of the house straight into the shed.

Mario looks around the shed, maniacally speaking to himself. "She won't leave me, never, I'll make sure of it...Now, where are you?"

He keeps looking around the shed, on shelves and in cupboards, ultimately finding the object he's looking for. He holds up the long-handled sledgehammer.

"Yes, you will do. She's not going to leave me, not until one of us is dead." Mario begins to cry. "Australian God, save me! Maria, hear me!"

He holds the hammer high into the air and then swings it around to smash all the wine-making equipment. He strikes the press, the fermenting tanks, glass containers and bottles. He gets to the barrels.

"Sorry, Mr Barrel, my old friend, I can't let you ruin my life."

Mr Barrel and his acquaintances, both empty and full, are hit relentlessly, pierced with numerous holes. Wine gushes out of the barrels, creating a symphony of burgundy waterfalls. He slips and slides around as other shed furniture and objects get the mad Mario treatment. Finally out of breath, he stops to look at what he has done.

"Ohh nooooooo! Noooooo!" Mario cries.

He slides over to one of the gushing barrels, holding his shirt underneath the cascading wine, trying in vain to capture the last of his vintage. Realising he is now losing all his crop, he hangs his head under the flowing wine to drink as much as he can. Wine spills all over him as he skids and glides amongst the haemorrhaging vats, crying over spilt wine, becoming more and more intoxicated, until his body collapses into a state of unconsciousness, bringing Maria's prediction of him drinking himself to death almost to reality.

A red sandstorm rages. Mario is a witness to all its ferocity as he sits on the ground, holding his hands up to his head, protecting his eyes from the stinging sand whilst trying to decipher the emerging image coming closer and closer towards him. As the storm subsides, the image becomes clearer. Macumba stands, majestically towering over the crouching Mario, and his stance and expression turn to a menacing fury as he holds up his spear ready to attack.

"No, Macumba! Don't kill me, I'm your friend...I'm your friend!"

Macumba strikes a fearsome image as he plunges his spear into Mario, who screams out in pain. Macumba pulls out the spear. Mario's fearful face turns to wonder as he stares at his open wound. Wine instead of blood gushes out of the lesion. Macumba stabs Mario several more times. Mario tries to block the haemorrhaging with the palms of his hands, to no avail; the wine continues to flow out, like the wine barrels. Mario looks to Macumba beseechingly as other tribal men join him. The sound of didgeridoos crescendos as the men start a tribal war dance. They are telling a story, like a stage performance, and Mario is the sole spectator; Mario is not sure if it is a welcoming performance or an intimidating one. Mario is still bleeding wine and confused as hell.

"Macumba, I'm still your friend," he shouts.

At this point, the Indigenous war dance turns into the Italian tarantella folk dance, and the sounds of the didgeridoo turn into accordions and tambourines. Mario is fixated on the bewildering yet comical scene. The image fades away to reveal government men taking children away from their mothers. A painful scream is heard. Maria chases down the men as they carry Elliot away. She is held aggressively by the men, and she cannot reach her son. Eventually, both of them are carried

232

away, crying and yelling. The ear-piercing shrieks are too much for Mario to bear. He is still on the ground, trying with all his might to rise, but he is unable to get up. There is a gravitational force holding him down.

"Don't take my son, don't take my wife, please, don't destroy my family!" He looks to his wounds, still spurting out wine. Macumba appears again. Mario implores him, "Help me, Macumba...please help me."

Macumba's stern face finally speaks. "You a good white fella, Mario, but you are a bad man!"

Helpless and hopeless, Macumba reaches his hand out to help Mario. He grabs for Macumba's hand but is unable to grasp it. Macumba disappears, and only a ghostly darkness remains.

Mario lays in a pool of dried-up grape goo mixed with vomit. He opens one eye enough to see a blurry vision of a pair of couture white-tipped shoes, and another pair of suede lace-up Oxfords.

"Is he dead?" asks Fred.

"No," answers Maria.

"You sound disappointed."

"God is testing me, I'm sure of it!"

"He's going to be alright. He a good man at his core, but he's created a shamozzle in the shed."

"Mmm. I'll clean it up later."

"Maria, he's smashed most of the wine bottles, but there's a few boxes in the corner that are untouched. Now, they're called Grange Hermitage and they're good bottles of wine. Put them somewhere safe, you don't want him getting to those as well. If he doesn't want them, give them to me."

"How do you know they are good ones?"

"There's a big deal about them in the newspapers, they've won lots of awards—hide them, don't let him smash them, and for God's sake, don't let him mix them with lemonade like we used to."

"OK, thank you."

Mario's wine-stained hand reaches out for Maria's white-tipped shoes; she quickly pulls them out of his reach.

"I am going to pray for him. I'm going to pray to his Australian God." With that, Maria and her white-tipped shoes walk away.

Fred's large hands grab Mario under his arms to pull him up. "Come on, mate, up ya get."

Mario mumbles something incoherent.

"You've done a right job on the wine gear, haven't you?"

"Sorry, Fred," whispers Mario.

"How are we going to make wine now?"

"No more wine. No more, my friend."

Fred drags Mario inside.

"What's wrong with Dad, Uncle Fred?"

"He's OK, Elliot, you just finish your homework, and I'll look after your dad."

"Oh, did he have another fainting spell?"

"He sure did!"

Mario sits in his usual position at the kitchen table, waiting to be served by Maria. The wine glass has been replaced with a cup and saucer, the jug with a teapot. Maria fills the cup with a nice warm brew and slides it over to him. She dishes up a plate of minestrone soup mixed with pasta and beans, just the way he likes it.

"Am I forgiven?"

"Sì," answers Maria.

"I've forgiven my father as well."

"Good."

"When I see him, I will thank him."

"What for?"

"For sending you to me."

Maria is touched and gives him a grateful smile. Mario takes her hand and kisses it.

"I will thank him and hug him, and then I will kill him after that!"

CHAPTER 22: THE UNWELCOME VISITOR

Mario has been sober for six weeks—not a drop of any type of alcohol has touched his lips since his hallucinatory bender. Maria once again sees the man she married. Mario is much more reasonable and agreeable than he has been the last few years, but he won't budge about staying in Australia; his mother and his hat are back in Italy waiting for him. He is determined to get the family cantina back up and running again, which would have happened already if not for his father's deception.

Euplio never receives a cent from his son again. Instead, Mario sends his mother nonperishable things, such as tea, sugar and coffee, as well as clothing items, linen and blankets. Antonietta never let Mario or her husband know that Maria had been sending her money—it is the secret shared between the two artful women. Antonietta uses half the money for food and half she saves and hides in the pantry cupboard, where she knows Euplio would never look. She manages the money well, and Euplio is none the wiser. He constantly complains about Mario not sending any more money, which Antonietta never comments on; however, she is secretly happy, as the feud with his neighbour over the water fountain has come to a halt at last.

With the items Mario is sending and the extra secret money, life in the little village of Bovino is improving for the Lanzani household. Antonietta assures Mario that all is well.

It is a glorious Sunday. Maria is preparing a picnic lunch for three, which could feed ten, as Mario tinkers in his shed. It is a special treat day, as they are due to meet Genaro and his children at the city park. Stella will join them after she closes the continental shop. Elliot is very excited, as the park in the city has amazing play equipment and paddleboats—he loves the paddleboats. He prepares his pirate hat and sword in readiness to act out his swashbuckling adventures with Lorenzo, Vincenzo, Immacolata, Concetta and Kevin.

There's a knock at the door.

"Who could that be?" Maria says to herself.

"I'll get it, Mum," shouts Elliot.

Maria continues to prepare the picnic feast as Elliot walks in with Pietro.

"H-h-hello, Maria."

Maria is surprised, but greets him graciously, then sends Elliot off to the corner store to buy some milk. She doesn't need milk, but she also doesn't need Elliot to witness his father's reaction to seeing Pietro. Elliot happily obliges. Maria knows that he will take longer than necessary, as he always does on his trips to the shops.

Pietro looks shabby and troubled.

"Are you alright, Pietro?" she asks with genuine concern.

"Is Mario here?"

"Yes, he is, but...um..."

"I—I—I need to see him. I'm in trouble, I need some help."

"He's outside in the shed."

"Can I go out there, please?"

"Of course...would you like me to come with you?"

"No, i-it's OK."

Mario is stacking the bottles of tomato sauce that have been made the week before; he turns to see Pietro standing in the doorway. There is a silence between them. Finally, Mario speaks.

"Are you not ashamed of yourself to come here?" he asks in Italian.

"Mario, please."

"You need to rub your face in a pile of shit—you will come up cleaner than you are now."

Pietro breaks down in tears and falls to his knees. Mario's stance towards his estranged friend softens as he helps Pietro up from his knees.

"Come...sit over here," Mario instructs, guiding the sobbing Pietro to a wooden crate. Pietro sits with his head lowered into his hands, eventually composing himself.

"Mario...I-I-I'm in trouble. I need your help."

"When did your problem become my problem?"

"It's not your p-p-problem, but as a friend, I thought m-m-maybe you could help me a little bit."

"What do you need, Pietro?"

"I need money. I p-promise I will pay it back."

Mario shakes his head. "I can't give you any money. I don't give money to anyone, no one at all."

"Please, Mario, I just need to pay Bastone back, and t-t-then I will be free of him."

Mario is incensed. "I told you! I told you, don't get involved with these men, why didn't you listen to me? Now who is the hippopotamus?"

"I know, I know! Please, please, I promise I will give him his money and I will be done with him."

"You will never be done with him! Not until one of you is dead, and most likely it will be you!" Mario's shouting is not helping the situation, and makes Pietro more agitated. He starts to shout back.

"I know you've got money!"

"I know I've got money, but I'm not giving it to you; my own father shafted me, and I won't let anyone do it again."

"Why won't you help me? I promise to pay it back, Mario, please!"

"You know why. I need to get the family back to Italy and restore the cantina, you know that. Now get out of my house, I don't want to look at you for one second more!"

Pietro finally accepts that Mario is not going to help him and no longer wastes his efforts pleading with Mario.

"*Arrivederci*, Mario...*B-b-buona fortuna*," he says in parting.

"Good luck, my arse. I'll make my own luck—with this." Mario wipes the sweat off his brow to indicate that it is hard work and not luck that makes a man successful.

Pietro turns to walk away, dejected, as Mario continues his verbal assault, only stopping when his old friend is out of sight.

Pietro enters the kitchen to say goodbye to Maria.

"Ciao, Maria," Pietro says as he kisses her on the cheek.

"Wait, Pietro," Maria instructs him. She looks outside to see where Mario is. She sees Mario scuttle to the back of the yard towards the chicken coop. As soon as she thinks he is out of sight, she reaches for the jar at the back of her condiment cupboard. Maria pulls out her nest egg container, takes out the contents—now quite a sizable amount of money—and hands it to Pietro. He can't quite believe his eyes. He breaks down crying again, but this time, it's tears of relief. He grabs both of her hands and kisses them. He can hardly speak, but he manages to eventually thank her.

"I hope it's enough," she says.

He nods, then hugs her, tells her she is an angel on earth, and leaves. Maria continues to prepare the picnic lunch as if nothing ever happened.

Mario is paranoid about the parcels of money he has hidden in the chicken coop, so he diligently digs them all up and stuffs his pockets with the notes. Maria calls him from the kitchen window, beckoning him to get ready for their outing. He calls back to her and says he will be there soon, then proceeds to fill the holes in again, the chickens clucking all around him. He is happy with his work; it looks as if nothing has disturbed the ground except scratching fowls. He collects the eggs and reenters the house, passing Maria, not mentioning his incident with Pietro. Maria doesn't ask. Mario doesn't have a safe, but he does have a pillow, and what's more secure than sleeping on top of your money every night for safekeeping? He shuts the door of the bedroom and carefully picks an opening on the side of the middle cushion lining, then puts all his pocketed money into the cavity; his pillow is now much fuller than it was, and much more comfortable, mentally more than physically.

The Lanzani family jump in the car ready for their day out. Elliot has his pirate gear, Maria has her large picnic hamper, and Mario has his clear conscience. They arrive at the city park to meet Genaro and his five children, Lorenzo, Vincenzo, Immacolata, Concetta and Kevin. Elliot and Genaro's five children quickly join each other to play on the park apparatus. There is even more equipment for Elliot to play out his fantasies than at the park he visits with Uncle Fred, with more participants to play along. Elliot and Kevin are about the same age; most times, it's them against the rest of Kevin's siblings. Maria keeps a close eye on all the children while Genaro and Mario engross themselves in their private conversation.

"Have you seen Pistola lately?" asks Genaro.

"Yes, this morning," says Mario, unimpressed. "He came to ask me for money."

"He asked me for money too."

"Did you give him some?"

"I don't have any money to give him, Mario. I've got five children to feed, and a business to run, and apart from that, Stella controls the money now, and I didn't want to ask her. She wouldn't give it to me anyway, because she thinks I would use it to gamble at the club...Did you give him money?"

"No, I'm not the Commonwealth Bank!"

"He looked in a bad way, though. I'm worried about him."

"It's his own fault. He should never have involved himself with those people. Everyone knew who they were and what they were," Mario says without any contrition.

"Yes, I know, but Bastone promised him a lot, and he believed it all."

"So, why should I fix his stupidity with my money?"

"Bastone promised him he would get him a recording contract, because his father knew a lot of people in the music industry. Pietro believed him. He was blinded by bullshit."

"Again, I ask, why should I fix his stupidity?"

"I would have given him the money if Stella would let me. Yes, she is the brains and the brawn," Genaro says with a chuckle.

Mario also laughs for the first time during the conversation.

Stella's arrival at the park is well advertised by her loud and boisterous voice thundering even over the children's chatter.

She stands by the wading pool with Maria, watching their youngsters in the paddleboats. Elliot and Kevin decide to act out a buccaneers' duel whilst standing up in their opposing vessels. Together, the two mothers scream out to the boys to sit down, fearing they will fall in the water—too late, both boys go down in a spectacular display. Luckily the pond is only three feet deep, but the day's outing ends earlier than expected.

CHAPTER 23: HAPPY LITTLE VEGEMITE

Maria prepares dinner for the family and sets aside a plate for Elliot to swap with Fred, ensuring it is a man-size portion, along with a couple of pieces of homemade bread. Elliot rushes in to collect his—or rather, Fred's—plate, then rushes back outside to wait for the exchange of dinners. Maria is curious. Why does Elliot like this Vegemite on soft bread with no crust so much? And what is so special about some mincemeat wrapped up in pastry, then dipped in sickly-sweet tomato sauce?

The exchange is made, and Elliot sits happily on the wooden crate eating his Vegemite-and-Cheese sandwiches with the crust cut off, speaking to Uncle Fred on the other side of the fence. Maria decides to find out what all this fuss over Vegemite is about.

"Hello, Fred," says Maria.

"Oh, hello, Maria," Fred answers from behind the fence.

"How is the pasta today?"

"Better than ever. Maria, you are a wonderful cook."

"Thank you, Fred."

"Elliot, can I try some of your sandwich?" she asks.

Elliot looks up to her in surprise, then hands her a quarter of the cut sandwich, reluctantly. Maria smiles at him as she bites into this black-and-gold filled white bread; her smile quickly turns into a twisted frown.

"Ohhhhh! Ohhhhhh, this is disgusting!" She spits out the half-eaten sandwich and throws it to the chickens—even they don't like it.

Elliot has a good laugh at his mother's expense, but Fred is worried that Maria will stop the food-exchange ritual for good.

"Elliot, how can you eat that? It's horrible, it looks like shoe polish and tastes like it too."

"I love it, and I wish you would buy it for me."

"I will never buy it for you. Fred, what are you feeding my son, is it poison?"

"Oh, Maria, yes, it is an acquired taste, but it's not poisonous—we've been eating it for years."

"What is it?"

"Umm, it's some sort of yeast extract? Actually, I don't know, it's just Vegemite."

"You have to be Australian to like Vegemite Mum, and I'm Australian," Elliot announces proudly.

Maria scoffs at the idea. "God help me," she says as she rushes back into the house to flush the repulsive taste out of her mouth with water. Elliot finds the whole incident very funny, but Fred is not so sure.

Mario and Maria are surprised by a visit from Genaro. They invite him in for a cup of coffee and some homemade biscuits, which he accepts with gratitude. He looks solemn, and after the general introductory greetings have subsided, he blurts out: "Pietro is dead."

Mario and Maria are shocked into silence. Finally, Genaro speaks.

"It was suicide. He hung himself...That's what the police

said, but I don't believe them."

Maria has tears streaming down her face, but Mario is stoic and pensive, still silent. Genaro continues. "It's funny to me that Pietro is found dead, and Bastone and Bambino have gone—they haven't been at the club since."

"Oh no, it mustn't have been enough," sobs Maria.

"What wasn't enough?" asks Mario.

"Oh, my prayers Mario, my prayers. I could see he needed help. I thought they would help him, but it looks as if they didn't." Maria covers her slip quickly with a white lie.

"Of course they weren't going to help him, Maria. This is the devil's work!" replies Genaro. "I think Bastone and Bambino killed him. What do you think, Mario?"

"I think we should give him a respectful funeral, bury him and get on with our lives."

"We can't bury him, we have to burn him," states Genaro.

"No, he can't be cremated, he needs to be buried," says an alarmed Maria.

"Sorry, Maria, you have no say. It was his choice. He said to me, 'If I die in Australia, burn me and scatter me into the ocean so I can float back to Abruzzo.' He has no family here; I could only contact a sister back in Italy, who wasn't very interested in what happened to him," says a teary Genaro.

"Poor darling. How did you find out?" asks Maria.

"The police rang me—they must have found my phone number somewhere—and they asked me about his family. I told them what I knew, but I didn't know much, so as the closest contact they had, I had to identify him. Stella is so upset."

Maria fetches her Bible and rosary beads, and places them in her bag. She bids Mario and Genaro farewell as she sets off to church to find some solace. The men sit at the kitchen table. Not much is said, but Mario offers Genaro a cup of tea.

"I need something stronger."

"That's all I got, sorry," says Mario.

The silence is deafening, and eventually Genaro leaves. Mario is alone; he breaks down crying, wishing he had given Pietro the money.

* * *

Pietro's service is a small, quiet affair, not the large five-hundred-plus mourners that ordinarily attend an Italian funeral. Under the circumstances, Genaro has decided to just invite a few of Pietro's closest friends, which includes his former band members, a few ex-colleagues, and Mario and Maria. A couple of *zozze*, however, manage to find out about Pietro's death, and crash the service. They stand quietly weeping in the corner of the crematorium, inappropriately dressed, but no one is particularly worried about that.

Maria doesn't feel overly comfortable being at Pietro's funeral, as she does not agree with cremation. In her mind, it will prevent the resurrection of his body after death, and the scattering of the ashes is impertinent; however, she loves Pietro, so if that was his wish, she will respect it. Mario isn't comfortable either, as he is struggling with feelings of guilt fused with grief and regret. Maria comforts him frequently, explaining that it was not his fault. Even if he did give Pietro the money, it would have been the same outcome; this is something she is certain of. Even at the funeral, Stella makes her presence known, screaming and crying loudly and uncontrollably as Pietro's coffin is lowered into the cremation chamber, almost throwing herself in with the casket. Genaro subdues her by pulling her away from the opening, Maria comforting her with her religious perception.

CHAPTER 24: PORT LINCLON

Elliot's pets now amount to three chickens named Cluck One, Cluck Two and Cluck Three, mainly because they all look the same, and he can't distinguish which is which, as well as the next-door neighbour's cat, which he calls Nosey, so when Mario brings home a rabbit, he is elated. Elliot calls the rabbit Bugs, but Mario tells him the rabbit's name is Yum. Elliot looks after Bugs/Yum, but eventually tires of him, as he doesn't think he is very interesting. All the rabbit wants to do is eat grass and hide in his homemade hutch, constructed by Mario with leftover wood and chicken wire. When Yum goes missing one day, Elliot isn't particularly upset, instead asking for a dog, which is vehemently refused. At that point, Elliot does get upset, arguing that he isn't allowed a dog or a television, not even a bike. Maria appeases him by promising that one day he can get the things he wants, but not now. Elliot protests and asks why he has to wait. Maria doesn't want to tell him it is because they will soon be returning to Italy and these are all long-term commitments that cost a lot of money that Mario does not want to spend. Instead, she suggests that he go to Uncle Fred's to watch a bit of television. Elliot marches off, still complaining that it is totally unfair.

Easter is the most important event on the Christian calendar.

For Catholics as devout as Maria, Holy Week is what they most look forward to every year, even more than Christmas. It is a celebration of the resurrection of Jesus, the foundation of Christianity. Maria is in her element. Good Friday is spent mostly at the church, and Easter Saturday is spent cooking up a feast for Easter Sunday lunch. Stella, Genaro and the family will be celebrating Easter Sunday with the Lanzanis, which makes Elliot happy, as there will be more cowboys and Indians to join him at the park for a new adventure. Yum is basting very nicely in the oven in a pot, surrounded by wine, tomato paste, natural juices and a concoction of herbs and spices. Most Italian families don't wait for the Easter Bunny to bring chocolate eggs; they eat him instead.

Mario walks into the kitchen with a parcel, and compliments Maria on how delicious the rabbit smells. She reminds him not to tell Elliot that it is his rabbit, or he won't eat it.

"OK, I won't say anything," Mario assures her with a devilish grin.

"And don't tell him it's the Easter Bunny either!" she stresses.

"OK, OK. Here, this parcel is for you."

"Hmm, who would be sending me a parcel? You open it for me, I'm busy."

Mario obliges by tearing open the small package, revealing a beautiful white opal, eight carats in size, displaying tiny fires from the depths of the stone as he holds it up.

"Oh my God, that is so beautiful, who would send me such a gift?" Maria asks.

Mario takes out a card with a picture of Jesus and the Mother Mary showing their sacred hearts. On the back of the card, the only word that is written is *Alesky*.

"It's from Alesky. But I thought he changed his name to Denis, and I thought he was in Port Lincoln—opals come from Coober Pedy. Ahhh, I can't keep up with that man," says Mario.

"Still, that was very nice of him. He must have heard we were leaving. You should get in contact with him and thank him before we go back home."

"This would be worth quite a bit," Mario says as he holds the fiery stone up to the light.

"You're not selling my opal!" Maria exclaims as she snatches the precious stone from Mario's hand and puts it safely into her pocket; she also takes the card, with the image of Jesus and Mary, which she also thinks is precious.

* * *

Port Lincoln, a seaside town on the Eyre Peninsula of South Australia, surrounded by bright blue water and a magnificent coastline, has beauty reminiscent of the Croatian coast. It is a town full of convicts' offspring and European migrants, particularly from Croatia, who escaped the Yugoslavian communist government. The dry summers and mild winters, similar to the Mediterranean climate, make the Europeans feel like they are home. It is a rough-and-tumble, hardworking township—just the way Denis May likes it. When Denis began speaking Croatian and sharing stories about the Dalmatian coast, the local Croatian community realised that he wasn't Australian—he was one of them, and he was welcomed with open arms.

Marko Brankavic escaped the Titoism rule in 1960 the same way Denis did in 1949—boarding a ship in the middle of the night, sailing to Italy as a refugee and eventually emigrating to Australia. Denis's journey started in Bonegilla, but Marko went directly from Melbourne to Port Lincoln, where his uncle, Tomislav Brankavic, had arrived ten years earlier with his wife and family. Denis, who at the time was known as Alesky Gulan, fled to Croatia and worked as a fisherman in a small Dalmatian coastal village until the opportunity to find a new world away from Europe finally presented itself. Marko is ten years younger than Denis, but the similarities are uncanny—he escaped a war-torn Europe with a pregnant wife. The only difference is that Marko's wife and unborn child escaped with him, and he now has a three-year-old son and another child on the way. Although this makes Denis's bad memories of Lubijca come flooding back, the bond between the two men is very strong.

Tomislav also shared stories about Croatia with Denis and realised they had mutual friends from the same fishing village. When Tomilsav arrived in Port Lincoln, his boat-building and fishing skills secured him a job with a small boat-building and repair business; within five years, he bought the business. Both Denis and Marko, along with Tomislav's son and two daughters, work for the business, which he named Anka Boats and Fisheries. Tomislav likes Denis a lot, as he is hardworking and smart, often solving problems that no one else can. Within a year, he agreed to allow Denis to marry his eldest daughter, Nada; Denis seems to have a habit of marrying the boss's daughter.

Nada is much younger than Denis, but she looks much older than she is; the pair don't seem mismatched at all. Nada is the complete opposite to Lubijca in appearance, but she still has a lovely disposition, and Denis adores her, especially now that she is carrying his child.

Anka Boats and Fisheries's main business is boat building and repairs; however, when it is southern bluefin tuna season, Denis, Marko and Tomislav's son, Ante, spend weeks out at sea catching the great torpedo-shaped, silver-bellied fish, which can reach up to 2.4 metres in length and weigh up to 250 kilos. It is hard and dangerous work, as the tuna are caught by hand with the pole and live-bait method, the fishermen standing on the edge of a boat, bare to the elements, flicking their catch up one by one onto the deck. In the 1960s, tuna fishing is the fastest-growing industry in Port Lincoln; there is plenty of work for many skilled and unskilled fisherman. Many drifters come to the South Australian fishing town looking for work, amongst other things.

Nada's morning sickness has not limited itself to just the morning, so by the afternoon, she isn't in the mood for any more drifters coming into the Anka Boat and Fisheries office looking for work. But one particular drifter isn't looking for work; he is looking for Denis May. As hard as Nada tries to get rid of him, he insists just as hard that he should see Denis, who is in the boatyard discussing new-and-improved boat designs with Tomislav, Marko and Ante.

"Denis, come to the office, there's someone here to see you," shouts Nada.

"Who is it?" Denis shouts back.

"I don't know, he said he's a friend of yours."

Denis begrudgingly stops his discussion to see who is so insistent on seeing him. He walks into the office and looks at the drifter, then blinks, looking again to make sure his eyes are telling his brain the truth.

"H-h-hello, Alesky," says Pietro.

"Denis."

"Hello, Denis."

The surprise subsides, and Denis gives Pietro a hug.

"What are you doing here?" asks Denis.

"I—I need your help."

"I thought you didn't trust me?"

"At the moment, y-y-you're the only person I can trust."

Pietro signals to Denis to follow him outside. Once there he says "I don't want to s-s-speak in front of that mean lady."

"Hah, that mean lady is my wife."

"Oh, sorry."

"Are you sorry she's my wife?"

"No, no, no, s-sorry I call her mean, I'ma sure she is a very nice wife."

"She is."

"A-and that's your baby?"

"Yes."

"Congratulations," Pietro says, switching to Italian. Denis switches to Italian too, as he replies.

"Thank you, now, what do you need from me?"

"I-I-I'm in big trouble, and I need your help. Please, come with me." Pietro guides Denis to his car. "Alesky—um, I mean, Denis—they say i-i-in life sometimes you kick, and sometimes y-y-you get kicked," counsels Pietro as they approach the car.

"That's very true, Pietro."

"This time, I kicked." Pietro opens the boot of his car. "I kicked very hard," says Pietro, this time without a single stutter, as he reveals a dead body with a single gunshot wound to the head. Denis just stares, not saying a word for about two minutes, which makes Pietro increasingly nervous, until Denis finally speaks.

"Good hit, not much blood...Did you do it?"

Pietro just nods his head and starts to cry.

"It's your first kill?"

Pietro nods again, not able to speak. Denis closes the car boot.

"Who is he?" asks Denis.

"I-it was self-defence," Pietro manages to say.

"I'm sure it was. We have work to do. Get in the car, wait for my pickup truck and follow me," instructs Denis.

Denis rushes inside the office to inform Nada that he won't be home for a few days, and not to worry about him; before Nada can say anything, he is in his pickup truck, waving to Pietro to follow.

Pietro is unsure of what's going on, but he has no choice but to rely on Denis. He follows the rusty red Ford truck that looks very much like the Henry that Willy used to drive; this reminder of simpler times puts a smile on Pietro's face. Denis's simple 'follow me' turns into a twelve-hour drive through the night to Coober Pedy, stopping only for petrol and refreshments.

At the first stop, they fuel up both vehicles and then sit in the nearby diner for a meal and a smoke.

"OK, Pietro, this is where you need to tell me what happened and who is permanently sleeping in the boot of your car?"

With a mixture of fatigue, shock, and unresolved surreal emotion, Pietro drops his head into his hands in despair. "You k-k-kill someone a-and all the life drains out of you," Pietro sobs.

"Your first kill is always hard. It's something you really don't get used to, it's to be avoided whenever possible."

"It's not my only kill!" Pietro says grimly.

Denis is surprised. "And you said I was the criminal?"

"I know...but you are, aren't you?"

"I told you; it depends what side you're on."

The two men share a grim laugh, but then the mood turns serious.

"What happened, Pietro?"

Pietro takes a deep breath and recounts his story in a surprisingly controlled voice.

"The man in the boot is called Bambino, and the car belongs to a man called Bastone, who at this moment is hanging dead in the shed of my house. They are part of the Melbourne 'Ndrangheta—the Calabrian Mafia."

"I know what the 'Ndrangheta is...You've stepped in a big pile of shit, you know," says Denis.

"I know, but it was me or them. I chose me. What would you do?"

"I would've done the same, but now we need to clean the shit off your shoe...Tell me more."

"Mario warned me not to get involved with these men, but I didn't listen—they were promising a lot of good things, and I believed them."

"Where do they sit in the organisation?" asks Denis.

"Bastone was the illegitimate son of a major enforcer who they call Mr Fluff."

"I've heard of him. They say he floats around like the clouds, but watch out for the thunder and lightning when the storm comes."

"Yes, and Bambino's father is in jail for killing his mother. Mr Fluff died last year, along with the other main man; from what I understand, there was a power struggle to fill the top spots. At the time, I owed them money and they were getting heavy with me. Well, Bastone was getting heavy. Bambino was weak, he just followed Bastone—whatever he told him to do, he did. I was having trouble getting the money. Bastone said if I did a hit for him, the debt would be repaid. I didn't want to kill anyone, that's not me...that used to be not me. Anyway, I asked Genaro and Mario to lend me the money, to save my life—Genaro couldn't give me the money, Mario wouldn't."

"Is Mario still here? I thought he would be back in Italy by now."

"No, that's why he wouldn't give me the money. His father spent all the money he was sending to him on lawyers for some stupid argument with his neighbour."

Denis couldn't help but laugh.

"It wasn't funny for Mario, he was really angry about it. That's why he wouldn't give me the money...but Maria did."

"Maria?" said Denis, surprised.

"Yes, she gave me a can full of money that she had. I don't think Mario knew about it."

"Ahhh, Maria...smart, beautiful and kind. I always said she was too good for him."

Pietro agreed and continued his story. "I offered to repay the money, but then Bastone said no, it's too late. I offered more money than I owed him, but he still refused. He had gone a bit crazier than he already was before his father died. He banged the gun on the table and said, 'You do the job or you will be the job.' He gave me a bus ticket to Melbourne with instructions for the hit. I said, 'Yes, OK,' just to get him out of my house, but I was never going to do it, I couldn't. So I think, think, think what to do. For one week, I slept at the side of my house waiting for them to come. They did. I left the door open, Bastone went into the house, Bambino stayed outside as the lookout. I shot Bambino with the gun Bastone gave me, and Bastone shot the cushion sleeping in my bed. Then when

Bastone came out, I choked him with my rope, then hung him in my shed to make it look like suicide. He looks a bit like me and was my size, so I thought by the time they found him, he wouldn't be as recognisable, the police could think it was me. I exchanged his clothes with mine, took his wallet, gun and clothes and put them in the boot of his car with Bambino. Then I left my home, my car, and my life."

"You're not as stupid as I thought you were," says Denis.

"Mario told me you changed your name, he got a postcard from Port Lincoln, so I knew you were here. You were the only one I could think of who could help me. Can you help me?"

"How well did you clean the house? Did you leave anything that's not supposed to be there?"

"I don't think so. I got rid of the cushion and the guns—they had silencers, so no one would have heard anything. The blood from Bambino was on the dirt; I got rid of that. I left everything of mine, I only took the money that Maria gave me, and I drove to Port Lincoln hoping to find you, and I did...Can you help me, please?"

"Yes, yes, Pietro, I wouldn't be here with you if I wasn't going to help you, calm down. How sure are you that they will think Bastone is you?"

Pietro shrugs his shoulders. "I spoke to Genaro before it all. I told him if anything happens to me, I want to be cremated. I wanted to get rid of the body."

"OK, well, we'll have to wait and see. I'll keep my eyes on the death notices."

"I told him to scatter the ashes in the ocean so they could float back to Abruzzo."

"They'll be floating to Calabria with any luck," says Denis. Denis is pensive; the cogs in his head are turning at double speed.

"From what you have told me, they were low-level mobsters...Now that the main men are dead, and with the power struggle happening, they may not even be missed. The 'Ndrangheta will have bigger problems to deal with, so you may be in luck...but you will need to change your identity, your look, even the way you speak, the way you think. You will need to become someone else. Can you do that, Pietro?"

"I need to get rid of all the shit from my shoe."

"That you do, mate, that you do!"

Denis and Pietro finally arrive in Coober Pedy. Pietro is dog tired, but Denis seems to be running full throttle on adrenaline, his mind a ticking clock.

"Stay in the car, I just need to get some supplies," orders Denis.

"Can you tell me where we're going?" asks Pietro warily.

"We are going to your new future."

Pietro nods as he takes this chance to catch a few Z's. He wonders why Denis always has to speak in riddles, but he is grateful for his help.

Denis bangs on the car to wake Pietro.

"Come on, follow me, just another ten minutes or so."

Once again, Pietro follows the red pickup, hoping that ten minutes doesn't turn into another twelve hours. Twenty minutes later, the red pickup stops near the side of a sandstone hill surrounded by a dusty red desert, pitted with open shafts. Pietro watches Denis unload the pickup. He signals for Pietro to stay in the car as he carefully gathers a supply of explosives together with jerry cans of petrol. Pietro is alarmed when Denis jumps in the car and orders him to drive to the farthest away shaft. They step out of the car with the dangerous supplies in hand.

"Open the boot, Pietro."

Pietro obliges, for a moment hoping that the dead body has disappeared, which it hasn't. He desperately wants to ask Denis what he is going to do, but decides against it. Denis floods Bambino's final resting place in the back of Bastone's car boot with petrol, then douses the interior and exterior of the car. When Denis is satisfied with the coverage, he picks up the empty petrol and explosives.

"OK, let's go."

Pietro follows Denis for about ten metres.

"Run!" calls Denis as he lights up the wick of a stick of dynamite and throws it in the direction of the car. The blast is deafening and dynamic, and as the fire engulfs the car, pieces of metal fly up like a volcanic eruption, landing on the hot red desert sand.

"J-J-Jesus Christ," shouts Pietro, "you're going to have everyone here now to see this!"

"Nah, there's an explosion every second day around here," says Denis, standing very proudly as he watches what is left of the car burn.

"That's the end of Bambino, and that's the end of Pietro Pistola. Your name now is Alesky Gulan."

"W-w-what?"

"Your name is Alesky Gulan now, and you are a Polish national."

"B-b-but—"

"It's the only identity I have left, you have no choice."

"I d-d-don't know how to speak Polish. I know nothing

about Poland."

"You don't need to speak Polish, you need to speak English with an Australian accent. Work on that. I told you, everything about you needs to change...Do you understand?"

"Yes."

"Alright, I think we need some rest, and then we got some cleaning up to do when the fire goes out...Don't worry, trust me—Alesky."

"Do I have a choice?"

"Nope."

Pietro sleeps like he has never slept before. He awakes disoriented, eventually comprehending that he is in a cave alone. Then, he remembers he is in Coober Pedy, an Aboriginal name which roughly translates to "white man in a hole", and that's exactly what Pietro is, a new white man in a hole, now named Alesky. He rises from his frontier living quarters, which are even worse than he experienced in Bonegilla, and exits the dugout. The heat of the desert jolts him back to recent events. In the far distance, he sees Denis near the skeleton of Bastone's burnt car, speaking to a couple of Aboriginal women. The conversation surprisingly carries clearly to where Pietro stands, but he doesn't understand what is said, as Denis speaks to them in their native tongue.

"My God, now he can even speak the Aboriginal language?" Pietro says to himself.

Denis waves at Pietro and calls him over. He walks tentatively towards the group. Pietro nods respectfully to the two women as they look him up and down, then say something in their own language to Denis. He laughs, then translates the statement to Pietro.

"She said you're a big man, so you will be able to dig a lot of dirt."

Pietro is confused, his silent, expressionless face begging for an explanation. Pietro is introduced to Milly and Kirra, the two Aboriginal women, as Alex.

"I've agreed with Milly and Kirra that they will noodle the dirt you dig if you pay them for any opal they find," he says to Pietro, who is still very confused. The women give Denis a big smile and wave the two men goodbye, then he explains to Pietro.

"You need to stay here in for a while, lay low, get used to being Alex. This is my site, so you can mine for opals for a few months until the tuna season starts, then you can come back to Port Lincoln."

"I don't know how to opal mine!" responds Pietro.

"Don't worry, I'll teach you. It's not hard, you just need muscles, which you have, and dynamite, which I have. Whatever you find underground, we'll go fifty-fifty, whatever the ladies noodle out of your dig, you pay them for."

"What do you mean 'noodle', isn't that a pasta?" asks Pietro.

Denis laughs. "No, no, 'noodle' in Coober Pedy means they sift through the dirt you dig from the shaft to find small bits of opal."

"Oh, OK. So you come here to mine all the time?"

"I was here for a couple of years. I found some good opals and I made a good living, but then I heard they needed fishermen in Port Lincoln, and I wanted to be near the water. I love it there, my family is there now. I still come here for a few weeks a year in the off season, but it's more of a hobby now. Tomislav's business is growing quickly, and he needs me there more and more now. How much money do you have?"

"I've still got the three hundred pounds Maria gave me."

"Good, we need to go into town and buy you a cheap truck, and you'll live here in the dugout for a while, but right now, we have to get rid of all this mess."

Denis looks around at the car skeleton and all the debris. "All of this needs to go into the open shafts, including any bits of Bambino. Nothing gets left out in the open—we bury the past and hope nothing comes back to bite you in the arse."

"I-I-I'm very, very grateful to you," says an emotional Pietro.

"Get your very grateful self busy, mate, before it gets too hot."

When all the debris is cleaned up, the men drive into the town of Coober Pedy for more supplies and a secondhand 1951 Holden Ute that has air-conditioning built in via the two holes in the passenger door. The Ute was corroded, it had holes, it rattled continuously, but it worked, was cheap, and did the job of transporting Pietro wherever he needed to go.

Denis left Pietro to return to Port Lincoln and to his own devices. Pietro was to ring Denis each week from the pay phone outside the Coober Pedy General Store to report on his opal-mining progress and for Denis to relay any information he might hear about the situation Pietro left behind.

Pietro is very surprised by how much he likes opal mining; it makes the black cloud that has been following him around for the past months more bearable. When Denis tells him during the weekly phone call that Pietro "Pistola" Mancini has been cremated in a small funeral service attended by his friends, he feels even more at ease.

"Good, looks like Genaro came through."

"Yes, he's either very smart or very stupid, I'm not sure

which yet," replies Denis.

"All I-I-I know is that Stella is the smart one in that relationship."

"Well, it's lucky for you that she didn't identify the body. By the way, I'm a father, to a little boy."

"*Auguri*, Papa!"

"Stop speaking Italian."

"O-O-OK, sorry, I get confused."

"My little boy is half Ukrainian Jew and half Croatian Catholic. How confused do you think he's going to be?"

"Which one is you?"

"I'm the Ukrainian Jew—Denys Maykaporvic, or Denis May here in Australia."

"I'm s-s-sure he will be as resourceful as his father."

"Hopefully he won't need to be. He was born in a good country and won't have to go through what I have. We are very lucky to be here in Australia, never forget that."

"I'm lucky to have you as my friend. Thank you."

Denis was dismissive of Pietro's display of emotion and ended the conversation, reminding him of what he needed to do to change his identity. Pietro was happy that Denis had given him a glimpse into his past; he saw this as a sign of trust.

* * *

It is a lonely life in Coober Pedy for Pietro, the new Alesky Gulan; the only company he has is Milly and Kirra as they noodle the dirt he dug from the shaft, and the resident lizard that lives with him in the dugout. Pietro becomes so friendly with the lizard that he begins to swat flies for it and leave them on the ground for it to eat. The lizard even sleeps at the edge of Pietro's sleeping bag. He finds himself conversing with the lizard, which he calls Cicco, every day. Pietro thinks, surely he is going mad, speaking to a lizard, but it is better than speaking to Saint Peter.

He lives a very rudimentary frontier life in the dugout most days, but once a week, he goes into the town, stays at the local hotel, has a shower, and cleans himself up for a night on the town. Everyone in Coober Pedy knows him as Alex, and no one asks him any questions; it is a town of many secrets, many rumours, and no absolute truths. If he has opals, he sells them raw or gets them polished and ready for jewellery settings. Much of what Milly and Kirra noodle is potch, but every now and then, they strike good opal chips, which Pietro buys from them, as agreed. The two Aboriginal ladies speak very little English, and Pietro doesn't speak any of their language, but when it comes to business, the universal language of money keeps them on the same page.

Milly and Kirra are finding a good amount of opal chips with increasing frequency, so Pietro knows he is close to a good vein, but he needs to blast into the rock. He is nervous about using explosives, so before he does anything, he plans to telephone Denis just to make sure he is doing it right.

When Pietro phones, his excitement about finding a potential vein of opal is not matched by Denis. Instead, his tone is very solemn and to the point.

"You need to come back to Port Lincoln," says Denis.

Pietro taps the phone to make sure he's hearing right, then questions him. "You want me to come back to Lincoln?"

"Yeah."

"Why? I'm just about to find a good vein, I'm sure of it!"

"I need you here for the tuna season. You can go back after."

Pietro senses that it's a demand and not a suggestion, and thinks twice about protesting any further.

"Are you alright?" Pietro asks.

"Well, I have good news for you, but bad news for me."

Pietro remains silent.

"Which one do you want to hear first?"

"I'll let you choose," answers Pietro.

"There was an accident with one of the tuna boats, we lost seven crew—my friend Marko and my brother-in-law Ante were two of them."

"Oh, I'm sorry to hear that. So, tuna fishing is dangerous?"

"Not any more dangerous than you with a stick of dynamite in your hand."

Pietro has a bit of a chuckle at how true that statement is, and decides immediately that he is not going to refuse this man who has done so much for him.

"OK, I'll come back straightaway."

"Do you want to know the good news?"

"Yes, of course."

"There have been some murders in Melbourne, they're calling them the Victoria Market murders, and the papers are saying that they are just family disputes. The government denies that it has anything to do with organised crime and says that the Mafia does not exist in Australia, but we know better, don't we?"

"Yes."

"This is good for you, because if they are fighting amongst themselves, they're probably not going to be looking for a couple of low-level enforcers."

"Yes, that is good, that means I'm safe."

"It means you're safe for now.   Don't ever let your guard down.   And you still speak with that stupid Italian accent—work on that."

"OK, mate, see ya soon," says Pietro, unsuccessfully attempting an Australian drawl.

CHAPTER 25: SOLD

Mario has gotten sober and smarter; his premium choice of beverage is now Earl Grey tea, brewed for a minimum of five minutes, with a dash of milk and two sugars. Wine is no longer an option. His chauvinistic expectation of being served by Maria has not changed, and he waits patiently in his usual chair at the kitchen table for his pot of afternoon tea.

Maria has sent Elliot to the corner shop to buy a box of Earl Grey, as they've run out. They wait for Elliot to return.

Elliot walks along the pathway to his house with a packet of tea as instructed, and a bag of mixed lollies. Maria gave him a little extra money; it was unspoken, but he understood that he could spend it on a treat for himself. Her stance on Elliot buying sweets has changed, so he never refuses an errand to the shop, and he never hurries. He has his straw cowboy hat on his head, cap guns in the holster firmly tied around his waist, his hand deep in the mixed lollies bag he's just purchased. Elliot passes the "For Sale" sign. It doesn't mean much to him, as it has been up for six months, but it seems different now. He does a double-take, and realises there is a large "SOLD" banner across the sign. He is pensive, and suddenly, like a bolt from the blue, he comprehends what the sign means. He becomes increasingly angry and runs into the house.

"You sold the house! I told you I'm not living in a shoe!" Elliot shouts at his parents.

"*Amore mio,*" pleads Maria.

"I'm not going to Italy. You can go, I'm staying here!"

"Elliot!" roars Mario.

Elliot throws down the box of tea and bag of lollies and runs outside in tears, followed by Maria, who is followed by Mario. Elliot is much too fast for the both of them. By the time they reach the front of the house, Elliot is nowhere to be seen. Maria is in a panic; she darts next door to the Brackenridge house.

"Fred...Fred!" she bawls, knocking furiously on the door.

Fred, hearing the ruckus, runs to the door immediately, opening it to a frantic Maria.

"What's wrong, Maria?"

"Is Elliot here?"

"No, what's happened?"

"He's run away...He was very upset about going back to Italy. I don't know what to do—should I call the police?"

"No, not yet, I think I know where he might be. I'll talk to him, you and Mario stay here."

Fred calmly exchanges his slippers for some closed shoes, then puts on his hat and jacket and shuffles past an anxious Maria and Mario.

"Don't worry, it will be fine," Fred assures them.

He hobbles down the road, his war wounds bothering him more and more these days, but nevertheless, he soldiers on to the *Bonanza* battlefield. He reaches the playground where he and Elliot usually play out their Western games; Elliot can't be seen. Fred is not deterred.

"Elliot? Elliot, come on, little mate, where are you?"

There is no answer, but Fred sees a glimpse of a straw hat

268

inside the wooden fortlike structure.

"Come on, Little Joe, we need to catch us some varmints."

From the wooden structure comes a teary reply: "I'm too upset to catch any right now, Uncle Fred."

"Now is the perfect time to catch them, your senses are heightened, and they won't be expecting you."

There is a long pause before Elliot jumps up, all guns a blazing. *POP-POP-POP-POP!* goes the cap gun.

"Hands up, varmint!" hollers Elliot.

"You can't catch me, I'm too smart and too fast for ya, lawman!"

Fred starts to run and Elliot chases him around the park.

Fred has a short break while Elliot reloads another round of cap strips into his gun. *BANG-BANG-BANG* sounds the gun, and Fred runs away faster; there's more shooting, and Fred falls to the ground. Elliot laughs uncontrollably as he hovers over him, continuing to shoot. Fred clutches his hat and groans.

"Gotcha, ya varmint!" shouts Elliot.

Elliot lies down next to Fred and puts his arms around him.

"You're so funny, Uncle Fred."

Fred groans again, then, in a very low and strained voice, he says, "Elliot, run and get me some help."

Elliot springs up, surprised, not really understanding the situation.

"I need help. Please, go get your dad or Auntie Reenie, quick."

"Did I shoot you for real, Uncle Fred?"

"Seems so, go run."

Elliot kisses him on the forehead and runs as fast as he can back to the Brackenridge house. Maria and Mario are relieved to see him as he dashes past them in a flash.

"Elliot," shouts Mario.

"I'm not talking to you two," Elliot shouts back.

He bursts into the neighbour's house as his parents follow him. Irene sits comfortably in her chair, watching television. The door slams open, and Elliot rushes in hysterically.

"I shot Uncle Fred! I shot Uncle Fred!"

"What are you talking about, child?" answers Irene, exasperation in her tone.

Elliot pulls on her arm. "Come on, come with me, quick... please!"

Irene follows him out of the house. He runs much too fast for her, or his parents, but they all follow him as quickly as they can.

When they reach the park, Irene sees Fred, who is motionless on the ground. She freezes for a second as she watches Elliot tickling him.

"Come on, Uncle Fred, you can get up now, the game is over—when you get tickled, you have to wake up, *pleeease*, Uncle Fred."

Irene walks slowly up to the pair of pretend cowboys. She stares at Fred for a moment, then kneels down next to Elliot. She gently takes Elliot's hand and clasps it tightly, leading him away from Fred to allow the paramedics that have just arrived to attend to him. A few minutes pass, then one of the paramedics gives a sympathetic head shake to Irene. She understands that Fred has departed.

Mario and Maria stand back, watching the scene unfold, shocked and teary-eyed. A small crowd begins to gather as Fred is moved inside the ambulance. Mario picks up Fred's hat, which has been left on the ground, and holds it close to his chest. Flashes and snippets of the wonderful times they shared play like a movie trailer in his head. He has only just begun to accept the death of Pietro, and now he has to deal with Fred's death; he is devastated, but in a strange way, he finds comfort in holding Fred's hat.

Irene takes a huge breath in and releases some built-up tears. Elliot takes her hand.

"Auntie Reenie, did I kill Uncle Fred?"

"No, you didn't." Irene sniffs.

"Good, when is he coming back?"

"He's not coming back, Elliot. He's going to Heaven."

"Oh, my mum says that's a really nice place."

"Well, your mum would know."

"They better have beer and sausage rolls there!"

Irene begins to laugh and cry at the same time, but she also wears a huge smile as she bends down to give Elliot a hug. Elliot hugs her back tightly.

"You're such a good boy. It must all come from your mother's side of the family."

Mario and Maria watch as Irene and Elliot embrace. It is a tender and moving moment. Mario fiddles with Fred's hat. Maria turns to him.

"Did you take a photograph, Mario?" Maria says to him.

Mario thinks for a moment. "I took an X-ray, Maria. I looked inside."

Mario walks up to Irene and Elliot, who are still embracing. He stands at a distance, respecting their grief, until Irene finally looks at him. Mario offers Irene Fred's hat. She gives him a warm smile.

"You keep it, Mario. I've noticed you don't have a hat. He would have liked you to have it."

Mario is very touched and almost breaks down. His inner conflict, the death of Fred, and Irene's unexpected thoughtfulness is just too much for him. He nods his head in appreciation, then grasps Elliot's hand and leads him back to Maria, who eagerly hugs him.

"*Amore mio.* Let's go home."

Something compels Mario to place Fred's hat upon his head; it fits perfectly.

Wearing Fred's hat must have altered Mario's thinking. The day after Fred dies, he nullifies the contract for the sale of the house and tells Maria to unpack all the suitcases—he has decided they are to remain in Australia. Their future resides in their son, and Elliot happens to be Australian. They will one day return to Italy to reunite with their families, but only for a holiday. Elliot, of course, is ecstatic.

A few weeks later, Elliot arrives home from school. He drops his coat and bag at the door, and enters the lounge.

"Hello, Uncle Fred," he says.

The picture of Fred on Maria's wall of death does not answer, but that is of no consequence. Maria told him that Fred can still see him from Heaven and that he lives in his heart. Elliot questioned that: how could Fred be in two places at one time? Maria was stumped at first, but then she explained that Fred's soul was in Heaven, but his spirit was in the hearts of all who loved him. Elliot was satisfied with that, as he did love Uncle Fred very much.

It's 6 p.m., dinnertime, and Elliot closes his homework book and runs into the kitchen.

"Is it ready, Mum?" he asks impatiently.

"Yes, *amore mio*," she answers as she plates up a piece of steaming hot lasagne.

Elliot takes the plate outside and waits patiently near the hole in the fence.

I hope she hasn't forgotten, Elliot thinks. After a moment, he becomes deflated at the prospect that Irene has forgotten and he places the plate of lasagne on the ground. This pleases the nosey neighbourhood cat, who has a nice time licking the lasagne.

Maria watches from the kitchen window, noticing Elliot's dispirited posture. She quickly puts her plan into action. The puff pastry is taken out of the fridge, ready for the mince meat mixture to be added. She learnt to make sausage rolls at the seminary, for Elliot's sake, as she knows how much he likes them. She anticipated that Irene would forget the food exchange date she made with Elliot and prepared a disappointment strategy, just in case. After all, Irene has more to worry about than a made-up tradition between her late husband and a seven-year-old boy.

Elliot stares at the hole in the wooden fence; he is beginning to get hungry. He looks to the plate of lasagne in horror and shoos away the cat happily licking the top layers of the lasagne sauce.

Suddenly, a sliding noise is heard. Elliot turns to the hole in the fence, through which a plate of sausage rolls appears.

"Oh, thank you, Auntie Reenie. Wait, you forgot the sauce."

"Oh, sorry," says Irene.

Elliot passes the plate back and waits for the sauce. He fixes the top layers of the lasagne to fill in the missing bits that the cat had licked. The plate of sausage rolls with just the right amount of tomato sauce reappears.

"Where's mine?" asks Irene.

Elliot slides the lasagne back through the hole, and Irene is none the wiser about the cat as she has her first taste of Italian food.

"This is delicious!" she exclaims. "Do you think your mum will give me the recipe?"

"Yeah, sure, but don't worry, I'll swap with you anytime."

Maria sees such glee on Elliot's face as he bites into the sauce-smothered sausage roll, she returns the puff pastry and mince mix back to the refrigerator, placing it next to the Vegemite jar, ready for another time.

CHAPTER 26: HELLO AND ARRIVEDERCI

It is time for Mario to stop trying to divert the path of his fate and make peace with Miss Destiny. He stands with Maria, together with other Italian nationals, including Genaro and Stella, as he reflects on the events that have brought him to his current position. It is 1967, the decimal currency is in its second year of having replaced the imperial pounds, shillings and pence. Change is a moving constant. Mario has been living in Australia for nearly fifteen years, and today, he and Maria will change from being Italians to becoming Australian citizens, something he once thought would never happen. Change is always difficult for Mario, but today Miss Destiny has convinced him that this course correction is the right one. Maria doesn't believe in destiny, preferring to trust in the divine, saying: "It's God's will."

All the foreign candidates place their hands on the Bible in the crowded Immigration Department of the Homeland Office. Maria wears the dress she wore the day she arrived in Australia, and Mario is sporting Fred's hat, which he wears with pride. Together, they pledge their allegiance to their newly adopted country.

"From this time onwards, under God, I pledge my loyalty

to Australia and its people, whose democratic beliefs I share, whose rights and liberties I respect, and whose laws I will uphold and obey." All the candidates recite the pledge.

The master of ceremonies doesn't really know if everyone says the affirmation correctly, as with the different accents all mishmashed together it sounds more like the hubbub of a marketplace. However, he is confident they all understand what they are saying and everyone is excited about the day.

"I'm sure you all appreciate what a privilege it is for you to become Australian, each of you having something to contribute to this great land. You may ask, can I love another country? The answer is yes. It's the same as loving two children—they are different, but you love them the same. Congratulations to you all, and good luck for your future."

The master of ceremonies swears them all in as citizens, and each New Australian receives their citizenship certificate.

Maria looks at her certificate proudly and says, "Thank you, Australian God."

They all congratulate each other.

"Mario, that's a nice hat," says Genaro.

"*Grazie*. Thank you."

"We can't call you 'Mario *sensa capello*' anymore, we have to call you 'Mario *con bello capello*' now."

Everyone who understands what Genaro is talking about laughs.

"Hello, Australian Mario, *arrivederci*, Italian Mario," Maria says teasingly.

"You're Australian now, Dad, like me!"

"Yes, I am, now let's go home and eat some pasta!"

"How about a sausage roll?"

"No thanks."

"A Vegemite sandwich?"

"No way."

"Come on, just one!"

"Do you want to kill me?"

Mario holds Elliot's hand. It's time to go, so he leads him out of the hall towards his new car, a very stylish 1963 EJ Holden, which has replaced the dented Vanguard. He bought it secondhand, of course.

Mario does not return to Italy, nor does he ever eat a sausage roll or Vegemite sandwich. He still writes to his mother, and his father lives on. When his mother got word that Mario and his family were to stay in Australia, she cried for a week, but he assured her that they would see each other again one day. His father still asks for money, which Mario refuses to give. His mother decides to send his hat, which she kept so carefully for his return, to his new home in Australia. Now Mario has two hats, and he never goes out without a hat on his head.

With the money Mario saved for the Bovino cantina, including the notes he kept in his pillow lining, he buys a small plot of land in the McLaren Vale region south of Adelaide, with a few established Shiraz vines and a small cottage in need of repair. He no longer works two jobs, instead accepting a position with General Motors Holden as a supervisor on the production line. His weekends are spent at the vineyard attending to his crop and fixing up the cottage as a weekend holiday abode, using leftover hardware discarded from Holden. Mario ceases drinking wine, but he continues making it, experimenting with small batches of different varieties of grapes and blends. He now respects the "liquid passion in a bottle", and no longer abuses it as he has done in the past. The wine is so good that he begins selling to friends and acquaintances. Maria no longer lies about working at the seminary; she only lied about it when she started, so God will surely forgive her for that. The seminary becomes one of Mario's best customers, nearly always purchasing the bulk of what he produces.

Elliot misses his Uncle Fred, but he often visits Auntie Reenie. Santa Claus has finally given him a television for Christmas, but he still sits with Irene watching television and eating sausage rolls with sauce, although she draws the line at giving him beerstaches. Mario misses Fred as well. His relationship with Irene has become amicable and respectful, and he tilts his hat to her if she happens to be in the front yard attending to her roses, but he never goes out of his way to seek her out, instead leaving the friendly neighbour interactions to Maria.

* * *

A glistening new Ford Falcon XP Fairmont sedan rolls up to the curb of the Lanzani house. Mario, who is out the front washing his own car, takes notice of the beautiful vehicle. Two men step out.

"Hey, you overprivileged Australian," Denis shouts to a startled Mario.

Mario stops what he is doing and smiles as he recognises Denis. *But who is the man with him?* he wonders. Pietro has by now completely changed his look; thanks to the physical nature of tuna fishing and a more abundant diet, his body is even more built up than ever, and his head is as bald as a boiled egg. They approach Mario and all shake hands, Mario none the wiser that he has just greeted his old friend.

"So, you're an Aussie now?" Denis says with a Cheshire cat

smile.

Mario laughs. "Yeah, mate."

"Is Maria here?" asks Denis.

"Yes, she's inside, come say hello."

They enter the house to a welcoming Maria. "And who is your friend?" Maria directs her question to Denis.

The stranger gives Maria a gift-wrapped box along with an envelope. "My name is Alesky Gulan."

Maria drops the gift and envelope and stares into the stranger's eyes. She immediately recognises them.

"Oh, *mio caro Dio*...Pietro!" she screams.

Mario looks to Pietro and then to Denis, then back to Pietro, not quite knowing what to do, what to say or how he feels. Is he ecstatic that his friend is alive, or bitterly angry at such deception? Maria begins to cry uncontrollably with happiness and confusion. Pietro hugs her, then directs her to sit down on a chair. Mario, too, sits down.

"Let me explain," says Pietro slowly, with an Australian accent and no stutter.

Denis helps himself to Maria's kitchen and makes a pot of tea for everyone. Mario is in need of something stronger, so he contemplates breaking out a bottle of Sambuca; he would if he could get out of his chair.

Pietro apologises profusely, then calmly explains the whole course of events that have seen him rise from the dead in front of them. Mario and Maria listen intently, their eyes, ears and brains working together to decipher all the entangled information. After the explanation, they all hug, and as the negative emotion is expelled, all that is left is joy. There are still some unanswered questions, but they are better off left that way. Mario, now able to remove himself from his chair, cracks open the bottle of Sambuca, and they all toast a long, healthy and prosperous life to Alesky Gulan.

"Did Genaro know about all this?" asks Mario. "He said he had to identify your body."

"No, I didn't tell him anything. He still doesn't know, and I want to keep it that way for now. I dropped some hints about being cremated and made sure that his phone number was in my wallet. I'm not sure if he genuinely thought it was me, or if he suspected something and just did what I asked. In any case, by burning me, he probably saved my life—you can't exhume ashes from the ocean."

"OK, we're all friends now, yes?" announces Denis. "Now you need to open your presents."

Maria opens the gift-wrapped box to reveal a set of opal earrings. She is very appreciative of the beautiful gift and gives Pietro aka Alesky a hug. He reciprocates by kissing her hand like a gentleman.

"Do you still sing?" asks Maria.

"Only in the shower. Do you still have the opal I sent you last year?"

"Yes, you are much too generous."

"Give it to me. I will get it made into a necklace for you."

"No, Pietro..."

"Alesky," he corrects Maria.

"OK, Alesky. These gifts must be very expensive, it's not necessary," says Mario. Maria agrees.

"Don't worry, me and Denis had a lot of luck mining opal in Coober Pedy, and now we are partners in a business called Anka Boats and Fisheries, which is doing very well. We've made our boats safer, they are selling very well, and the demand for southern bluefin tuna is growing each year."

"That is very good news, we're very happy for you."

"Open your envelope, Maria," says Denis.

Out of the envelope comes a folded piece of paper and a bank cheque for dividends to the amount of two thousand dollars, a small fortune. The paper is the title to a share of the Anka Boat and Fisheries company.

"This is much too generous, we can't accept this," exclaims Mario.

"With the money you gave me, I made you a shareholder of the company," Pietro states.

"But I didn't give you any money," responds Mario.

"No, you didn't, but Maria did."

Mario turns to Maria, even more shocked than when he first encountered a resurrected Pietro.

With wide, innocent eyes, Maria looks back at him and simply says, "It was God's will—the Australian God."